THE OTHER GWYN GIRL

NICOLA CORNICK

Boldwood

First published in Great Britain in 2024 by Boldwood Books Ltd.

Copyright © Nicola Cornick, 2024

Cover Design by Alice Moore Design

Cover Imagery: [Lee Avison] / Arcangel, Shutterstock and Alamy

Every effort has been made to obtain the necessary permissions with reference to copyright material, both illustrative and quoted. We apologise for any omissions in this respect and will be pleased to make the appropriate acknowledgements in any future edition.

A CIP catalogue record for this book is available from the British Library.

Paperback ISBN 978-1-78513-722-8

Large Print ISBN 978-1-78513-718-1

Hardback ISBN 978-1-78513-717-4

Ebook ISBN 978-1-78513-715-0

Kindle ISBN 978-1-78513-716-7

Audio CD ISBN 978-1-78513-723-5

MP3 CD ISBN 978-1-78513-720-4

Digital audio download ISBN 978-1-78513-714-3

Boldwood Books Ltd
23 Bowerdean Street
London SW6 3TN
www.boldwoodbooks.com

For Andrew, with love always.

PROLOGUE
ROSE – OXFORD, FEBRUARY 1650

A bitter wind blew down Magpie Lane, sending the snowflakes swirling. A single lantern, high on the wall of Christ Church College, cast a dancing shadow as we passed beneath it and slipped through the doorway into Merton College gardens.

Mother held me tight by the hand; in her other arm, she cradled the baby, who had wailed for the whole journey from our lodgings in Botley, her voice a thin, high thread, tiny but determined.

'Be quick, Rose,' Mother said, when I stumbled, tiredness and cold pulling me down. 'Nell will catch a chill if you dawdle along like this.' She sounded both cross and distracted. She always did.

I was five years old and could remember a time *before*, when it had been summer and we had lived in the country. Father had been there and the sun had shone every day. Now it was perpetual winter, Father had gone, and Nell had arrived.

The gardens were shrouded in darkness and the path was lost beneath the snow, but a lamp burned in a downstairs window. Mother released my hand and hurried towards it, a moth to the flame. I ran to keep up.

I saw her rap on the pane three times, sharply. A door opened and we were bundled inside.

'Why must Nell have her horoscope cast tonight?' I had asked Mother earlier, when she had told me we were to go out into the city that night. I had been warm, or at least as warm as I could be in our draughty garret rooms, and was drowsily contemplating my hot milk and my cot.

'Because the timing of such celestial matters is critical,' Mother had said sharply.

'Why?' I had pressed again.

'Because Mr Ashmole says so.'

'Why?'

'Why do you always ask so many questions, Rose?'

I think Mother had been tempted to leave me behind that night but feared that Mrs Culpeper, who owned the lodging house, might kidnap me and sell me in payment for our rent arrears.

Oxford was a dangerous place in the winter of early 1650; the Puritans had finally crushed the spirit that had made the city such a stronghold of Royalist support under the late King Charles I. Informers, spies and enforcers abounded. Masterless men roamed the streets. Old soldiers and their families were left to starve and the shadow of death stalked the narrow alleyways. People hid behind their shuttered windows on nights like this.

Except, evidently, there were those at the university who still lived in grand style. We were in a big, shadowy room, a library lit by candlelight, lined with bookcases and decorated with huge white heads carved from stone. It was a rich man's room, smelling of pipe smoke and the lingering scents of a roast dinner.

I stared about me, dripping melting snow onto the soft carpet beneath my feet, and then I saw the open fire and hurried towards it to thaw my frozen fingers. I climbed up into the huge armchair directly beside it and settled in, luxuriating in the heat.

'Rose!' Mother exclaimed, but the man who had come forward to greet her only laughed.

'The little maid knows what she wants and takes it,' he said. 'It is not a bad philosophy for life.'

'Rose rushes headlong towards everything,' Mother said. Her bitterness was clear. 'She does not think. She is just like her father.'

I loved my father dearly and could see nothing wrong in being in his image, but evidently my mother did not agree.

The stranger, however, knelt beside my chair to see me more clearly, affording me the chance to assess him too – he was a big man with a florid face and wide forehead, his eyes narrow and bright with intelligence, a reddish hue to his long curly hair and with fine lace at his neck and wrists. A gentleman of substance, then, the sort of man Father had once been, and a scholar too, which Father most certainly had never been.

'Well met, Mistress Rose Gwyn,' he said. 'I am Elias Ashmole.'

The name meant nothing to me, other than that this was the man whom Mother had said we must consult to draw up baby Nell's horoscope, but when he turned to a hovering maidservant and sent her away to fetch warm chocolate for me, I decided I would love him forever.

Meanwhile, Mother had taken the seat offered beside Mr Ashmole's desk, which was littered with papers of all kinds and books open at what appeared to be random pages. Nell, whose wailing had dropped to a low grizzle and then died away altogether, was now being admired. I could imagine her gazing at Mr Ashmole with her big blue eyes, wrapping her tiny fingers around his.

As I sipped my warm chocolate from the beaker the maid presented, I listened to his words: 'An elfin child, so sweetly pretty... You say you saw a star shooting across the sky on the night she was born? Some see that as a harbinger of doom, but I consider it a very auspicious sign. I will draw up her chart for you now...'

The combined effect of the soft scratching of Mr Ashmole's quill as he sketched the chart, the warmth of the fire and the comfort of the hot chocolate made me very sleepy. As I drifted in and out of dreams, I heard snippets of the conversation:

'Her sun is in Aquarius... She will be a lively and creative personality...'

Scratch, scratch, scratch.

'The moon... in the house of Cancer, the Crab...' Mr Ashmole's voice had a slight uncertainty to it, but then the confidence returned: 'A very loyal and passionate person...'

'Capricorn rising...' He let out a chuckle. 'A determined individual, then. Nothing will stand in her way.'

'I knew it!' Mother sounded excited. 'I knew she was destined for great things when I saw the star in the sky overhead on the night of her birth.'

'Like the baby Jesus,' I said.

Both of them looked at me.

'Well, perhaps not quite,' Mr Ashmole said. He peered at me over the top of his spectacles. 'Do you wish me to do your chart as well, little maid? When were you born?'

'I don't know,' I said, 'but I am nearly five years old.'

Mr Ashmole looked enquiringly at Mother.

'It was in the dark days of the summer of '45,' she said, 'when the King's fortunes had turned.' Then, lowering her voice, 'We do not speak of it.'

'I see,' Mr Ashmole said.

There would be no horoscope for me, then.

Scratch, scratch, scratch. I dozed.

'Scorpio in mid-heaven,' Mr Ashmole murmured. 'Oh, there will be challenges along her path, no question about it, but she will triumph over them.'

'I want her to be happy,' Mother said, suddenly vehement. 'I want her to be safe.'

'She will be more than that,' Mr Ashmole promised. 'She will be celebrated. And she will know a great love.'

'Oh, love!' Mother sniffed. 'I would rather hear that she will marry a rich man for his fortune.'

'I do not see a marriage...' Mr Ashmole cleared his throat. 'One must remember, madam, that a horoscope is not proscriptive, only a guide to the path the child might take...'

I slid off my chair and went to stand beside the desk, curious to see the chart he was creating. I was too short to see over the edge, so Mr Ashmole drew up a stool for me to sit on. I was disappointed that the horoscope, which had sounded so intriguing, was completely incomprehensible, no more than a wheel of squiggles, letters and odd symbols.

'Is it magic?' I ventured, tracing a finger over one of the drawings, which looked like a wiggling worm.

'No, little maid,' Mr Ashmole said firmly. 'It is science, not magic. It takes a skilled scholar to interpret a chart.'

I could not see that this would be of much use to baby Nell, who would not be able to read it, but I was glad it was not magic. Our father had shown me some magic tricks last summer when we were at Becote Manor, making ribbons and buttons disappear, and daisies spring from my ears until I was screaming with laughter.

'Always believe in magic, pet,' he had told me, but the only magic that had happened since then was that both Father and the manor had disappeared, apparently for good.

Mr Ashmole finished the horoscope with a flourish.

'I will have a clerk copy it for you tomorrow and deliver it to your lodgings,' he promised. 'The original will stay in my collection, of course, for the scholars of the future to study.'

This all sounded rather grand to me. Would scholars of the future be interested in my baby sister? But Mother seemed impressed and she reached into the hem of her skirt and took out a small bag of money. I heard the clink of coins as she held it out to Mr Ashmole.

'With my thanks, sir,' she said.

I wanted to cry out to her not to give the last of our money away, for I had had nothing but bone broth and gruel to eat for the past week, but Mr Ashmole, fortunately, refused.

'Dear madam...' He pushed the hand holding the money away gently. 'I would not dream of it. Keep your coins to feed your girls and in recognition of our shared loyalties.' He dropped his voice. 'I was very sorry to hear about Captain Gwyn. Out of respect for his father, the late Canon, I wish I could help you, but alas...'

He did not explain why the help would not be forthcoming and he was already crossing the library to usher us back out of the door and into the cold. The icy draught that wrapped around my legs was a shock that almost made me cry out. I could not imagine attempting to walk back to the garret in Botley through these snowdrifts.

Mr Ashmole, however, seemed keen to be rid of us now that the horoscope was cast.

'Remember, Madam Gwyn,' he called, almost gaily, 'there is a brilliant future ahead of your younger daughter. Have faith!'

Faith would not feed us, nor would it warm us, I thought, as the cold bit into my toes.

I remembered his words again when I was lying in my cot at our lodgings, Mother snoring beside me and baby Nell snuffling in her sleep like a little piglet. Fortunately, in St Giles we had met a carter trudging home with his two huge dray horses. He had exclaimed to find anyone out in such inclement weather and had given us a ride in the cart as far as New Osney, so we were not too chilled when at last we had arrived home.

Nell would have a brilliant future, but what about me? I drew the thin blanket up closer beneath my chin and decided that I would forge my own future. It would contain warm fires and chocolate and thick, cosy carpets.

* * *

The following day, true to his word, Mr Ashmole sent a clerk to our lodgings with Nell's horoscope in a scroll tied with a blue ribbon. Mother was in raptures and went to sit by the window to pore over it in the winter light. She did not see the other, smaller scroll that the clerk took from his sleeve and pressed into my hands with the whispered words that Mr Ashmole had decreed it was for my eyes alone.

I waited until Mother had gone out to beg for some stale bread to feed us, then I took her place on the window seat and unrolled it. As with Nell's chart, there were diagrams and curves, squiggles and letters, none of which made any sense to me.

I was disappointed, but not for long, for the cream ribbon that tied it suited my auburn hair very well.

Folding the chart, I put it away in the old treasure tin I kept beneath my bed whose only other contents were the knife my father had left me, the key to the fishing house at Becote Manor which Mother had told me I could keep because it was worthless, some battered wooden soldiers, a thimble and a shiny gold button.

When Mother wasn't looking, I also took the blue ribbon from Nell's scroll and hid it until she had forgotten about it, then took it out and cut it in half to tie my plaits. All in all, I thought I had done quite well by Mr Ashmole.

1

JESS – THE PRESENT, LATE MARCH

'Welcome to Fortune Hall!' the sign said. It was wooden, painted in a whimsical vintage style, with horseshoes, four-leaf clovers and various other good-luck symbols. Rather incongruously, it was hanging from a metal spike on the top of a steel gate that was about as welcoming as a slap across the face. It reminded Jess rather too much of the place she had left half an hour before – the open prison at Bright Hill, where her ex-boyfriend was currently residing at His Majesty's pleasure.

'I don't suppose you'll come to visit me again,' Jared had said, rather plaintively, when she had pushed back the plastic chair and got up to leave. 'Not that I blame you. It's all been a bit of a nightmare.'

'Especially for the people you defrauded,' Jess had agreed. Jared's self-absorption was extraordinary. Even now, after a high-profile trial and a conviction based on an overwhelming pile of evidence, he was still protesting his innocence and complaining that his life had been ruined.

Jess looked through the car window at the painted four-leaf clovers on the sign.

Luck. They said you made your own and, certainly, she felt she had been the architect of her own *bad* luck through being so oblivious to Jared's faults. For over two years, she had been taken in by his winning charm and the way he had made her mundane existence seem exciting. For once, her life had seemed almost as dazzling as that of her younger sister, Tavy. Except that it had all been an illusion.

Now, having said a final goodbye to Jared, she realised she didn't even feel sad, only angry and exhausted. Jess's losses – the flat she and Jared had once shared, her security, her savings and her self-confidence and faith in her own judgement – were all casualties of the mess, but they felt insignificant compared to the victims of Jared's investment scam. Elderly people had lost their life savings, students the means to fund their education, families their homes and plans for the future. Night after night, Jess lay awake, tormented by their stories and the desire to make amends.

Even though the police had cleared her of any involvement in Jared's criminality, she felt responsible. She felt she should have known.

Her sister Tavy's fame had meant that the whole case had been splashed across the news as well: 'Cheating trader brother-in-law of reality TV star Tavy Yates steals the dreams of thousands' was one of the less lurid, albeit inaccurate, headlines.

It was going to take her a while to get back on her feet. Coming to Fortune Hall was a stopgap, Jess told herself, a temporary measure to buy her some time and give her a place to hide away until she felt a bit more resilient. Tavy had suggested it, which was very generous of her under the circumstances. Under normal circumstances, Jess would have flatly refused as she and her sister were polar opposites in just about everything, and spending any time under the same roof as Tavy was bound to end badly. But since Jared, normal circumstances didn't exist any more and Jess felt a surprising urge to take refuge with her family. Like all her other ideas lately, she thought, it was probably a bad one.

She switched off the car, got out and walked towards the steel gates. They were set between two old lodge houses. Both were squat buildings, stone and foursquare, obviously empty. Through the blank windows she glimpsed fallen masonry and broken beams. The steel fence extended along the road for as far as Jess could see. It was even more secure than the prison had been. She almost expected to see security guards patrolling with dogs.

It was very quiet. Although the main road to Oxford was only a mile away, here, down this narrow country lane, there were no cars and no other signs of life – of the human kind, at least. There were plenty of birds singing and unidentified animals scuffling through the grass verges, although Jess could not see them. After living in London for the past three years, she found the quiet unnerving. It felt as though she could hear it; it was a presence and it made the hair on her neck rise slightly as though someone was watching her.

The gates were even bigger and more imposing at close quarters, the 'welcome' sign even more incongruous. Jess recognised it as the logo from the credits of Tavy's latest TV programme; her sister, a well-known style influencer and celebrity, was in the throes of redesigning a derelict country house for no other reason that Jess could see than that it was the latest in a long line of 'rescues' she had performed. Tavy's brand was to pick random neglected objects, whether abandoned kittens or vintage furniture, and give them a fresh start in life. Not that Jess watched many of Tavy's programmes, but she did know that her sister spent much of her life under a lens.

Someone *was* watching her, Jess realised. Two cameras were poised on posts above the gate, pointing beadily in her direction.

There was a shiny steel box with a bell on the wall by the gate. Jess pressed it. And waited.

The day was very still. No more than a hint of breeze stirred the bare branches of the trees. There was a whisper of spring in the air and clusters of primroses were growing wild on the bank inside the fence. Distant traffic noise came from the main road a mile away, blended with the drone of an aeroplane overhead and the cawing of whatever the big black birds were that clustered in the tops of the trees. Crows, rooks, jackdaws, Jess couldn't remember which was which. She didn't dislike the country, simply felt out of place in it.

'Fortune Hall.' The tinny voice from the metal box startled her. It sounded bored.

'Jess Yates to see Tavy Yates,' she said, adding, 'I'm her sister. I have an appointment.'

There was another agonisingly long pause. Jess pulled her coat more closely about her. The pale March sun had an edge of warmth to it, but here in the shadows, there was a chill. She got out her phone. If they didn't let her in soon, she would have to call Tavy direct. She hated doing that. Her sister always sounded in a mad rush and made her feel as though she was a nuisance.

There was a metallic clunk and a grinding sound, and the steel gate started to open. The 'Welcome to Fortune Hall' sign clattered against its spike. Jess ran back to the car, started the engine, thrust it into gear and shot through the gap before it could close again. She felt slightly out of breath as she watched the metal gate slam shut behind her.

'Trespassers will be prosecuted,' the sign at the side of the drive read. So much for the welcome to Fortune Hall. Tavy loved her fans, or so she always said, but, evidently, she didn't want them to get too close to her.

There was no one in sight, not even a building, nothing but a long drive lined with trees that disappeared over the top of a slight rise. Green lawns sloped away on either side, dotted with more trees. It looked like an expensively manicured golf course.

Jess drove slowly. Now that she was almost there, she felt a treacherous urge to turn around and flee back to London. Her friend Sammy had offered her a sofa to sleep on. At the same time, she had also offered her the advice that meant Jess couldn't accept it: 'This is a good opportunity to spend some time with your mum and your sister, Jess. You know how much you've regretted drifting apart from them.'

Jess paused, the view of elegant green lawns blurring suddenly and unexpectedly as her eyes misted with tears. She was tired and lonely and the memory of Sammy's words struck home. There had been no dramatic estrangement from her mother and younger sister, more a slow neglect. Tavy's life as a presenter and influencer had been a world away from her work at Canada Water Library in South London. They had had little in common as children and even less as adults, and after their father had died...

Jess clenched her hands around the steering wheel. *Focus*, she thought. *Breathe.*

A squirrel sauntered across the drive ahead of her and shot up a tree. She watched its bushy grey tail disappear and noticed that the trees were old, some with huge thick branches and hollowed-out trunks. A flicker of sensation feathered across her senses then, something that took her out of the tumble of nerves and preoccupations. Fortune Hall was on old land, a place with ancient roots that lay beneath Tavy's attempts to modernise and brand it in her own style. It had a life and an identity of its own that had existed centuries ago and Jess could feel the presence of that history all around her.

As the Mini crested the hill, Jess shook off the fanciful thought, only for it to return with greater force as she finally saw Fortune Hall over to her right at the foot of a slight hill, and beyond it a lake that gleamed silver in the faint spring sunshine.

The house was built of a grey limestone and should have looked dull, but it seemed to glitter in the light with the insubstantial air of a fairy castle. The basic shape was a rectangle, with two small wings attached that formed a U-shape around a modest courtyard. In a later period, someone had evidently added bay windows, a couple of balconies and some ill-advised turrets. The overall effect was of a house in fancy dress.

Then Jess saw the marquees on the lawn outside, the TV broadcast equipment, the lorries, lights and gantries, all the paraphernalia of filming, and when she looked at the house again, it had shrunk back to a plain, grey shell with no character, nothing more than an empty set for Tavy's series.

She parked a short distance away from the entrance and decided to leave her suitcase in the car for now.

The place was oddly silent; she couldn't see anyone from the camera crew and the door of the house, oak with studded ironwork, was firmly closed. No one came out to meet her.

Standing on the gravel, seeing the house at close quarters, Jess could see what had drawn Tavy to this particular tumbledown renovation project for her show. It looked so forlorn and dishevelled. Tavy's brand of taking something that was old or unloved and making it shiny and new again was perfect for this house.

There was no bell, so Jess raised her hand to knock at the door, but before she made contact, it swung open. Tavy was there, radiant in a scarlet, wide-legged jumpsuit with balloon sleeves. Behind her stood their mother in a floral playsuit, black tights and stilettoes, and behind *her*, an entire film crew, with cameras rolling.

'Jess!' Her sister enveloped her in a scented hug, teetering in high red platform heels. 'Welcome to Fortune Hall, babes. It's *so* good to see you again.'

Her silky fair hair brushed Jess's cheek and she hung on with determination even when Jess tried to break away from the hug. She'd never been big into public displays of affection, particularly with an audience, and there was a hell of an audience here. No one had warned her that her reunion with her sister would be televised.

The camera closed in on Tavy wiping a tear from the corner of her eye and lingered on Jess's face. It felt intrusive and wrong.

Jess stumbled backwards, almost tripping over the sumptuous multi-coloured rag rug on the polished wooden floor. What sort of expression she was wearing was anyone's guess – shock, horror, embarrassment, all three and more? She hadn't even brushed her hair and she was crumpled and travel-stained.

She hadn't seen many episodes of *Welcome to Fortune Hall* but she could imagine the voiceover for this one, that oleaginous actor Hal Price intoning, *'Can the stakes get any higher? Now it's not only the house that needs some love – can Tavy Yates work her magic on her own family, and heal the hurt? It's her biggest challenge yet...'*

Jess wondered how she could have been so naïve. She was the loser sister whose boyfriend had ruined so many people's lives. Tavy would pick her up, make her shiny and new again and her fans would call her a saint.

Never mind the house renovation, *she* was Tavy's latest rescue project.

2

ROSE – THE MARSHALSEA, LONDON, JULY 1671

This was the third time in my life that I had been in gaol.

The first time, I was thirteen and had stolen a loaf of bread so that Nell and I might eat. Although I was usually a quick and clever thief, that day I was slow and stupid. I was caught, imprisoned and branded with a 'T' on my wrist, to wear my shame publicly forever, so the judge decreed. Only the fact that I was a child restrained him from having me hanged.

The second time, I was fifteen and Nell was eleven. Our mother, who was habitually too drunk to turn a profit in her bawdy house, could not pay the rent and so we lost that roof from over our heads and were locked up for debt. By then, I was old enough to understand how to use any scrap of advantage I had. I sent a letter to the newly returned King Charles II asking for clemency on the grounds that our late father had supported him in the wars and lost his entire fortune in royal service. To my astonishment, the King ordered our release.

This time, the third, I was twenty-six years old and I was in gaol for treason. My crime was that I had been an accomplice in the attempted theft of the Crown Jewels.

Fortunately, there were several possibilities open to me before I was burned at the stake for my crime. I could plead marital coercion and blame everything on my husband. As he was a known highwayman and notorious villain, this had some authenticity.

I could claim I was quick with child, which I was – four months gone at least. The drawback to that would be that they could still condemn me to death after the babe was born and the mere thought of that turned my stomach to ice. No one and nothing was going to separate me from my child.

There was one more option. I could throw myself on the mercy of the one woman who might help me, the little sister from whom I had parted on bad terms three years before when I had married John Cassells and she had had the effrontery to tell me I was making a mistake.

'He's no good, Rose,' Nell had said bluntly. 'He's a wastrel. He'll come to a bad end and he will drag you down with him.'

How Nell would laugh to be proved correct. How I wished we had never argued over a man, least of all one as unworthy as John Cassells. But my pride was nothing compared to my life, and even more important was the future of my unborn baby. I had lost the last one. I would do everything in my power to protect this child, even beg Nell to help me.

I beckoned the gaoler over. She was a slovenly woman only a few years older than I at a guess, who spent half her time poking and pinching us for the fun of it and the other half drinking and flirting with the male warders. In my experience, the women gaolers were worse than the men, more cruel, more mean-spirited. It was a career of a sort for a woman who did not mind spending her days in the dank, stench-ridden bowels of the gaols, but living in perpetual dark had never appealed to me. The pay was but a fraction of a male warder so the females made up for it by stealing what small items they could take from their charges, beating us for the fun of it, pulling our hair. All of their frustrations had an easy target in the women in their care. This gaoler did not like me because I never tried to curry favour with her like the other women did, nor would I gossip. I suppose she had imagined that I would be a more tarnished version of my sister, a bawd and a bitch.

'Fetch the priest for me, if you please,' I said. I pressed a silver sixpence into her hand. Her eyes bulged a little when she saw it and I knew that if she had realised that I had coin hidden about me she would have robbed me of it before now.

'You planning on asking for the last rites, Your Majesty?' She laughed at her own wit, showing her blackened stumps of teeth. She called me 'majesty' or 'highness' all the time because of my crime. It amused her, but it had irritated me very quickly. 'Or perhaps you are intent on tying the knot?' she continued. 'Is there a gentleman here who takes your fancy? I can arrange a tryst if all you need is a quick swiving, for we cannot be sure if your husband is dead or alive, can we? You would not want to add bigamy to treason on the charge sheet, would you?'

'All I require is someone who can write,' I said coldly. It was a constant humiliation to me that I had no learning, our mother never having seen the need for either Nell nor I to be taught to read and write. She had not understood the importance of education, whereas I knew all too well the advantages it gave. With education, a man, or even a woman, could change their life. 'The priest, if you please,' I repeated. 'With a quill, ink and parchment.'

'Of course, your highness,' she said, pocketing the additional penny I offered and dropping a mocking curtsey. 'You have the manner of a nob, that's for sure, even if you have nothing else!'

I supposed that the gaoler was right. I did have a certain peremptoriness of manner and very little on which to base it. *'Never forget, girls, that you are the daughters of a gentleman,'* Mother had frequently told us when we were children. In practice, it had meant nothing at all since our father had died years before and we were nobodies. Yet perhaps I had cultivated an unconscious sense of authority alongside my criminal tendencies, or perhaps I simply had a managing nature. One of us had to be practical, and Mother was usually too drunk and Nell had her head in the clouds.

The priest came. I heard the clank of the iron door, the squeak of rusty metal on metal as it opened. A fresh breeze momentarily stirred the rank air of the cell, where twenty of us were huddled together in the corners like blind mice.

'Has someone else died?' the woman beside me asked, turning her face towards the lantern light, eyes wide with fear. She was shaking constantly, the ragged shreds of her gown rustling.

'No,' I said. 'Do not trouble yourself. All is well.'

In gaol at thirteen, the sight of such pitiful wretches had shocked me; now I was hardened to it and grateful that my spirit was stronger, but how much longer it would remain so was a moot point. I shuddered. I had to get out.

'Her over there,' the gaoler said, pointing to me. 'She was the one what called you in.'

The priest squatted beside me on the cobbled floor, close enough that I could smell him: a mix of pomade from his hair and old sweat from his dirty robes. My throat closed with revulsion, though I have smelled much worse in my time. He tilted his head towards me, the better to hear, for it was noisy with the shouts and screams of the madwomen and the chatter of the other girls echoing from the stone walls.

'Write this,' I said. I was pretending that I wanted a scribe because I was a lady; the truth of my illiteracy shamed me. 'Dearest Nell,' I began. 'Out of the love you bear me, I beg that you will help me now that I am in such dire need.'

I stopped. Was that too much? I could not be sure, although I could easily imagine my sister throwing back her head as she heard this appeal and laughing until she cried. She would know that the words were forced out of me; that I hated asking for anything from her as a point of principle.

'If not for me,' I continued, 'then I pray you to help me for the sake of the babe.' Nell was a mother too; I thought that that might stir some pity in her. 'I beseech you to plead with the King for me and free me from this place,' I said, whilst the priest's pen scratched across the parchment and he squinted in the pale light from the lantern, 'before both I and my baby perish.'

'A nice touch, mistress,' the priest said. 'Sure to melt the stoniest heart.'

'I am truly penitent of my crime,' I finished, 'and my gratitude will know no bounds.'

'Well put, mistress,' the priest conceded, showing his tombstone teeth in a grin. 'Who could resist? Do you wish to sign it with your mark?'

I hesitated, then took the quill and scratched a shaky cross on the letter. Shame stirred in me again that I could not even write my own name, and with it a fury that I had to pay this charlatan to put down my words, then pay him again to deliver them. He would charge dearly, particularly when he knew where the letter was going.

My money was almost all spent. I knew that when the priest had left, I would need to go out into the yard and beg for pennies from the passers-by who peered at us through the prison bars. We were the entertainment for the idle gawkers who came to jeer and crow over us, but we needed them too for their occasional charity paid for us to stay alive. The thought sent another rush of urgency through me. I almost pushed the priest away.

'Take it to number seventy-nine, Pall Mall,' I said, holding out a half guinea. I took a deep breath. 'Make sure it gets into the hands of Madam Eleanor Gwyn herself.'

The priest was so focused on the pale shine of the coin that for a moment the name failed to register with him.

It was the gaoler, listening in as usual, who gave a squawk. 'Nell Gwyn?' she said. She gave a cackle of laughter. 'Nell Gwyn! *She* won't help you! Don't you know they asked her about you when first Colonel Blood tried to steal the jewels? No one could believe you were her sister, she so witty and pretty, and you neither of those, and a criminal to boot! She said that both you and that fancy highwayman husband of yours were dead to her. *She* isn't going to want the likes of *you* bringing her down.' And she put her hands on her hips and laughed at the idea until the tears ran.

I was afraid that the gaoler was right, but I would not give her the satisfaction of admitting it. Besides, I did not know how much truth there was in her words. Gossip and rumour ran through the staff and inmates of the gaol like rats through a sewer, but not all of the information was accurate. In the six weeks I had been in the Marshalsea, I had heard that Thomas Blood had not only been pardoned of his crime in attempting to steal the Crown Jewels from the Tower of London, but that the King himself had received him and granted him estates in Ireland. It was said that he was lording it round court, full of swagger and pride. That in itself was so ridiculous as to be unbelievable to me.

I had heard that my husband John, who had been one Thomas Blood's accomplices, had either been killed or had absconded abroad, no one seemed to know which. And I had heard that until they found John one way or the other, I would be held as surety for him, as well as a conspirator in my own right. It seemed not to matter that Thomas Blood had been freed; I would not be. Such was the lack of logic by which justice was served in London, and being a woman, and a destitute one at that, I had no way to challenge it.

Well, I had one way. Through Nell's intervention, there was a small possibility I might be pardoned. But that would require so many things to go right, when lately everything had gone wrong.

The priest had gone, concerned perhaps that he might be robbed for his half guinea if he lingered in this nest of thieves.

'He'll cheat you,' one of the other girls said, looking at his retreating back as he scurried away down the corridor. 'He's no real parson.'

'He can be the devil himself for all I care,' I said, 'as long as he delivers the message to my sister.'

Her gaze swung back to me. She was staring, eyes bright in a face smeared with dirt. Lank strands of hair hung down to her shoulders. Her gown was torn. I felt sick all of a sudden to be such a figure of curiosity. I had always hated the attention that Nell revelled in. 'Nell Gwyn,' she said. 'Only fancy!' There was admiration in her voice, as though Nell was someone who had achieved something particularly fine in life, which perhaps she had.

I had long observed that whilst the nobility might be contemptuous of my sister's position as the King's mistress, the ordinary people loved her. They saw her as one of them, a girl from the backstreets of London who had risen to consort with the highest in the land. The truth was rather more complicated, but Nell, the consummate actress, played on their loyalty and support, especially now that the King had a new French mistress who was almost universally hated.

'What is she like?' the woman asked.

I knew she wanted an insight that no one but Nell's sister could give, a special glimpse into the secret life of a public figure, but my mind was blank. I thought of all the quarrels that Nell and I had had over the past twenty years and the way we had drifted apart, firstly because as we grew up the difference in our characters had become very apparent, and then, later, because John had forced such a wedge between us. How had we become so estranged? I wondered, feeling suddenly tired. Blood should have been thicker than water. I could only hope it would prove to be so now.

The woman was still looking at me expectantly. 'Nell cannot cook,' I said randomly. 'And she is the untidiest person I ever knew.'

The woman looked disappointed at such a banal response, but it was the best I could do.

I turned my back on her, leaned my head against the mouldy, dripping wall and closed my eyes whilst I thought about how I, who shunned attention as much as Nell loved it, had become the most notorious woman in London.

* * *

It had all begun back in January. It was a harsh winter. The shutters rattled with storms and the cold crept under the door of our tenement to freeze us in our bed. On the night I met Thomas Blood, however, huge snowflakes were drifting gently down between the misshapen chimneys and huddled roofs of London. They made the city look magical, hiding for a brief time the dirt and decay.

John, my husband, was in a good mood, that evening and for once it was not induced by drink.

'Your sister performs tonight in Mr Dryden's new play, *The Conquest of Granada*,' he said, seated by the fire, his clay pipe in hand. 'They are saying it is her last performance, now that she has produced a whelp for the King.'

Even though Nell and I were not close, I detested it when people spoke disparagingly of her, especially a man like John, who was far looser in his morals than Nell had ever been. For the sake of peace though, I held my tongue. I was tired of quarrelling with him and it felt as though that was all we had done these several months past.

'They are always claiming it to be Nell's last performance,' I said. 'It means they can charge more to see the play.'

'I thought we might go,' John said. 'The theatre and then a hot pie and a drink at the alehouse. What do you say, Rose?'

He got up and came over to enfold me in an enormous hug. His clothes smelled of damp, tobacco and sweat. I pushed him away, ostensibly because I had my hands full of dirty laundry, but mostly because, these days, I could not bear his touch, not after what had happened the last time he had been in his cups.

'You are very flush all of a sudden,' I remarked. 'How may we afford such indulgence?'

John seldom had any work, at least not honest toil, as he felt manual labour was beneath a man who claimed to be the heir to a baronetcy and had once been an officer in the King's army. I suspected he was no more a baronet than I was a duchess, and he had certainly never been a soldier. The only time he made any money was when he robbed travellers out on the dark streets at night. He called himself a highwayman and expected the respect due to such a villain, but, in truth, he could not ride and owned no horse, which made him no more than a common footpad.

'Ask no questions.' He tapped the side of his nose at me. 'I have a business arrangement with a gentleman. It promises to be lucrative.'

I sighed. Whatever it was, it was bound to be illegal, but at least there would be more money. Whilst I scrubbed floors and washed dishes in the inns, took in laundry and peddled goods in the markets to scrape together what pennies I could, winters were the worst times because John was too lazy to go out to rob people in the bad weather. This scheme, whatever it was, must be taking place within doors.

In the end, we did go to the theatre, I seeing no reason to refuse an outing that would involve a hot meal prepared by someone else. John, still in expansive mood, bought us seats in the pit and I was glad I had worn my best lace-trimmed bodice and embroidered skirt. I had never been able to compete with Nell in terms of looks, for I was taller and larger all round, with hair of a darker auburn and eyes of hazel. Nell, in contrast, was a pocket goddess with fiery red hair and bright blue eyes.

There was a buzz when we took our seats and John loved that, adoring being noticed as the brother-in-law of the leading lady, even though that leading lady scorned us both. For me, the memories of the theatre were different; I had not been sorry to put it behind me. Nell and I had worked there for Orange Moll when we were little more than children, selling fruit and sweetmeats. It had been Nell's pathway to the stars, but for me it had been no more than achingly hard work for the pittance of the few pennies Moll spared us. As I grew older and less winsome, the ladies stopped cooing over me, but some of the men still wanted to pinch my cheek and much more besides. It was a grubby world of powder and pretence. Nell saw the glamour in it, but I only saw abuse and manipulation.

Now, I watched the orange girls dart among the crowds, selling their wares and the promise of themselves, carrying messages from gallants to ladies; I smelled the remembered scent of the candle wax and sawdust, and felt the press of sweaty bodies. I heard the whisper run through the audience: 'It is Rose... Rose Gwyn... The sister who became a thief rather than a bawd...' Self-consciously, I touched the brand on my wrist, the indelible mark that condemned me as a criminal. It could be hidden but it could never be erased.

Nell was superb, of course. The torches dimmed, she sauntered on to speak the prologue, and the house immediately went wild. She lit up the stage with her wit and her presence. For a few brief hours, the theatre was a magical place that carried us all away from our humdrum cares. I was not immune to Nell's skill, only deeply envious of it. I always had been, ever since I had realised that she had the ability to act, and, as such, to escape, whilst I had the quick wits but no talent.

Nell did not so much as glance my way. I felt the sense of regret rise when I thought about our quarrel. I had been enamoured with the idea of marriage and the pretence of respectability it brought with it, and I had not wanted to hear Nell's assessment of John's character. It was doubly annoying that she had been proved correct about him. John was indeed a bully, a braggart and a drunkard, as I had discovered for myself all too quickly.

At the end of the evening, the cheers threatened to bring down the rafters, the thunderous clapping making the building shake to its foundations. We applauded too and Nell bowed and kissed her hand to everyone, dazzling, the darling of the crowd, and yet as far removed from me now as she could possibly be. She had that talent of giving the impression that she was still the same as everyone else and people loved her for her lack of snobbery. You could see it in their faces. They thought she was one of them, but I knew better. She had left us all behind.

As the good-natured crowd spilled out into the snowy street, looking for a link boy to light them home or, in the case of the nobles and gentry, their carriages in the melee outside, John slipped my hand through his arm and steered me towards The White Hart Inn. Covent Garden was full of people with the same idea, all jostling to get out of the cold and continue the evening's entertainment.

At the side of the road, a brazier glowed warm and filled the air with the sweet nutty scent of chestnuts. Further along, another vendor was offering hot baked apples. John grabbed one in passing and tossed a few pennies to the street seller as though he were a lord. He bit into it heartily and swore when it burned his mouth. I was afraid he might turn back to berate the man who'd sold it, so I tugged on his arm and quickened my step.

'We shall be fortunate even to get within doors,' I remarked, brushing the snow out of my eyes and shrinking more deeply within my cloak. It was cold and I needed hot food to warm me. 'All the world seems to be out on the town tonight.'

'Thomas will have secured us a place,' John said confidently, his bad temper forgotten. 'No one refuses him.'

I had some curiosity then to see this man with whom John had entered into business and who could apparently secure a spare seat in a busy alehouse.

As we entered, John pushing his way forcefully through the crowd, a man equal in height and bulk to him rose from a table right beside the fire and gestured to us to join him. I recognised him, having seen him once before, preening and parading himself at Whitehall with the infamous Duke of Buckingham. It was Colonel Thomas Blood, a soldier and adventurer who was said to do the duke's dirty work for him, a man without morals or conscience.

'Why, it is Colonel Blood,' I said. I shot John a glance. 'You are in deep waters now, are you not?'

John's hand gripped my arm almost too tightly. I sensed bluster in him but also nervousness. Thomas Blood was a man who would make most other men quail, and women too. I felt a shiver of revulsion run down my spine.

'Be nice to him,' he hissed at me, dragging me behind him through the crowd.

Thomas Blood was all smiles as he stood to greet us and kiss my hand, pressing his wet lips against it for rather too long. 'A rose indeed,' he murmured, smiling into my eyes. 'A pleasure to meet you, mistress.'

'This rose has more thorns than sweet flowers,' John said, and roared with laughter at his own witticism as he gestured for me to sit beside the man on the settle by the fire.

I cast him a sharp glance. I didn't trust him and was suspicious about this encounter. Was Thomas Blood looking for a mistress? It would not be the first time that John had tried to whore me out, though I had told him before in no uncertain terms that I would not do it. John had seen it as just another way to make money when times were hard despite the fact that I was his wife. Such niceties, I had discovered, did not count with him. And there were men who would offer good coin to be able to say that they had bedded the sister of the King's whore.

The colonel grinned and raised a hand to summon the barmaid, who darted over with plates piled high with steaming beef pudding. My mouth watered. I resolved that if I needed to walk out in high dudgeon, I would take the pie with me.

'I might have guessed as much,' the colonel said, sloshing ale into the beaker beside him, 'from Madam Eleanor Gwyn's sister.'

John and he, in great good humour, dug into their pies and seemed in no hurry to tell me the detail of their plan. I decided not to ask. The food was, for the moment, more important.

Around us, the chatter and bustle of the ale house swirled, the air thick with beer and the rich smell of meat. No one paid us much attention. Thieves and criminals were common here. A highwayman sat in the corner by the door, smoking a clay pipe and counting his gold; a couple of dishevelled gentlemen played cribbage over by the privy entrance. Peg Cherry, the barmaid, was leaning over the next table to pour the customers more ale, tossing her black curls as she flirted with them, her breasts almost falling out of her gown. Both John and Thomas Blood were staring at her cleavage like a pair of youths whose tongues were hanging out.

'So, mistress,' Blood said, dragging his gaze from Peg and wiping the back of his hand over his fleshy lips, 'you will be wondering what this is all about.'

'In your own good time, sir,' I said, but the sarcasm passed directly over him, which was probably just as well.

He belched several times and patted his belly, which was straining at the gold buttons of his waistcoat.

'My friend and I—' he nodded to John '—have a plan to rob the Tower of London and steal the Crown Jewels.'

I almost spat out my mouthful of ale.

Colonel Blood slapped me on the back as I choked. When I had got my breath back, I glanced over my shoulder instinctively to see if anyone had overheard him, but everyone was intent on their own business.

'I beg your pardon,' I said, eyes streaming. 'I thought you said you planned to steal the Crown Jewels. But surely no one could be so foolhardy.'

John shifted on the bench, looking a little uncomfortable at what he perceived to be an insult, but fortunately Colonel Blood seemed to take it as a compliment on his daring.

'No madness, I assure you, madam,' he said, 'but a cunning plan for the highest of rewards.'

At least a dozen reasons came swiftly into my mind as to why stealing the Crown Jewels would be anything but a cunning plan. I did not voice them. There was no point; neither man would listen and John would only become angry to be called a fool. I bit down hard on the inside of my mouth to stop myself blurting out my thoughts. I knew I could be impulsive and I knew the price I paid for it.

'You need not know the details of course,' Blood said carelessly, taking another swig of his ale, 'for I doubt they would make sense to you, and a woman can never hold her tongue, so best you know nothing other than your own part in this.'

'*My* part?' I almost choked again at the implication that I should have a role in this ludicrous scheme. It was one thing to keep quiet whilst John ruined his life but quite another to be forced to participate in my own downfall.

'Aye, madam.' Blood leaned close to me all of a sudden, his hectically flushed face only inches from mine, his breath foul. 'I need someone on watch on Tower Pier on the day of the robbery, someone who can sound a warning if anything goes awry, provide a distraction, perhaps, should we need to affect an escape. Can you do that?'

'I could,' I said, 'but—'

'There is no option of refusal,' Blood interrupted. 'John will explain that to you if you do not understand.'

I did not dare glance at my husband. I could sense he was wound as tight as a vice, as tight as the anger I also sensed wound up in Colonel Blood. Men like that were dangerous on so many levels, physically large and strong, given to violence. We women walked a tightrope beside them. I already knew what would happen if I refused. The last time I had defied John, he had beaten me, and after that, I had told him I would kill him if he laid a hand on me ever again. If I failed to do his bidding now, I would have to make good on that promise, and if I killed him, I would be hanged for it.

I felt the familiar weight of fury and frustration settle inside me. I was trapped. Digging my nails into the palms of my hands, I tried to calm my racing heart. My mother had married the son of a gentleman and had imagined herself set up for life as a result. How illusory that had turned out to be and how swift our fall into the gutter. Nell had scrambled her way out of poverty via the theatre, ruthlessly using all the talents she possessed to climb the ladder to freedom. She might live in comfort now, but that was entirely dependent on the whim of the King. And I had married John, tired of fending for myself and thinking him a strong man who would protect me, only to realise that I had to protect myself *from* him. It was a mistake that haunted me.

I had no illusions that John would share any of his ill-gotten gains with me even if he were able to pull off this ridiculous theft, but it did occur to me that for once we might have some money and I would be able to steal a part of it when John was insensible with drink, and run away to make a better life for myself. It was not much of a plan, I knew that, but it was something, and it was enough to pull me out of my torpor and inspire me to fight again.

'Very well,' I said. 'I will play my part.'

'Of course you will,' Thomas Blood said, bellowing with laughter. And he and my husband set out to get roaring drunk.

I left them when Thomas was three sheets to the wind and regaling a keen audience with boasts of his exploits in the Dutch Wars and John was fondling Peg Cherry, who was perched on his lap regardless of the fact that I was sitting next to them. I trudged back to Three Kites Alley through the falling snow, the cold piercing my boots, and I reflected as I went that this foolish plot would surely never come about for neither John nor Colonel Blood had the discretion needed to keep a secret. In that I was wrong, and in another matter also, for I should have been more suspicious of the whole affair. I should have wondered at Thomas Blood's complacency, for even for a man so confident in his own negligible abilities, he seemed strangely relaxed about a plot that anyone with any sense could see was madness and would never succeed.

Now, within the dank and dripping walls of the Marshalsea gaol, with the shrieks and screams of the mad and starving around me, I went over once again the circumstances that had brought me here and reflected that I should have realised from the start that it was not a simple case of robbery, but a deep and complicated game of treason and betrayal that I had been drawn into. Yet it is easy to be wise after the event, and after the event, it is also too late.

3

JESS – THE PRESENT

'Well done, babes,' Tavy said, flashing Jess an approving smile. 'You're a natural on TV! I'm sorry I didn't warn you beforehand that we'd be filming your arrival—' she spread her hands appealingly '—but with the show, it's all about authenticity. You'd have reacted quite differently if you'd known, all stiff and awkward, and we would have had to have done endless retakes.' She shrugged one slender scarlet-clad shoulder, put down her e-cigarette and exhaled a grapefruit-scented cloud. 'Anyway, it was great. You were great.'

The camera crew had packed up for the day and gone home, leaving just a few of Tavy's team: Ed, her PA, and Francesca, her psychic, who was an intense woman clad all in black who had greeted Jess with the slightly chilling words, 'I sense some dissonance in your aura.'

Jess, Tavy and their mother were sitting in what Tavy referred to as the parlour, a small room at the side of the house, with an open fireplace and panelled walls. It was clear that the renovators hadn't got this far yet – it looked like something from the denouement of an Agatha Christie novel where the suspects were assembled in a room with mismatched velvet chairs and sofas, threadbare curtains and hunting pictures with dead pheasants. It was also very cold and there was an odd atmosphere. Jess disliked it intensely.

'I'm not sure I want to be in the show, actually,' she said, feeling it was important to make this clear to Tavy from the start. 'It's not my thing. And with all the horrible publicity there's been around Jared's arrest, I'd just rather hide away quietly.' She stopped. She'd seen the look that had come into Tavy's eyes and the stubborn set of her jaw. Jess recognised it from their childhood. It meant that her sister was determined to get her own way and wasn't prepared to consider any alternative point of view. After a moment, though, Tavy shrugged again and drew on the e-cigarette.

'See how you feel after the weekend,' she said easily. 'There's no need to decide now.' She swung around to gesture to their mother, who was sitting in an armchair flicking through a magazine. 'Mum's loving being involved, aren't you, Mum?'

Mrs Yates looked up, smiling. Her eyes, a paler blue than Tavy's, were soft and kind, albeit a little vacant. 'It's great, hon. I love it here.'

Tavy made an 'I told you so' gesture.

Jess bit her tongue. Their mother had been Tavy's most successful rescue so far. After the death of their father from a heart attack ten years before, Una Yates had self-medicated with alcohol and tried to take her own life. Tavy had paid for her to get the best treatment and, gradually, Una had emerged into some semblance of normal life again, if it was in any way normal to be a part of Tavy's celebrity entourage. Jess admired her sister for the determined way she had helped their mother, but she wished it hadn't all taken place in the media spotlight. It felt as though every inch of their family life was mercilessly exposed for profit, and now she was going to be added to the soap opera.

She put down the mug of coffee that Ed had made for her. It was cold now and couldn't ward off the chill in the parlour, which Tavy and their mother both seemed strangely immune to. Perhaps she was the only one who felt an odd atmosphere here and perhaps that was only because she was so tired and felt dislocated from everything that was familiar.

'I had another project for you I thought you'd be interested in.' Despite saying they wouldn't discuss Jess's future role any more, Tavy had returned to the subject almost immediately. The impatient tapping of her foot in the red stilettos told Jess she was determined to get her sister to agree. 'The history of the house is really interesting. There's a story Nell Gwyn lived here, although there are no records to prove it.' Tavy tossed her hair over her shoulder. 'I thought it would be fun for you to look into it – find out more about Nell and her connection to Fortune Hall. She's a great character – the producers are really keen to include a bit of educational content, but nothing too heavy. They thought Nell might be an interesting angle.'

So now Tavy was co-opting a three-hundred-year-old celebrity into her reality show, Jess thought. But she didn't say anything because actually the idea did have a sort of appeal to her. She'd studied history and had worked at the Bodleian in Oxford and at the British Library for a while. The toxic mess around Jared's arrest had led her to resign from her latest library position so she could take some extended time to sort her life out, but books and history were still her big passions. This was the first time in months, apart from when she had first seen Fortune Hall, that she had felt a flicker of interest in anything.

'That sounds good,' she agreed. 'Perhaps I could dig around in the history of the estate, that sort of thing?'

'Be my guest,' Tavy said. It was clear she was bored with the idea already. 'You could start in the library,' she added. 'There's a stack of old stuff in there that I'm sending to a house clearance firm to sort out.'

'You're sending *books* to a house clearance company?' Jess felt shocked. 'But if they're old, there might be something valuable!' Then, seeing Tavy's look of utter indifference, she added quickly, 'At least let me sort through them all first to check.'

'Do whatever you like,' Tavy replied, waving the matter aside, 'but you'll have to be quick because they're taking them away sometime next week.'

There was a knock, and Ed stuck his head around the door. 'Apologies for the interruption,' he said, 'but Ethan Sterling is here about the plans for the orangery.'

Tavy checked the delicate gold watch on her wrist. She looked intensely irritated. 'Damn it, I don't have time to talk to him. Did I tell you to ask him to come today?'

'Yup,' Ed said. He grinned, unabashed. 'Bad time, huh?'

'It's never a good time to see Mr Sterling,' Tavy said. 'Get rid of him for me?' Then, in an abrupt switch of tone, 'And could we have some more coffee and cake, Ed? I need some carbs, but don't tell the fans!' She gave him a flashing smile.

'Sure,' Ed replied.

Tavy had not thanked him, Jess noticed, switching her attention away from him the minute the door closed and dropping the practised smile. It seemed to Jess that she didn't see Ed as a real person, just an incredibly efficient part of the machinery. It had been Ed who, when Jess had arrived, had extracted her from Tavy's iron grip on camera, arranged for her bags to be brought in and shown her where the cloakroom was. He'd been a lot more friendly than the rest of Tavy's 'people', especially Francesca. In the midst of all the madness, Ed seemed like the only sane person around. Jess rather liked him and didn't like seeing Tavy treat him – or anyone, for that matter – with such dismissiveness. As for Ethan Sterling, whoever he was, he'd obviously got short shrift as well.

Tavy's bright blue gaze was narrowed on her in a speculative way and Jess realised her sister was still thinking about how she might present her on screen. She looked down at her faded jeans and striped sweater and felt sharply self-conscious. Tavy always looked amazing, but Jess didn't want to be dressed by her. She didn't want to be restyled the way their mother had been.

'I'll gladly do some historical research,' she said, to divert her sister from raising the subject of the documentary again, 'but you also said in your texts that you wanted me to act as housekeeper here. Perhaps you could give me an idea of what that will entail? Then I'll go and settle in and let you get on with all the other stuff you've got to do. We can catch up properly later.'

'Oh, Ed will tell you all about the job,' Tavy said, brushing it aside. 'He's been dealing with all the domestic side of things.' She stretched luxuriously, like a cat. 'But I'll show you to your room before Mum and I head off for the weekend.'

'What?' Jess stared at her. 'You're going away?' So much for her cosy plan for the three of them to sit down together over the weekend and start to reconnect as a family, away from the camera's gaze.

'I'm not here very much at all, to be fair,' Tavy said. 'It's a job, you know? And not one I'm really enjoying.'

Jess's mouth dropped open. 'I thought you lived here,' she said. 'In the programme, you say you do.'

Tavy gave her trademark belly laugh. It sat oddly with her fragile appearance but her fans seemed to like the contrast and it was one of the things about her that was in fact the most authentic. Jess could remember her laughing like that when they were children, doubled up, eyes sparkling with mirth. It wasn't so funny now, though.

'You thought I lived in this building site in the middle of nowhere?' Tavy dried her eyes. 'What, with no gym and pool?' She pulled a face. 'Nah, it's not my sort of place at all.'

Jess shut her mouth with a snap. The dream of cosy family time withered a little bit more.

'Mum chose the house,' Tavy was saying, 'because I don't really mind which crumbling ruin we do up as long as it's proper old and will look great when it's finished.' She shrugged. 'Anyway, part of the deal with the TV company is that Mum and I stay at the Old Bank Hotel in Oxford when we film down here. I'm travelling all over the place with other projects as well at the moment.' She turned away, fiddling with her phone, her hair falling across her face, hiding her expression. 'We're not going to be seeing that much of each other,' she added slowly. 'I'm so busy, you see.'

Una looked up from the magazine, more at Tavy's change of tone than the words. 'Tavy's a big star,' she said happily. 'Everyone wants her to do stuff.'

Jess realised she'd misread the situation entirely. Tavy had reached out to offer sisterly support, but it hadn't been so that the three of them could spend time together. She was getting a free member of staff, and as a bonus she'd also planned on incorporating Jess into the TV show. Win-win. As for their mother, she'd hugged Jess after Tavy had and said, 'How are you, pet?' but whilst Jess was trying to think of a reply, she'd drifted away.

Even though she felt hurt and snappy, Jess decided to go for upbeat. There was no point in provoking a quarrel. She'd only just arrived. 'Well,' she said brightly, 'I'm still grateful for the bolthole and the job. It'll tide me over until I get back on my feet.'

Tavy nodded approvingly. 'That's the spirit,' she said. 'Now that rat Jared is locked up, you can get on with your life.'

Jess swallowed hard. 'I'm really sorry about the way you were dragged into the newspaper stories,' she started to say, but Tavy wasn't going there. She brushed the words aside.

'Not your fault, babes,' she said. 'As soon as they found out he was related to someone famous they were bound to use that angle.' She toyed with her phone, clearly keen to avoid a difficult conversation.

Jess felt a sharp pang of regret that they had drifted so far apart. Or perhaps they hadn't been that close to begin with? She and Octavia had always been like chalk and cheese, Tavy the sparkling wit, talented at acting, singing, dancing, the performer, all glitter and surface gloss. Jess felt exhausted when she compared herself to her sister. She was the older, duller one, the one who couldn't even claim to be sensible and responsible any more since she had made such a hash of her life. She pushed the thought aside, not wanting to dwell on it.

'Is there a specific reason why you need a live-in housekeeper,' she asked, 'given that you're not here all that much?'

'It's the insurance,' Una said suddenly, looking up from a spread of the Princess of Wales's ballgowns that she was peering at in a magazine. 'Someone has to keep an eye on the house twenty-four/seven.'

'That's right.' Tavy smiled at their mother as though she had said something particularly clever. 'I pay a security firm to patrol the grounds, but legally I have to have someone living here whilst the building work's being done in order for the insurance to be valid. The house-sitting agencies charge a fortune and the last couple who stayed here walked out because they said the place had a spooky vibe. To be fair, Francesca agrees. She says several people have died here – at least three in the house and one in the lake,' she added matter-of-factly.

'That's very specific,' Jess commented. 'But when a house is five hundred years old, I'd expect that.' She wasn't a great believer in the supernatural, but even so, stuff about death and hauntings was not what she wanted to hear when she was going to be alone at Fortune Hall. 'I suppose if the renovation doesn't work out, you could always make a show called Tavy's Haunted House instead.'

'Hey, that's a cool idea.' Her sister brightened. 'I'll talk to my agent about it.' She pulled a face. 'To be honest, the renovation is dragging on because of planning laws and building regulations and boring stuff like that. We hadn't anticipated it would be so slow.' She rolled her eyes. 'That's why Ethan Sterling keeps hanging around. He's the historic buildings consultant for the council, or something tedious like that, and he's determined to keep to the letter of the planning consent. The lawyers told me they had it all sorted, but clearly they don't, and it's costing me a fortune.' She tapped her fingers thoughtfully on the arm of the chair. 'The haunted house thing might be a way to change tack, or even get out of the show.' She yawned. 'It's boring me, to be honest.'

'You always did have a short attention span,' their mother said unexpectedly. 'Jess was the steady one. You always wanted excitement, Octavia.'

Irritation flashed across Tavy's face, quickly dismissed. 'Yeah, Mum,' she said, 'you're right. Being steady didn't do Jess much good, though, did it?'

Ouch. Jess repressed a wince at her sister's insensitivity. Her mum went back to her magazine.

Tavy rolled her eyes at Jess. 'Francesca says that this is the wrong project for me,' she said moodily. 'I wish she'd had that insight earlier. I'd already signed the contract with the TV company when the message came through.'

Jess resisted the urge to make a sarcastic remark about the spirits and their sense of timing. She knew it was going to be hard not to rise to Tavy's provocations. It was lucky she'd already decided to start looking for a more permanent job as soon as possible.

'I don't know where that coffee and cake has got to,' Tavy grumbled, getting up. 'Come on, Jess, I'll show you round.'

'Is there any heating?' Jess asked. She wished she could decamp to the hotel in Oxford as well, but that was definitely not on offer. She was cold, tired and hungry, but Tavy had given her a roof over her head and at least the strings that turned out to be attached didn't seem too onerous.

'There's an open fire in your bedroom,' Tavy said. 'You remember all that fire-lighting stuff from the Guides, right?'

She wasn't joking, Jess realised.

Jess followed her sister out of the parlour and down a stone-flagged corridor. She hadn't quite got the hang of the layout of the house yet. The impression of a mysterious warren of rooms was accentuated by the general air of dishevelment, with peeling paint, wires hanging down from the ceiling in a concerning manner, and ladders propped against the wall. Jess, who had acted as health and safety officer for her department in the British Library, shuddered.

They went down the long corridor into a room that was a jarring contrast to all the dark wood and stone, with steel appliances, white cabinets and a big farmhouse table.

'My kitchen,' Tavy said happily and with no sign of irony, though Jess doubted she ever made even a sandwich for herself these days. 'Isn't it gorgeous?'

It was. It also had an Aga that was giving out waves of warmth. Jess thought that if the bedroom was too cold, she might sleep next to it, like a dog.

Ed came in just as Tavy was grumbling about the lack of coffee.

'Sorry,' he said. 'Ethan wanted to see the orangery. He has a few questions about your plan to turn it into a swimming pool complex, Tavy.'

'I'll bet he does,' Tavy said. 'Mr Sterling always tries to stop me doing what I want.'

'It's my sole purpose in life,' a voice from the doorway said.

Jess spun around. The voice was deep and resonant with a natural air of authority. It also held an undertone of sardonic amusement.

A man was standing in the opening, hands in the pockets of his fleece jacket. He was not exceptionally tall, a little above medium height, but he filled the space by giving the impression of durability. Beneath the fleece, he wore a crisply ironed white shirt. A pair of chinos and boots completed a look that set him apart in Tavy's high-end kitchen with its dazzling white surfaces and vases of tiger lilies. He had wind-blown dark hair and green eyes in a face that was strong and compelling. Jess understood immediately why Tavy would dislike him. There was something very solid and unmovable about him; he would not let her sister get her own way, and Tavy hated opposition.

He was also a lot younger than Jess had imagined from the way that Tavy had referred to him as 'Mr Sterling'. Although there were lines of experience at the corners of his eyes and bracketing his mouth, he wasn't the elderly historian she had envisaged, not by a long chalk. He was perhaps in his early thirties, only a few years older than she was. The most disconcerting thing about him, however, was that he seemed familiar to her. She was absolutely certain they had never met before and yet, as soon as she had seen him, she'd felt a curious pang of recognition, as though she had known him for years. Judging by the arrested look in his eyes, quickly veiled, he had had the same reaction to her.

'Coffee, Ethan?' Ed broke the silence, pressing the button on the shiny Barista Express.

'No thanks,' Ethan said. 'I'll head off now. But I'll be back tomorrow to finish the appraisal so I can get Ms Yates—' again the note of sarcasm '—a quick and thorough report.'

'My housekeeper will be here to deal with it.' Tavy didn't even look up from her phone. Jess started to wonder if the antagonism between them was actually based on attraction. Ethan Sterling was hot, albeit not Tavy's usual type.

'Housekeeper,' Jess repeated, trying not to feel to peeved at her sister's dismissive tone. 'That would be me.' She stepped forward. As Tavy clearly wasn't going to introduce them, she'd do it herself. 'Jess Yates.' She extended a hand and risked a smile. 'I'm Tavy's sister.'

Ethan's grip was firm and brief. The sense of recognition was much stronger as soon as he touched her and it was all Jess could do not to react. What was wrong with her? She felt as though she had had too much sun.

'How do you do, Ms Yates,' Ethan said. This time, there was no indication he had felt the same shock of affinity that she had.

'Call me Jess. Too many Ms Yates can be confusing.' Jess smiled at him. She didn't want to get off on the wrong foot with Ethan just because Tavy was churlish to him.

Ethan's mouth curved into a faint answering smile. 'Good to meet you, Jess,' he said. He took out his phone. 'Is 10 a.m. tomorrow convenient for the orangery survey or is that too early?'

'It's fine,' Jess agreed. She doubted very much that she'd be sleeping in. The combination of a strange house and everything that was on her mind would keep her awake for sure, and hopefully by the morning, the strange effect Ethan had on her would have disappeared. She was probably just tired.

Ethan nodded, raised a hand in farewell to Ed, and walked out. Tavy finally looked up from the phone.

'I hate that guy,' she grumbled.

'No, you don't.' Ed gave her a mug of coffee. 'You just don't like people who get in your way.'

Ed certainly had her sister's number, Jess thought. That made the dynamic between them more interesting. Jess wondered if Tavy was aware of how much Ed liked her. It was clear to see in the way he watched her. But Tavy was so self-centred, maybe she took it for granted, or perhaps she hadn't even noticed Ed's admiration. With his warm brown eyes and ready smile, he was very cute, but Jess reflected that Tavy would want much more than that. She was, after all, dating Hunter Blake, who was a menswear model. And a supercilious prat, in Jess's view.

Una wandered into the kitchen. 'I just met Ethan going out,' she said. 'He's lush. He'd be great in the TV show.'

'Mum!' Tavy looked deeply irritated. 'He didn't want to be in it, remember?'

Jess met Ed's eyes and he smothered a grin. 'Let me show you where everything is, Jess,' he said.

Una, humming under her breath, started to make herself a ham roll. Evidently, Tavy's disapproval was water off a duck's back to her.

'Your mum's a dab hand at anything to do with food,' Ed said, watching as Una packed in layers of salad between the ham. 'She makes the best toasted cheese.'

'She used to run a pub, back in the day,' Jess said. 'It won awards.'

'No way!' Ed looked stunned. 'I did not know that.' He had a fabulous Geordie accent that drew out every syllable. His gaze lingered longingly on the sandwich for a moment and then he snapped back to attention. Jess wondered if he hadn't had time for lunch. 'Coffee grinder, hot chocolate maker, waffle machine.' Ed pointed them out to her.

'I only need a kettle and a fridge,' Jess objected.

'The pub in the village serves great food,' Ed noted. 'It also does breakfast at the weekends, if you want to give it a go tomorrow. We're never here to try it,' he added, 'but the guys on the gate say it's good.'

'That would be the security guards?' Jess asked. 'Are they here all the time?'

'Twenty-four hours,' Ed replied. 'It was part of the agreement with the villagers. They were afraid Tavy's fans would run amok, so we promised to have a permanent crew on hand.'

'I love my fans.' Tavy looked up from her phone briefly. 'Everything I do is for them.'

'Sure, you do,' Ed said dryly, 'just not when they break in and picnic on your lawns or take bits of the house away as souvenirs.'

'As long as the security people know I'm here,' Jess said, 'and don't try to arrest me.'

'I've told them all about you,' Ed said, 'so that's fine. The key safe is there; all the keys are labelled. Just make sure the house is secure whenever you go out. The code for the gate and all the other details are on that list I've left you, along with my number for any emergencies.'

'Wow,' Jess said, smiling. 'That's efficient.'

Ed blushed endearingly. 'I'll take you through the rest of the stuff on Monday – the housekeeping duties and so on,' he said. 'I'm sorry we're all away this weekend.' He glanced at Tavy, but she was still focused on her phone. 'Tavy has so much in her schedule.' His shoulders slumped a little.

'It's okay,' Jess said quickly. 'I know how busy she is. This way, I get chance to settle in whilst the film crew and the builders aren't around, anyway. And Ethan will be here for a while tomorrow, right? Is there anything I need to do to help him or will he just get on with the survey on his own?'

'For God's sake, don't help him.' Tavy looked up suddenly. 'And don't offer him a cup of tea. He doesn't deserve it. I've just had an email from the lawyers saying that he's objected to me ripping out the panelling in the library.' She glared at Ed as though it was his fault. 'He says it's seventeenth century, so you'd think it would be ready for a refresh. I want white book-shelves and lots of glass.'

Jess saw the telltale tightening of the muscles around Ed's mouth before he smiled again. 'I've left you a copy of Tavy's schedule for the next week,' he said to Jess, ignoring her sister, 'and I'll text you if it changes at all, but as

it is, we should be back on Monday to film some more scenes in the garden
– assuming the weather's nice.'

'Thanks so much,' Jess said, taking the sheet and scanning the dizzying
list of interviews, travel, parties and club openings and TV scheduling her
sister was undertaking. 'This is so helpful.'

'He's just doing his job,' Tavy said, with an edge to her voice now.

'Your bedroom is on the first floor, up those stairs on the right,' Ed
continued. 'I've taken your bags up.'

'The backstairs,' Tavy added. 'Servants' quarters.'

There was a very awkward silence.

'There's an ensuite bathroom.' Ed rushed to bridge the gap. 'Actually, it's
the only bedroom with modern plumbing at the moment.' He checked his
watch. 'Tavy, not to hurry you, but are you ready to go? The show in Oxford
starts at nine and you've got the pre-party to get ready for. Hunter will be
here in a minute.'

On cue, there was the sound of wheels on the gravel outside and a car
door slammed. The front door opened, impatient footsteps echoing
through the hall.

'Hi, hon!' Tavy greeted the newcomer with a megawatt smile. 'I'll be
ready in two minutes.' She gestured to Jess. 'You remember my big sister
Jess, don't you, Hunter?'

'Yeah, of course.' Hunter gave Jess a nod, his gaze sliding over her with a
complete lack of interest. If Ed was the boy band type, Jess thought, Hunter
was off-the-scale *Love Island* perfect, with the stubble, the white teeth and
the artfully tousled fair hair. He checked the heavy gold watch on his
suntanned wrist. 'We're already running late, babes,' he said to Tavy, a
slight edge to his voice, sounding irritated.

'They'll wait for me,' Tavy said. '*Us*,' she amended, on seeing his frown.
She waltzed up to Jess and approximated air kisses two inches from both
cheeks. 'See you next week, Jess. Have a lovely evening. Mum!' she yelled
over her shoulder as she strode down the hall. 'You coming?'

Ed hung back for a moment. 'Sorry to abandon you,' he said.

'No problem,' Jess replied.

'Ed!' Tavy's voice echoed down the corridor. 'Come on! You're going
with Mum in the taxi.'

Ed pulled a rueful face and raised a hand in farewell. 'See you soon, Jess.'

The front door closed. There was the sound of voices; the doors of the car slammed. The engine noise faded. And suddenly it was just Jess and the brightly lit kitchen and the ghosts of Fortune Hall.

4

ROSE – LONDON, MAY 1671

On the morning of the seventh of May, when the robbery was to take place, I was out with my orange barrow, down on the River Thames by the Tower at seven o'clock. It was a breezy morning, with a cold-edged wind coming off the river. I had pushed the fruit cart down the narrow lane that led to the Iron Gate, with the squat bulk of St Katharine's by the Tower to my left and the close press of tenements to my right, houses whose upper storeys overhung the road and shaded out the early-spring sunshine.

People were already out and about their daily business. Every so often I remembered to call out, 'Buy my oranges, four for sixpence!' No one did, though a street urchin attempted to grab one as I passed and I swatted him away like a fly. The oranges were old and rotting; I could not blame any customer for seeking out fresher ones, but I had not wanted to spend much money on something that was mainly for show. They rolled around the wooden barrow as it creaked over the cobbled street.

This plan is madness. It will never work.

How many times had those words echoed around my head over the past few months as Colonel Blood's plot unfolded? How many times had I hesitated on the verge of telling John I would have nothing to do with it? And then, in March, I had discovered that I was with child again, and had felt both elated and terrified. It changed everything, for now I had another life to defend and nurture. A miscarriage had robbed me of my last pregnancy and nothing was going to take this baby away from me. I would do whatever was needful to protect it.

So here I was and now that the moment had come, I felt a sick dread in the pit of my stomach. I knew that the jewels were lightly guarded, for Thomas Blood had prepared his ground well, visiting the Tower on a number of occasions and befriending the custodian and his wife to allay suspicion. Nevertheless, it was still an utterly foolhardy plot and I could not believe it would succeed.

The clock on St Katharine's Tower chimed the hour as I turned my little cart onto the wharf, passing the great iron gate that led to the Tower precinct. I saw John immediately; he was acting the part of groom, standing by the water gate, holding a handful of lively nags. That meant that Thomas and his two accomplices were already within the Tower. My heart sped up. If all went according to plan, they would tie up Talbot Edwards, the keeper of the jewels, make good the robbery and be away before any alarm was raised.

People milled along the edge of the river, which looked innocent and blue in the sunshine, reflecting the little fluffy white clouds that scurried overhead. To my right, the huge bastion of the Tower soared, with its ramparts fifteen foot thick and dizzyingly high; to my left, boats jostled at anchor. There was a smell of fish mingled with rotting weed from the thick green slime of the river. It caught in my throat, making me turn away from my fellow street vendors who were selling mackerel and flounders, two for a groat. I felt sick enough with my pregnancy as it was; I had no wish for the stench of dead fish to make me feel worse.

My role was simple. I was to keep watch, to alert John if I saw any soldiers approaching and to aid Thomas Blood's escape, if necessary, by creating a diversion. If matters went badly awry, I was to hide the jewels and take them away. I prayed hard that neither action would be necessary.

I was alive to every sound, every movement, holding my breath, waiting. John loitered, looking bored. He seemed nowhere near as on edge as I.

'Buy my oranges, four for sixpence!' I called. Nobody did.

A rival cherry seller called her wares, five cherries for a groat, sweet and juicy.

I strolled along the wharf, amongst the milling crowds, turned when I reached the end of the jetty, and started back.

'*Treason! Murder! The Crown is stolen!*'

Even though I was more than half-expecting it, the shout made me jump almost out of my skin. My heart started to race even faster. Heads were turning as the cries drew louder and closer.

A buzz arose from the crowd, a murmur that anticipated violence. I heard running footsteps and then a shot. Someone screamed. Men were barrelling through the throngs on the wharf now, roughly pushing people aside, beating a path with their swords and pikestaffs. There were soldiers in their black and red livery, and other men who had joined the fray. Everyone was jostling and shouting. A fight broke out; I heard the thud of a fist making contact with flesh and then the splash as someone fell into the river.

I stood transfixed. There was no requirement to create a distraction. Already, there was so much confusion around me that there was nothing I could add to it.

A priest ran towards me in cloak and cassock, his vestments flying, his boots thundering on the jetty. I realised that it was Thomas Blood.

As he passed my orange barrow, he opened his hand with a lightning-fast flick of the fingers. Something fell from his grasp in a rainbow sparkle of colour and disappeared amongst the oranges. My heart jumped. He gave me a huge wink as though this was no more than a monstrous joke, and then he was past.

'Out of my way, woman!' A burly yeoman warder pushed me aside. The barrow tilted dangerously and I righted it and started to push forward along the wharf, moving in the opposite direction from the hue and cry. Glancing back over my shoulder, I saw that the priest had been wrestled to the ground. From beneath his cloak spilled out the Crown of England, a sad and sorry-looking flattened piece of metal that appeared to have been squashed with a mallet. The crowd gave a gasp of shock and excitement.

'It was a gallant attempt!' Thomas Blood shouted. 'It was for the Crown!'

John, I noted, had leapt onto one of the horses and was galloping off up

St Catherine's Street. He made no attempt either to help or wait for his comrades.

I turned away hastily and sped up, the little cart bumping and creaking over the rough surface of the wharf, the oranges bouncing. By the time I had reached Petty Wales and the Ram's Head alehouse, the disturbance was far behind me. My arms and legs ached from the effort of pushing the wretched barrow over the uneven ground, so I rested against the alehouse wall for a moment to catch my breath. The urge to search amongst the oranges to see what was hidden there was almost overwhelming. It felt as though I might have imagined the whole thing, so quick, so furtive had Thomas Blood's actions been. Could I really be pushing a fruit cart that was hiding some of the Crown Jewels? And if so, what the devil was I supposed to do with them? Thomas Blood and his associates had been captured. Had John been arrested as well by now? God forbid I should be caught with a barrow full of jewels. I shivered, my mind a tangle of panic.

I straightened up, rubbed my aching back, and set off again, uphill towards Leadenhall Street. There was nothing for it but to get home safely, find out what had happened to John and decide what to do from there. Already, my feet were sore and the sun was starting to get hotter as it rose higher in the sky. I took a deep breath to steady myself and wished for good luck to speed me back to Red Kite Yard.

For a while, I made good progress, slipping unnoticed through the alleys, just another orange girl amidst the other hawkers, animals, carts and carriages. I refused two offers to buy some of my oranges and refused another to buy my body for an hour. I'd never sold myself, not even when I was starving. Nell had called me a fool for being so fastidious, and I think she thought I considered myself better than she was. 'A woman needs to use every advantage she has,' she had once told me, but it was not that I thought myself more virtuous than she was, but simply that I hated sexual congress. I'd seen and heard too much of it at a young age when our mother had worked in Madam Ross's brothel, and I'd tried it and found it wanting. All that huffing and sweating and panting, slapping of bare flesh and grunting and groaning... I was happy to avoid it as much as I could.

'It is not so bad with a man who knows what he is doing,' Nell had tried to console me when I had confided in her, but I did not see that as much endorsement of her lovers and no incentive to take one of my own. It was bad enough having to submit to John's conjugal demands.

I tried not to think about John as I wended my way through the alleys and passageways of London. If he had been caught along with Thomas Blood and his other men, then there was not much hope for him. The terrible thing was that I felt so little grief at the thought of John arrested and hanged for treason; whatever love I had thought I had for him when we wed was long expended, damaged beyond saving from the first moment he had raised a hand to me.

Just off Fleet Street I paused for another rest, for my arms were burning with the effort of pushing the barrow by now – I swear those jewels had added a hundredweight to my load. I ducked into the shade of the alley behind Belasyse Court, where it was cool and quiet. I had not thought to be troubled by anyone there, especially not early in the morning, but then the back door of a coffee house burst open and a couple of youths spilled out into the lane, aided by the boot of the landlord behind them.

'Begone and don't come back here!' the man bellowed, kicking them into the rubbish and slamming the door behind them.

The two youths sprawled on the ground for a moment, then staggered to their feet, swearing and shaking themselves like dogs. The expensive linen and velvet of their attire was stained with wine and what looked like vomit. I recognised their sort at once; arrogant sprigs of the aristocracy still drunk from the previous night. One of them picked up a stone to hurl at the window of the coffee house, but the other caught his arm and tilted his head in my direction, a sly look in his eyes. I stiffened. They were between me and the entrance to the alleyway, which was a bad mistake on my part, but I had huddled into a dark corner to enjoy the deep shadow. Now, they came in close, crowding me, and I could smell the sweat on their bodies and the stale wine on their breath. I did not move.

'How much for a quick one, sweetheart?' the first youth slurred. He glanced at his friend. 'Both of us together? Here, in this neat little corner?' He leaned a hand against the wall, trapping me.

The other youth giggled. He picked up several of my oranges and attempted to juggle with them, crossing his eyes against the glare of the sun over the rooftops.

I was horrified to see that in the bottom of my barrow, one of the emeralds from the Crown Jewels was glinting in the light. Fortunately, the youth was still too drunk to notice it. His balance was tipsy and he dropped the oranges, which only served to make him giggle all the more.

'A guinea says you will be too limp to take her,' he said to his friend. 'You always suffer from brewer's droop.'

'Devil a bit,' the other retorted, reaching for the ties on his breeches.

I sighed. I hated having to deal with drunk and spoiled noblemen, but needs must. I reached for the knife concealed in my garter and held it turned inward up my sleeve. Neither of them noticed. The second lad was chasing oranges over the cobbles and the first one was staring at my breasts as he fumbled with his crotch.

'Thank you for the offer, kind sirs,' I said sarcastically, 'but I would rather eat a rancid mackerel than service either of you, separately or together.'

The orange juggler's mouth dropped open and he turned bright red. I think he was genuinely shocked. The other, though, was the dangerous one. I had recognised it the moment I had seen the anger seething in his eyes.

'Why, you bitch!' he said, almost pleasantly. 'You'll be sorry you said that.' He grabbed my arm and dragged me down to the ground, resting his full weight across me, his foetid breath on my face. He had taken me by surprise and I had banged my head on the wall as I fell, which put me in an even worse mood. One of his hands was across my mouth to prevent me from screaming, but that did not matter. I had no wish to draw attention to what I was about to do. He was asking for trouble and I would oblige him.

I hooked my foot around the back of his leg and rolled him beneath me so that I was sitting on his chest, his arms were trapped under him, and my knife was at his throat. I was so quick and he was so befuddled, that it was almost too easy. He tried to push me off, but I dug the blade in, just enough that a thin trickle of blood joined the other stains on his linen collar. Behind me, I heard the other youth give a squeak of fear.

'Get her off me, you fool!' my prisoner yelled at his friend. He thrashed around some more, but by now I had pinned his legs beneath the wheels of the orange barrow and he struggled in vain.

'Listen to me, you self-important little popinjay,' I said. I rested my not-inconsiderable weight more heavily on his chest and felt him struggle for breath. 'Don't try to bully an orange girl ever again. If you do, it will go badly for you.'

I dug the blade in a little deeper. More blood ran. His eyes bulged. I waited a few more seconds for the lesson to sink in. Then, as I was about to let him go, I heard steps in the alleyway behind us.

'Sir!' the other youth was calling out now in a thin, frightened wail. 'Sir, please help us! We are being attacked!'

I jumped up and spun around. I was accounted quick on my feet, but even I was too slow compared to the newcomer. His sword – a proper soldier's sword, not an aristocrat's toy – was at my throat before I had barely turned to confront him.

'Much as it pains me,' the man who was holding the sword said, 'I cannot permit you to kill Lord Swinton. It would cause too many difficulties.'

His voice was low but very firm. I raised my gaze from the sword's blade to his face. He was tall; I had to crane my neck to look at him and that was dangerous with the shining blade less than an inch away.

I judged him to be older than I by about nine or ten years and he had dark hair that fell to his shoulders beneath a battered, broad-brimmed hat. His eyes were dark as well, the same chestnut brown as his hair. There were lines about them that came with experience and weathering, like the tan of his skin beneath his stubble. His expression was as hard as the line of his jaw. He wore the russet coat and black boots of an officer and spoke with the flat, authoritative tones of a man accustomed to having his commands obeyed.

'Drop the knife,' he said.

I was angry, but I did as I was bid. If it hadn't been for the jewels, I would have abandoned the cart and run there and then, and I was so quick, I could have got away, I think. But now I was caught, trying to decide what to do, and the lost seconds also lost me any advantage.

Lord Swinton scrambled to his feet, brushing cabbage leaves and pigeon droppings from his trousers. 'The woman is a thief,' he said virtuously. 'She tried to rob and murder me! She should be arrested—'

He got no further. The soldier sheathed his sword carefully, turned fully towards Swinton and hit him once, directly and with ruthless precision. Swinton went down again amongst the cabbage leaves and lay there, blinking in shock.

'Don't say another word,' the soldier said.

'Sir!' The other youth foolishly grabbed the soldier's arm, releasing him immediately as the man turned his hard gaze upon him. He backed away. 'You should not hit him,' he gibbered. 'He is the son of the Duke of Creighton!'

'I am aware of who he is,' the soldier said. 'He is also a knave. If the duke has any difficulty with the situation, he may take it up with me. Colonel Guy Forster.' He bowed ironically. 'I may be found at Lord Craven's house in Drury Lane.'

'Colonel Forster!' The boy's Adam's apple bobbed. I could have sworn he turned several shades paler. 'Lord Craven's house...' He edged further away. 'Jamie, get up! Come on!'

'You heard your friend,' Colonel Forster said to the dazed youth. 'Off you go. And keep your hands to yourself in future.'

They went in a flurry of swearing and cabbage leaves.

Colonel Forster bent down to retrieve my knife and in the same moment I saw a great big ruby red stone sitting atop one of the oranges, glittering at me. Damn those jewels! They seemed to have a life of their own. Quick as a flash, I grabbed the ruby and pocketed it. It was so heavy, it seemed to weigh me down and, at the same time, it felt as bright and dangerous as a beacon. Colonel Forster was looking at the knife in his hand and also, thoughtfully, at me. My face felt flushed with guilt.

'Who are you,' I said quickly, to distract him, 'and who is Lord Craven, that his very name strikes fear into those arrogant little sprigs of nobility?'

He smiled then, a smile of genuine amusement that made me blink. It transformed the austere lines of his face into something much warmer and more approachable. I reminded myself that I did not want to approach him. On the contrary, I should be running away from him.

'I am merely a soldier in the King's service,' he said easily, 'but Lord Craven...' He hesitated. 'Lord Craven is the richest man in London and as such he owns half the aristocracy. They borrow money from him, so—' He snapped his fingers. 'He could snuff them out in a moment.'

I smiled wryly to imagine having such power. Or such fortune.

'And you, mistress,' Colonel Forster asked. 'How do you come by such a dagger as this?' His gaze narrowed. 'Did you steal it?'

He had my measure, right enough, and he had only just met me.

'No,' I said, seeing no point in false outrage. 'It was given to me by my father.'

'It bears the coat of arms of the Gwyn family,' Colonel Forster observed.

'My father was Captain Thomas Gwyn who served under Lieutenant Colonel Sir Thomas Dallison in Prince Rupert's Regiment of Horse,' I said. I spoke without pride, for whilst I was glad my father had served the last king, I saw nothing to celebrate in the man himself. The knife, my dark red hair, my solid build and a talent for cards were the only useful things I had inherited from him.

'I did not know that Mistress Eleanor Gwyn had a sister,' Colonel Forster mused. His dark gaze appraised me again and it was easy enough to read. I had seen that look many times before. *You are nothing like her... She is dainty and witty and pretty enough to appeal to a king. Whereas you...*

'I am the other Gwyn girl,' I said. 'Rose. Rose Cassells.'

He tipped his hat to me and smiled. 'A pleasure to meet you, mistress.' He offered the knife to me, handle first. 'Would you have killed him?' he asked casually.

'No,' I said, stowing the dagger back in my garter, 'I only wished to get away. He tried to force himself on me and I wanted none of it.'

His mouth tightened. 'Young cubs like that need to learn a few hard lessons.' He looked at me and a smile lightened the grimness in his eyes. 'That was a neat trick you pulled, though, to gain the upper hand.'

'You saw it?' I was startled, for he must have been watching for longer than I had imagined. What else had he seen – jewels glinting in the sunshine amidst the oranges? I had to put an end to this conversation and get away with my contraband. 'It was easy enough with a lad young and small,' I said. 'I could not pull such a trick with you.'

'No.' His smile had a wicked edge now which made me blink. 'You will need to try something different to gain the upper hand with me.' He took an orange from the cart, gave me a nod and strolled away.

* * *

It was a long walk back to Red Kite Yard and for most of that journey I thought about Colonel Guy Forster and how differently my life might have turned out had I married a man of integrity rather than a villain like John Cassells. John called himself a captain and that had turned my head at first, but it soon emerged that he had never served.

I gave myself a shake. No more foolish dreaming. My mother had married a real soldier and he had left her penniless and despairing. If there was one lesson I had learned in life, it was that I could rely only on myself, and that was precisely why the red jewel was in my pocket. When the time came, that ruby would be my key to a better life.

John was waiting for me when I got home. I pushed open the door of the lodging house carefully, for it was quiet – too quiet for midday. He was sitting by the side of the empty grate, an equally empty bottle dangling from his fingers, his face pale and blotchy with sweat. I assumed he was drunk, but as he got slowly to his feet, I realised it was fear that gripped him. His eyes were bloodshot and wild.

'They captured them all,' he said. 'Blood, Hunt and Perrot. All taken by the guards. And now those bastards will betray me without a qualm.'

I noticed that he had no concern for me and no interest in how I had managed to get away. He was too wrapped up in feeling scared and sorry for himself. Anger pricked at me.

'Then you had better take the remaining jewels and run away,' I said. I pushed the barrow towards him crossly. I was hot and bone-tired, and although I had not really expected him to care about me, conversely it still upset me that he did not. 'You can scrabble in the cart for your prize. I am going to fetch a drink from the alehouse.'

He barely paid attention to me. His fear had sparked into excitement when he realised that I had saved some of the loot. He was already throwing the oranges out of the cart in his haste to find the other jewels.

My patience with him, such as it was, snapped. I felt sick with loathing and anger, gripped with fear. 'Get rid of them,' I said from the doorway. 'Hide them, sell them, give them away, do whatever you choose. I care not. I always said it was a foolish plan and now I want no more to do with it. Nor with you, for that matter. You will drag me down no further. Leave and don't come back here.'

He looked up briefly, his eyes glinting now with greed. 'But, Rose,' he said, 'this will change everything! Our fortunes are made!'

'I want no more to do with it,' I repeated. 'I will disclaim any knowledge of both you and the jewels.' The ruby, a heavy weight in my pocket, branded me a liar, but that was different. That was for the baby's future.

John's temper flared. He knocked the ale flagon aside and it smashed on the earthen floor. He overturned the table on top of it; one of the legs splintered as it collapsed. Eyes glittering with fury and drunkenness, he stood looking at me with loathing. 'If they arrest me, I will name you too,' he taunted.

'They have nothing on me,' I said. 'No one saw me at the Tower. And if either you or Thomas are so lost to honour that you implicate me, I will plead marital coercion, being forced to obey my husband in all things.' I gave him a bitter smile. 'You should like that, John. It gives you an authority you do not possess.'

They were defiant words, but inside I was quaking, not so much through fear of John but from a sick feeling that there was a net of a different sort closing about me now. For all my bold words, I knew it would be hard for me to get out of this unscathed.

The fresh, cold air outside was a relief after the foetid fumes of drink and violence. I needed to clear my head and think. I knew Thomas Blood was taken – I had seen his capture myself. John had said that the others had been arrested alongside him. The sensible thing would be to take the advice I had given John and run away and lie low until it became clear what was going to happen.

The difficulty was that there were very few places I could hide. I had no family, other than my mother and Nell, and no friends whom I could trust. The sort of people I knew were the sort of people who would turn me in for a reward, no matter how small. I thought of throwing myself on Nell's mercy, but I was reluctant to bring trouble to her door and afraid that she would turn me away, leaving me even more wretched than before.

I bought a half-pint of ale and a cold pie from the chop house and ate it as I walked along Little White Lyon Street. It banished my hunger and quenched my thirst, but I felt uneasy and on edge. Word was buzzing along the lanes of the attempted theft of the Crown Jewels, each story more lurid than the last. The gossip was that Thomas Blood was in the Tower of London and refusing to answer for his crime to anyone but the King himself. That would be typical of Blood's arrogance, I thought. I listened intently but heard no word of any missing jewels; perhaps in all the mayhem, the authorities had yet to discover that some had gone astray. I touched the ruby in my pocket superstitiously for luck.

Eventually, when the sun had passed behind the tower of St Martin's Church and the shadows were lengthening in the street, I stood up and started to head for home to find out what had happened to John. I suspected that, despite the danger, he would probably still be in the tenement, unconscious with drink, or perhaps down the alehouse celebrating with Peg Cherry. Maybe I should turn him in to the authorities myself. It was an appealing idea.

I had decided that, regardless of what John did, it would be best for me to disappear for a little while, get out of London and take refuge somewhere that would be safe for me and for the baby. The only place I could think of was Becote Manor. After the Restoration, the King had taken it from the parliamentarian who had stolen it from our family and had given it to Nell. This had grated with me, given that I was the elder and my father's heir, but then Nell was the King's mistress and I was nothing. So, I held my tongue and tried not to mind that, beyond repairing the roof and installing a caretaker, she had done nothing to improve it. Perhaps I was feeling nostalgic for my childhood and had some plan to recreate that life for the baby. I was sure I would be able to square the matter with Nell, who had more important concerns than lending me one of her ramshackle estates.

The one thing I needed to do before I begged a place on a cart to Oxford was to collect the very few possessions I had back in Red Kite Alley, including my precious store of coin. I knew it was dangerous, so I waited

until it was dark and then reconnoitred the alley and surrounding warren
of streets thoroughly before I risked approaching. No one ever noticed me –
I was indistinguishable from every last one of the women who thronged the
lanes of London, whether they were street vendors, prostitutes or washer-
women. Unlike Nell, I had never wanted to stand out and knew how to
make myself invisible, drawing my shawl up to hide my hair, moving from
shadow to shadow like a wraith.

There was no sign of John when I approached the tenement, but it was
clear that someone had been there looking for him. Even from a distance, I
could see the broken door hanging by one hinge, and as I crept closer,
peering through the doorway, I saw cupboards and chests emptied, plates
smashed, chairs overturned. I was incensed to see that my favourite blue
and white china chamber pot was in shattered pieces on the cobbles. It
hadn't been worth much, but I had liked it. All the fabric of my life, such as
it was, had been carelessly thrown in the gutter.

I almost jumped out of my skin when there was a touch on my arm, but
it was only my neighbour, old Widow Fry. 'They came looking for your
John,' she whispered in my ear as I ducked into hiding under the lintel of
her door. 'Soldiers! Dozens of them! He was long gone, but they ransacked
the place.' Her filthy nails plucked my sleeve urgently. 'They are looking for
you too. They asked me if I knew where to find you, but I told them nothing.' She looked virtuous. 'You should run, my dear,' she said. 'Run and
hide, before it is too late.'

I pressed my hands to my aching head, trying to think. So, the hue and
cry was up, but it seemed that John had escaped, presumably taking the
remaining jewels with him. I did not give much for his chances of staying
free, not with a band of soldiers pursuing him, but that was his problem. I
was going away.

I went inside, stepping through the debris of broken pots and sticks of
furniture. I could take very little with me and there was nothing worth
saving here. But upstairs, on a tiny shelf in the disused chimney, I found my
coins still safely hidden and grabbed the bag thankfully. Then I went back
downstairs to retrieve my treasure tin, the one I had kept since I was a girl.
It too was hidden, under a loose board in the shed that housed the privy.
But as soon as I took it out, I realised something was wrong. The lid had

been prised open and something was missing among the old buttons and trade tokens and battered toys.

It was the key to the fishing house at Becote Manor.

I sat back on my heels as I tried to work out what had happened. I had not realised that John had known about the tin, but he did spy on me and he was the only person who knew about the manor house apart from Nell and our mother. Perhaps he had had the same idea as I, to take refuge there.

I bit my lip. The last thing I wanted to do was to be reunited with John at Becote. Damn him for stealing my key, but thank goodness he had not known where I had hidden my gold...

'Mistress Cassells?'

In my preoccupation, I had forgotten to be vigilant and now my heart jumped into my mouth.

I recognised that voice. I scrambled to my feet, almost knocking over my meagre lantern in the process. The pale light illuminated the face of Colonel Guy Forster, all the hard planes and angles I remembered. It also illuminated the bright blade of the sword in his hand.

'Damnation,' I said. 'It's you.'

He smiled. 'It is a pleasure to see you again too. And now you are under arrest.'

5

JESS – THE PRESENT

After the noise of the last car had died away, Jess stood for a moment in the silent kitchen with the strange sensation that she had travelled back in time. Without Tavy glued to her phone or Ed demonstrating the coffee machine, it was as though she was in a time bubble; even though the shiny surfaces of the modern kitchen winked back at her, she felt that if she stepped over the threshold, she would be in a different era entirely. It was a disconcerting sensation.

With a quick, sharp sigh of impatience, she went out into the corridor. It was wreathed in shadows and, behind her, the brightness of the kitchen immediately seemed to dim. She fumbled for the light switch and felt a ridiculous sense of relief when it came on. It was a bare bulb, though, which only served to make the pools of darkness starker.

The light for the servants' stair was even worse, an ancient yellow bulb beneath a filthy flowered lampshade that matched the frayed carpet runner. There were bare boards on either side. Clearly, she – the poor relation – was as much a servant in Tavy's world as the endless parade of housemaids and footmen had been in previous centuries. Tomorrow, she decided, once she had had her meeting with Ethan Sterling, she would go shopping for a few home comforts.

At least the bedroom was clean. Ed, presumably, had made sure that there were fresh sheets on the bed, and although there was an open fire, there was also an efficient electric heater that had taken the chill off the space. Heavy red velvet curtains framed mullioned windows on two sides and a soft rug beside the bed was a nice touch. Jess unpacked her meagre belongings and put them away in the heavy walnut wardrobe and matching chest of drawers, where they almost vanished.

She felt strangely tired – emotionally exhausted, perhaps – but, at the same time, wired from events of the day and the strong coffee. She decided to go and make herself some food, do a quick check that the house was secure and then watch television for a bit, trying to instil some sense of normality before she attempted to sleep. Tomorrow, she would orientate herself properly and work out which passageways led where, which rooms were open and try to get a sense of the grounds as well.

As she went back into the kitchen, she reflected wryly that it was clear which bits of the house were important to Tavy and which were not. The kitchen needed to be as high concept as possible. Tavy, like their mother, had always loved food and cooking, although these days it seemed other people did that for her. There was a grand dining room, where Ed had told her the film crew assembled every Monday to discuss the plans for the week. She'd find out all about that in a couple of days. There was another reception room that was all white paint and huge chandeliers, the room everyone had been crowded into when she had arrived. Then there was the very opulent downstairs cloakroom, because, as Tavy had said, 'I'm not using the Portaloos like everyone else.' Upstairs, there was one bedroom in the process of being decorated: 'Tavy's Room' as it was known in the programme, which, it turned out, she never visited, let alone slept in.

Somewhere in the house, a clock chimed. Jess jumped. She hadn't heard it before, but perhaps that was because there had been other people and noise all around. She was about to switch on the TV to give some semblance of company when her phone rang. She'd expected it to be Sammy, whom she had texted earlier to say she'd arrived safely, but to her surprise she saw it was another friend, one of the few who hadn't dropped by the wayside when Jared had laid waste to everyone's lives.

'Hey, Jess,' Lucy Brown said. 'How are you? I've discovered you've been holding out on me – I hear you're staying just down the road from us near Beckett.'

'Lucy!' Jess felt the now-familiar mixture of pleasure and embarrassment that she experienced when dealing with old friends. She was so acutely ashamed of her involvement with Jared and although she knew most people didn't blame her for his behaviour, some people did. Plus, she very much blamed herself. 'I only got here today,' she said, by way of excuse. 'Who told you?' Then, 'Oh, it *is* lovely to hear from you, Lucy.'

'You too.' Lucy's voice was warm and sincere. They had met through mutual friends in London, in what seemed to Jess after all that had happened to be another life. Lucy had been a musician in those days and so her social life had been fragmented between concerts all over Europe and the UK. They had caught up rarely, but when they did, they had talked for hours. It was one of those friendships that they could pick up exactly where they had left off, with no sense of anything changing. But now, Jess was aware that rather a lot had happened since they had last spoken.

'I'm sorry I haven't been in touch for ages,' she started to say, but Lucy dismissed that.

'You've had a lot on your plate,' she intervened firmly. 'Look, let's get together soon, shall we?'

'I'd love that,' Jess said truthfully. Suddenly, she felt a lot less alone. She'd known that Lucy and her fiancé were living somewhere nearby, but she had hung back from making contact first. She felt a warm sense of gratitude that Lucy had got in touch.

'Whenever you're ready,' Lucy said. 'Finn and I are only a few miles away in Knightstone. I just wanted to say how much we'd love to see you. But I guess you've got a lot going on at the moment with Octavia and your mum there.'

'Not so much,' Jess said involuntarily. 'I'm on my own here until Monday. Tavy's got a very full diary.'

'What?' Lucy sounded outraged, which Jess found heart-warming. 'She invites you down and then abandons you in the haunted mausoleum?'

'It's not that bad,' Jess found herself defending the house, which, only a few minutes before she had been thinking was creepy and too quiet. 'I mean, I knew Tavy wanted me to be the housekeeper here, so this is part of my job, and Fortune Hall just needs some TLC, doesn't it? I don't think it really is haunted...' A scent of orange blossom wafted gently through the room and Jess looked round to see where it was coming from, but the vase of flowers on the big farmhouse kitchen table were unscented calla lilies.

'That's fair enough, I suppose.' Lucy sounded slightly mollified. 'But nevertheless I don't like thinking of you rattling around there on your own. We're away this weekend or I'd invite you over straight away, but perhaps we can meet up next week?'

'That would be great,' Jess said. 'Don't worry about me in the meantime. I'm going to go shopping tomorrow and start finding my way around. I've got plenty to do.'

'Okay.' Lucy still seemed slightly concerned. 'We'll be back on Sunday night, but if you need anything in the meantime, give Ethan a call. Ethan Sterling. He's a friend of Finn's and he lives just up the road from you.'

'We've already met,' Jess said. 'He came round to see Tavy about some aspect of the renovation.' She hesitated. 'I've never met him before with you and Finn, have I? Only he seemed familiar.'

'I don't think so,' Lucy said. She sounded intrigued. 'Familiar, how?'

'Oh, it's nothing,' Jess said hurriedly, thinking that if she started talking about a sense of affinity, Lucy would think she'd already developed a crush on Ethan. 'I must have confused him with someone else.'

'Difficult to do,' Lucy said dryly. 'Ethan is pretty memorable.'

Jess laughed it off. 'I've got an appointment to inspect the orangery or something with him tomorrow. But if I need any help in the meantime, I won't call him. Somehow, I can't imagine him dashing out here to rescue Tavy Yates's sister.'

Lucy laughed. 'Yeah, I'd got the impression they don't get on. Ethan's very discreet, but it wasn't hard to work out. He used to love his job until he had the gig as Tavy's historical consultant foisted on him. Now he's in a permanent bad mood. Probably because Fortune Hall used to be in his family until his grandmother was forced to sell up about ten years ago. The house has been going to rack and ruin ever since.'

'Oh God,' Jess said, 'I see.' She felt a wayward pang of sympathy for

Ethan. 'That must be hard for him. I suppose the most positive way of looking at it is that Tavy is trying to give the house a new lease of life.'

'I'm not sure Ethan sees it that way,' Lucy said, 'but you'll have to argue that out with him. Actually, I think he might finally be ready to let go of Fortune Hall – or Beckett Manor, to give it it's proper name. He's got a complicated history with it – wonderful childhood family holidays, you know the sort of thing – but now Tom's gone to college, Ethan could travel, or do something for himself—'

'Wait,' Jess interrupted. 'Who's Tom? Ethan's partner?'

'Sorry,' Lucy said ruefully. 'I'm chattering on because I'm just so pleased to be talking to you, Jess! Tom is Ethan's younger brother,' she added. 'Ethan brought him up after their dad died. Anyway,' her voice lightened, 'Ethan will tell you all about it when you get to know him. In the meantime, I'd forgotten that you've got twenty-four-hour security at the hall, so if anything happens you can call Ted Cutler out. He's the head security guard.'

'I suppose you know him too,' Jess said. She was starting to believe the old adage that everyone knew everyone else in the country.

'Ted used to deliver the milk around here,' Lucy explained, 'but he had to give it up when he got sciatica. He's got a lovely superannuated German shepherd dog called Zelda.'

'Superannuated, eh?' Jess was smiling despite herself. 'I get the feeling neither of them would be that quick in an emergency.'

'Maybe not, but don't tell Tavy,' Lucy said. 'Ted needs that job to pay for his youngest to get through vet college. I don't want her sacking him because he's not up to Tavy's hot bodyguard standard.'

Jess wondered how many times she would hear the words 'Don't tell Tavy,' during the next few weeks and months. She had a feeling that her sister, always so preoccupied, didn't know a quarter of the stuff that was going on around her. 'I'll look forward to meeting Ted and Zelda,' she said. 'Thanks so much for ringing, Lucy. Now go off and have a great weekend and I'll look forward to seeing you both next week and catching up on all your news.'

After Lucy had rung off, silence settled over the house again. Jess switched on the TV and the room filled with the technicolour brightness and sound of a reality show taking place somewhere that looked generically hot and sunny. The shots of beaches and palm trees made her long fiercely for a holiday. Then she remembered that the last time that she and Jared had been to the Caribbean, his part of the holiday had probably been paid for using someone else's savings, and she felt sick. Quickly, she changed channels, only to find Tavy staring at her out of the huge screen. It was one of her sister's previous 'rescue'-type shows, where she had allegedly helped to rehome rabbits, hamsters and other cute, furry creatures. Seeing Tavy looking winsome as she cuddled a rabbit whilst trying not to chip her nail polish made Jess feel a bit sick in a different way. On her third attempt, she found a programme about the Tudor dynasty and settled down with relief.

The fridge yielded all sorts of delicious food. It did cross Jess's mind that Ed had probably ordered most of it to keep Tavy sweet during filming. However, as she tucked into a bowl of miso and butternut soup with crusty bread, she felt no guilt whatsoever. On Monday, she would talk to Ed about a household budget since she was fairly certain Tavy would have nothing to do with that.

The Aga made the kitchen feel cosy and there was a lovely wooden rocking chair beside it, which Jess thought would make a nice place to sit and read in the evenings when she was on her own. Perhaps in a few weeks, this solitary job might feel a bit less strange, assuming she lasted that long. She had lived alone in the flat in London for a couple of months after Jared had been sent to prison, but her time had been focused on finding a buyer and packing up. Besides, it had been in a busy street in Shoreditch. It was nothing like Fortune Hall in either size or location. But she didn't mind her own company; in fact, living with Jared had been exhausting sometimes, given his preference for filling every moment with company and activity.

She made a few calls to Sammy and a couple of other friends just to let them know she was settling in, and then the combination of the soup, the warmth and the long day set Jess yawning so much she decided she would go to bed after another quick look round. She wasn't sure if she would sleep in such an unfamiliar place, but she was so exhausted that perhaps she would.

She took her mug of tea with her and went down the corridor into the entrance hall. There were two locks on the big oak front door and two bolts, all of them modern. The doors from the dining room to the hall and to Tavy's posh drawing room were also locked – Ed had told her that the film company stored their gear in there so that made sense, but Jess made a mental note to find out where there was a key in case of emergency.

The parlour opposite was sunk in gloom and she had no real urge to go back in there, but she flicked on the light switch and noted that all the mullioned windows were firmly shut. She considered drawing the curtains as it felt very exposed to have the blank windows staring out into darkness, but then she thought the curtain rail looked so rickety it might fall down if she gave it a tug, so she left it.

That just left one other door off the passageway down to the kitchen and Jess hadn't seen inside that room yet. She guessed it must be the library and she was aware of a tingle of anticipation as she turned the knob and stepped within.

Once again, the gothic nature of the room struck her. There was nothing but bare bulbs in old gilt brackets, branches and branches of them along the walls, draped with cobwebs like a scene from a Dickens novel. They illuminated shelf after dark wooden shelf of dusty books set between old oak panelling.

Jess felt her heart leap, as though there were secrets here waiting to be uncovered. She remembered Tavy's description of how she wanted to redecorate: *'I want white paint and lots of glass!'* Surely that would be sacrilege in such a beautiful and historic room.

Empty cardboard boxes were stacked beneath the shelves, testament to the imminent removal of the contents. She drifted along the shelves, touching the spine of one book lightly, brushing the dust away to read the title of another. Even with the most cursory of glances, she could see that there were some real treasures here: ancient editions of plays by John Dryden, Shakespeare's sonnets, *Don Quixote* and *The Pilgrim's Progress*. They mingled with early twentieth-century copies of *The Fox and the Hound* and *The Turf*.

Blowing several centuries of cobwebs off one volume, Jess saw that it was a collection of poetry. She opened the book and waited for the scent she loved, the combination of vanilla and time past. This book, though, smelled of a faint mixture of sweet cherry, old furniture and woodsmoke. It was so distinctive that for a moment she felt she could almost reach out and touch the past it had come from, four hundred years before. She could see a man, sitting before the fire, his head bent over the pages, engrossed. The light was behind him and the shadow of a woman slipped across it for a moment and he looked up and smiled...

Jess came back to herself, the book still in her hands, and looked at the page it had opened at.

> *'But true love is a durable fire,*
> *In the mind ever burning,*
> *Never sick, never old, never dead,*
> *From itself never turning.'*

She smiled a little as she recognised the words of the poem by Sir Walter Raleigh. She'd studied sixteenth- and seventeenth-century literature at college and loved the way it resonated even after five hundred years. Not that she and Jared had had that sort of connection.

A few of the letters were underlined with the palest smudge of old ink. A sheet of paper slid from between the pages of the book, gliding down to the floor. When she picked it up, Jess saw it had carefully formed letters of the alphabet written on it. The parchment was thin, almost translucent, and the ink so faded, it seemed to disappear before her eyes. Below the rows of letters was another quotation:

> *'My love for you is ever true.'*

Not a childish sentiment, even though it was written in a wavering hand that looked like a child learning to write. Some of the alphabet letters were underlined. Checking back in the poem, she realised the same ones were underlined in both: R O S E.

Was it a name or a reference to the garden? she wondered. It felt as though there were a lot of surprises here amongst the ancient texts of the library, texts which, she knew, Tavy was about to bundle up and send off to the house clearance people. Jess was going to have to work quickly if she was to have a chance to look through them all. And what would she do with the gems she found? It was unlikely Tavy would want them on her new glass shelves, but Jess was damned if they were simply going to be given away. She pinched the bridge of her nose. She'd work that out when the time came.

A proper sense of excitement stirred in her for the first time since she had come to Fortune Hall. Here was something she was both interested in and good at: books. Sorting them, cleaning them, cataloguing them and reading them, of course. She wasn't going to part with anything from this room before she had had the chance to take a thorough look at it.

Holding the poetry book against her heart and her mug of tea in the other hand, Jess went out and closed the door. She felt warmer inside now, as if she had formed a bond with Fortune Hall and its history.

Out in the hallway, she realised that the parlour door was open, which was odd, as she was sure she had closed it firmly. As she went across to shut it, she caught a flash of light glancing across the parlour windows, like the beam of a torch. Her heart raced before common sense asserted itself. It was probably Ted, the security guard, and his dog Zelda on an evening check-up of the grounds.

She went across to the bay window. The clouds that had been hanging around all day had gone now that night had fallen and the sky was a clear, starry dark blue with a sliver of new moon. From here, Jess could see across the sweep of lawn to where a thread of water gleamed in the distance – the lake she had caught sight of when she had arrived. She touched one hand to the cobwebbed, diamond-paned glass, feeling rather like a character in a costume drama as she peered out to see if she could catch sight of Ted and Zelda.

Something moved in the darkness again, drawing her eyes to the huge oak tree on the edge of the carriage sweep, close to the house. Beneath it, she could see a tall dark figure, clothed all in black, looking upward into the boughs of the tree. The hairs on the back of Jess's neck rose as a chill fluttered down her spine. The moonlight, falling through the bare branches, illuminated the man's face in black and white, turning into a carving that looked as austere as a statue in a church. And as Jess stared, trapped for a split second in the moment between seeing him and screaming, he turned his head and looked directly at her.

Jess gave a screech and dropped the mug of tea. It bounced off the window seat and onto the wooden floor, rolling against the skirting board, breaking into several pieces and showering liquid everywhere.

She expected the figure to run away, but instead of doing anything so furtive, he came out from under the tree and walked directly towards the window with a strong, confident stride. Jess made a grab for the phone in her pocket, but by the time she'd got it out to call the police, he was tapping on the windowpane. She looked again, and this time she recognised Ethan Sterling. Now she felt a total idiot.

She tried to open one of the windows, but it stuck fast. She tried a second one, fumbling it because her hands were still shaking.

'You scared the hell out of me!' she said without preamble.

'I'm sorry,' Ethan replied. He sounded genuinely contrite, but Jess wasn't in the mood for apologies. The adrenaline was still coursing through her, encouraged, it seemed, by the unwarranted pleasure she realised she was taking in seeing him again so soon.

'You were checking up on me, I suppose,' she said. 'Making sure I wasn't ripping out the panelling in the library under the cover of darkness.'

She saw his teeth flash in a grin. 'Actually, I was—'

'Or perhaps you're here because Lucy sent you to keep an eye on me,' Jess continued. 'I don't need a nursemaid, thank you. Nor do I appreciate you creeping around at night!'

'I'm sorry,' Ethan said again. 'I should have let you know—'

'Please don't do it again,' Jess said, still feeling ruffled.

'I won't,' Ethan replied. 'I promise.' He took something out of the pocket of his jacket and held it out to her. 'The thing is, I have a licence for species protection. It gives me permission to check up on the Bechstein's bats that are roosting in the oak.' He gestured towards the tree he'd been standing under when she first saw him.

'Well, you don't have a licence to disturb me!' Jess said. She was on a roll. She had been very calm, she thought, dealing with Jared and all the crap that had gone with that, and then discovering that Tavy had just dumped her here. But enough was enough. Even if Ethan had a perfect right to be there, he'd given her a fright. The fact that she was inexplicably attracted to him only made it worse.

Then she realised how ridiculous she must sound, leaning out of the window like an angry Juliet berating Romeo. Her temper deflated. She gave a sharp sigh.

'Sorry,' she said. 'I overreacted.'

'That's okay,' Ethan replied. 'Like I said, I should have warned you I'd be here. I'm very sorry to have startled you.' He slid the licence back into his pocket. 'If you want to double-check that I'm safe to have around, Ted and Zelda can vouch for me, the dog in particular. She really likes me.'

Jess felt a reluctant smile starting. 'That's okay,' she said. 'I believe you. I think we've got off on the wrong foot, what with you and Tavy being at loggerheads.' A thought occurred to her. 'Does she know you come out here when she's not around?'

She saw a shadow touch Ethan's face. 'No,' he said, and for the first time there was an element of constraint in his voice. 'I'd really appreciate it if you didn't tell her. I'm on the level, and the wildlife around here needs me to keep an eye on things, but Ms Yates would probably try to have my licence revoked if she knew.'

He didn't say anything else to try to persuade her and Jess appreciated that. She could make her own judgements.

'I'll look forward to hearing more about the wildlife tomorrow,' she said, 'when you come to check out the orangery. Now I think you'd better go – assuming the bats are doing okay.'

Ethan's eyes gleamed with amusement. 'They're doing fine,' he said. 'Thank you. I'll see you tomorrow.' He raised a hand and then melted back into the shadows of the oak tree as silently as he had appeared whilst Jess closed the window and retrieved the pieces of her empty mug.

The encounter with Ethan had left her with a sense of anticipation about the next day and, in an odd way, reinforced the sense of warmth and connection she felt for Fortune Hall. She decided not to analyse that too much.

She made sure that the parlour door was properly secured this time, tidied up the kitchen and prepared a hot-water bottle, then, yawning, made her way up the servants' stair to bed.

Lying in the dark, feeling both alert to a strange place and exhausted at the same time, Jess thought about what Lucy had said about Fortune Hall once being in Ethan's family, and how it might feel, not only to have to give up that claim but also to see someone else with no sentiment for the house, no understanding of it, try to turn it into something completely different just for a TV show. And then, rather to her surprise, Jess fell into a deep and dreamless sleep.

6

ROSE – LONDON, JUNE 1671

I had thought about Colonel Guy Forster a lot during my incarceration in the Marshalsea. Naturally, I blamed him for it. Had he not been so cunning as to guess that either John or I might return home under cover of darkness, and had he not waited silently, hidden, to apprehend me, matters might have been very different. But he *was* cunning and clever enough to wait when he had seen the jewels in my orange cart earlier that day. He had followed me home and later come back to catch me.

I had not tried to persuade him to free me on our short, swift march to the prison. I had said nothing at all, for I knew he was a man who saw his duty as supreme and would not be swayed from it. He had held me tight by the arm, so I could not escape, and occasionally when I had glanced up at his face, I could discern nothing but grimness there, as though my arrest pained him in some way, though surely it pained me more. At least I still had the bag of coin, now sorely depleted after paying the priest to carry my message to Nell, and the ruby, both of which I had managed to hide down my bodice when I had begged the colonel to turn his back so that I could relieve myself in the privy before I was dragged off to gaol.

It felt as though time trickled past slowly whilst I waited to see if my plea to Nell had been successful and I tried to rein in my impatience. I knew it might take days, weeks even, if she were out of town with the King. I did not permit myself to think my approach might fail, for I knew how close I was to despair.

An hour went by or perhaps two, and then the gaoler was there, kicking me awake from my half-sleep. 'On your feet, Your Highness. The governor wants to see you.'

Not Nell, then, come to my aid, but potentially more trouble. I knew I should not have drawn any more attention to myself, but I burned with frustration to be locked up and forgotten.

The gaoler escorted me down the dingy corridors, up a rickety wooden staircase and into to a room that smelled of stale wine and old rot. It did, however, have a proper window and I lapped up the sudden brightness from the dazzling sun as it illuminated the dancing dust specks.

'Mistress... Cassells, is it not?' The governor of the Marshalsea, Sir Thomas Wolverton, was a large, fleshy man who had grown fat on bribes and good living. 'Ah yes.' He steepled his fingers. 'I understand that you have sent a plea for help to your sister, Mistress Eleanor Gwyn. That was, I venture to suggest, a foolish move. You should place your trust in the law, Mistress Cassells, rather than try to circumvent it.'

Clearly the gaoler had told him, but I suspected she had only spoken up after the letter had gone because she had taken my bribe and thought there might be more money from that source. Sir Thomas was annoyed that my plea had got out, but I felt a huge wash of relief because it meant that now I had a chance. The guards had not stopped the messenger. They had not torn up the letter. I had hope.

'I have done nothing wrong, sir,' I said, stretching the truth a little, 'and yet I have been abandoned here with no chance of release. I merely asked my kin for aid as I am four months gone with child and in desperate need of help.'

Sir Thomas's cold blue gaze assessed me, flickering over the slight bump of my stomach. I could not tell what he was thinking, although I knew I would certainly appear filthy, smelly and unkempt. After a moment, to my surprise, he gestured me to a seat on the hard wooden chair in front of the desk.

'I am sorry that you feel your case neglected,' he said. 'The mills of English justice grind slowly – but with compassion and fairness, of course.'

I managed to repress a snort of disagreement. There was very little that was just about English justice, as far as I could see.

'I heard that Colonel Thomas Blood and his associates had all been pardoned,' I said. 'I hoped that my sister could persuade the King to extend the same generosity in my own case, especially in view of the fact that I am a woman, and was only following the bidding of my husband.'

Sir Thomas gave a thin smile. 'It seems you are also a lawyer, Mistress Cassells, with the same quick wit as your sister is reputed to possess.' He sighed and sat back in his chair. 'Who knows what Madam Gwyn might be able to persuade His Majesty to do? We all know how quixotic he is. We shall have to wait and see.' He toyed with his quill, watching me. 'In the meantime, I have news for you – sad news, I fear – of your husband, Captain John Cassells. His body was found in the Fleet ditch this morning. He had been stabbed. Tragic, of course—' he viewed me from beneath his bushy brows '—but not an unexpected end for a criminal such as he on the run from the law.'

I pressed my fingers together even more tightly and said nothing. I had always doubted that John had the wit and the resource to escape and reinvent himself, even with jewels in his possession. A different man could have fled overseas, taken on a new identity and lived like a king, but John was too lazy and stupid for that and now he was dead. I did not feel the slightest pang of sorrow about it, other than that that he had squandered much of his life on drink and debauchery. I did not even feel particularly shocked; I had known John would meet an ignominious end.

'His parents have taken his body to prepare it for burial,' Sir Thomas said.

'*Parents*?' This was sufficient to distract me from my mental images of John's bloated and stabbed body lying in the Fleet. It was not that I did not imagine he had any parents; he had once told me he had had a gentry upbringing but had said that his family had disowned him when he had joined the army. As with all of John's tales, I had taken it with a pinch of salt, but it could have been true. I knew he had had nothing to do with them whilst he was alive. 'Well,' I said, recovering my self-possession. 'It is good to know John will not be thrown into a pauper's grave.'

Sir Thomas's rheumy blue eyes narrowed on me. I could see a gleam of calculation and spite in their depths. He tapped a document on his desk. 'Sir Grey and Lady Cassells also have a plan that might benefit you, my dear.'

For a moment, my heart soared at the thought that John's parents might be prepared to help me escape this place and offer a home to me and the baby. It was only for an instant, but I had a vision of a country house of honey stone and green lawns, a laughing baby taking her first tottering steps, a sense of peace and security and love.

I snapped out of the dream just as Sir Thomas brandished the document beneath my nose. It was a letter, the handwriting a spiky, angry script. 'You will need to read it to me,' I said.

He looked contemptuous. Shame at my illiteracy curdled in my stomach again. What sort of fool was I to imagine even for a second that Sir Grey and Lady Cassells, who sounded high and mighty to me, would give a home to a daughter-in-law like me, raised in a bawdy house, a criminal in her teens, living hand to mouth on the streets? It would be difficult enough for them to live down the loss of their son in so vulgar a fashion. More likely they would pay for me to live quietly and make no scandal. But that would do very well, as long as the baby and I were safe.

I straightened my spine as Sir Thomas picked up the letter and started to speak.

'Sir Grey Cassells writes that, as the younger son, John was never expected to inherit. However, the death of his older brother from plague last year without any issue meant that John would have been heir to the baronetcy and what land and fortune came with it.' He looked at me. 'Which is not much, in all conscience, for the Cassells have little money and an overweening pride. But as it seems you and their son were legally wed, no matter how much they deplored the match, they are prepared to take your child when it is born and raise it as their heir.' He put the letter down. 'This should be some comfort to you, mistress, if you are condemned to death for treason. The child will not suffer for your sins.'

'No!' The word was wrenched from me. I felt sick. The room blurred and tilted in front of me. I pressed my hands to my stomach as though that way I could protect my baby from those who wanted to steal her away from me. She was the reason why I had swallowed my pride and written to Nell; she was the reason I had vowed to escape from John; she was the reason I had allowed myself to become entangled with Blood's stupid plot in the first place, to provide for her, for us. I would never, ever hand her over, least of all to people who cared nothing for her.

But, like a whisper, the words slid into my mind: *If you are dead, you cannot protect her... Is it not better for her to have a comfortable life than an orphaned upbringing on the streets that would be worse than yours?*

'No,' I said again, more softly but with more determination. 'They cannot have her. The King will pardon me. Nell will help me.' If I said it strongly enough, I thought, the words would come true. I could make myself believe them.

But the spectres of my imagination tormented me: the King did not care; the law was perfectly capable of hanging one man for a crime and allowing another to go free. It happened every day. Nell would not raise a finger to help me, she would not wish to be dragged down by my disgrace, nor give that weapon to her enemies to use against her. I would be imprisoned until my daughter was born and they would take her from me a moment later and I would never see her or hold her...

With sheer force of will, I pushed the panic down. 'It will not happen,' I said, rising to my feet, 'and you may tell Sir Grey and Lady Cassells so.'

'All they have to do is wait,' Sir Thomas said. 'They are the child's closest kin, after you.'

'I have a mother and a sister too who would dispute that,' I said fiercely, and saw him smile to see how much he had discomposed me. People such as Sir Thomas throve on the pain of others; I realised that it was one of the things that he enjoyed the most about his work. 'In a day, two at the most, Nell will procure me a pardon and send to free me.'

Sir Thomas gave me his cold smile. 'We shall see.' He got up from his desk and walked over to the door, throwing it open. The ever-present shadow of the gaoler fell across me. 'Escort Mistress Cassells back down to the cells if you please,' Sir Thomas said. 'Make sure no harm befalls her – yet. Sir Grey and Lady Cassells are prepared to pay well for her child.'

'What about the letter to Madam Gwyn?' the gaoler asked.

Sir Thomas flicked his fingers as though he were brushing away a troublesome fly. 'No matter. The King will not involve himself in so trivial a matter, and even if he does, there's many a slip twixt the cup and the lip, as they say. Take her away.'

7

JESS – PRESENT DAY

Seeing Ethan again in the daylight was an odd sensation, Jess found, as though their conversation in the moonlight the previous night had created some sort of intimacy between them that did not really exist. As she watched him climb out of the Land Rover and walk across the gravel to the front door with his long, rangy stride, she reminded herself that they were little more than new acquaintances. Yet that felt odd and inadequate when her intuition was telling her that there was an elusive sense of affinity between them.

She wasn't sure that she liked the sensation. It made her feel vulnerable. After Jared had been arrested a year ago, she hadn't dated at all. She'd been so miserable, so full of self-loathing and with no confidence in her own judgement, that the last thing she had wanted was to embark on a new relationship. Even though she had started to feel a bit more robust in the past few weeks, it was still early days and a sudden and mysterious attraction to Ethan, no matter how hot he was, was unexpected and puzzling. Jess decided to try to ignore it. Ethan and Tavy clearly weren't on good terms and she was only here for a few weeks, or months, at the most, and there were a hundred good reasons why she should avoid becoming involved with Ethan Sterling.

A German shepherd, that Jess guessed must be Ted's Zelda, bounded after him with the energy of a much younger dog.

'Hi,' she said, opening the door to Ethan's knock and trying to sound neither too chilly nor too welcoming. 'Come in. How are you?'

'Good, thanks.' Ethan smiled at her. 'Is it all right for Zelda to come in? Ted's having a day off, so I'm looking after her for him, but she can wait in the car.'

'It's fine,' Jess said, giving Zelda's silky ears a stroke. 'I love dogs. She's not pure German shepherd, is she?' she added. 'There's a lot of gold in her fur and she's very fluffy.'

Ethan laughed. 'You're right, she's a Golden Shepherd, German shepherd crossed with golden retriever.'

'Which makes her even less effective as a guard dog, I imagine,' Jess observed, as Zelda pressed confidingly against her to encourage cuddles and waved her feathery tail back and forwards.

'But a great judge of character,' Ethan said, smiling. 'She likes you.'

'I'm sure she likes everyone,' Jess said dryly. 'She's a friendly dog. Would you like a coffee?'

Ethan followed her into the hall and took off his coat. 'Coffee would be great, thanks.'

Jess was very aware of him as he and Zelda followed her down the corridor to the kitchen, but she was also aware that Ethan's attention was not on her but on the house; on all the changes, large and small, that Tavy's builders had already made to a place that, she assumed, he had known from childhood.

On impulse, she turned and asked: 'How does it feel, coming to Fortune Hall these days? Is it very strange?' And then she blushed deeply, annoyed with herself for asking such a personal question when only a minute earlier she had reminded herself that she barely knew him.

Ethan, though, looked surprised but not offended. 'Someone has obviously acquainted you with my complicated connection to the property and its history,' he said.

'Oh...' Jess reached for the kettle whilst Zelda settled beside the Aga with a contented sigh. 'Lucy mentioned it. It's not a secret, is it?'

'Nothing is a secret in a village like Beckett,' Ethan said wryly. 'It's common knowledge that my grandparents lived here and generations of the family before that.' He paused. 'It is difficult to see changes to the house,' he added carefully, 'but time marches on, doesn't it? These things happen.' He took the chair Jess indicated. 'My gran should have sold up years before she did,' he said, 'but like a lot of old people who are attached to the places where they've lived for so long, she couldn't bear to move.' He made a slight gesture as though brushing away a memory. 'It took an accident where she ended in hospital to force her to realise she couldn't manage any longer. I was fresh out of college and offered to come and run the place for her – I'd always loved it, even as a kid, and I chose to study architectural history for that reason – but the real issue was the cost, of course. We couldn't afford it any longer and it's a money pit. It was a working farm back when my granddad was alive, but that's not viable any more.'

Jess put a pod in the coffee machine. 'That must have been so tough for her to accept,' she said. 'I can only imagine what it must be like to be wrenched from a home you've loved for years. It was bad enough—' She stopped. She'd been about to say how difficult she'd found it packing up the flat she had shared with Jared and uprooting herself after the court case, but she didn't want to talk about that with Ethan.

He had waited politely for her to finish the sentence, but when she didn't, he picked up smoothly, as though there hadn't been a break in the conversation. 'So, we sold the house ten years ago and since then it's been passed from developer to developer, getting more dilapidated each time. People want the land, and they think they can convert the house into heritage flats and make a fortune, but then they run up against the restrictions in the planning rules.' He stopped and took the cup of coffee Jess offered. 'Thanks.'

Their fingers touched and Jess felt again that shock, like a jolt of electricity raising the hairs on the back of her neck. She almost dropped the mug.

Get a grip, she told herself, glancing across at the neatly parcelled-up newspaper package that contained the broken shards of the mug she'd broken the previous evening. She didn't want Ethan decimating her entire stock.

Ethan's expression, when she dared to glance at him, was perfectly bland. He took a gulp of the coffee. 'Ah, that's good,' he said. 'I was up early doing some more species protection work. I needed that.'

'Bats, again?' Jess asked.

Ethan laughed. 'Birds this time. Apologies again for scaring you last night.'

Jess smiled too. 'It's okay,' she said. 'I think I'd managed to scare myself, actually. I'd been in the library and was blown away by some of the old books I found. Poetry by Sir Walter Raleigh and Shakespeare's sonnets... I felt such a strong connection to the past in there that I could almost imagine I'd stepped back in time.' She blushed, remembering Jared referring to the way she could sense an atmosphere as 'freaky'. She'd only mentioned it to him the once.

But Ethan was looking intrigued. 'Well, if anything can transport you to another place, it's books,' he said. He looked at her thoughtfully. 'From the way you talk, it sounds as though they are your thing?'

'I worked at the Bodleian Library in Oxford after I graduated,' Jess explained, 'then at the British Library when I moved to London. So yes, I suppose you could say that.'

It was the first time, she thought, that a man had actually looked interested when she had mentioned her profession, rather than glazing over at the word 'library' or even 'book'.

'Very cool,' Ethan commented. 'Isn't working at Fortune Hall a bit of a come-down after the Bodleian, though?'

Jess laughed. 'I'm between jobs at the moment,' she said as casually as she could. 'I'm taking a break to sort out my personal life.' She fiddled with the handle of her mug, very aware of Ethan's speculative gaze resting on her. 'I'm only here to house-sit really,' she added, 'but I've told Tavy I'll sort through the books in the library before the house-clearance people come to take them away.'

She saw Ethan's mouth tighten. 'I see,' he said politely. 'Well, that makes sense. I saw Ms Yates was starting to box them all up in preparation for redesigning the room.'

Jess wondered whether Ethan had heard about Tavy's demand for white shelves and plenty of glass. Very probably he had; perhaps he had had to give permission for any changes to the structure of the room. She winced at the thought of the builders ripping out all the beautiful panelling and oak shelving. No wonder Ethan sounded a bit grim.

'I'll make sure nothing valuable gets thrown away,' she promised. 'I thought I might approach some of the antiquarian booksellers in Oxford if there is anything really old or rare; with some contacts still at the Bodleian, I should be able to get a recommendation of someone good.'

Ethan's expression relaxed. 'It's none of my business,' he said, 'but I'm glad to hear it. Some of that stuff is really old. My grandmother inherited a lot of the books along with the house and some of them are first editions. I'd hate to think of them simply being thrown away.'

'Is there an inventory somewhere?' Jess asked. 'That would be a help. And why are the books still here? I mean, didn't your family want to keep them?' She stopped, feeling the colour flare in her cheeks. 'Sorry,' she said. 'That was rude of me—'

'It's fine,' Ethan said. 'It's a fair question.' He sighed. 'When the house was put on the market, my dad thought it would be good to pitch it as a heritage property complete with contents. All the furniture, fixtures and fittings were included. So were the books, some of the paintings and other stuff. He took a few pieces, but he wasn't really interested.' He paused. 'There was a lot going on in my parents' lives at the time, so I think he was just glad to offload everything. I was desperate to get my hands on the books and some other bits, but Dad wouldn't keep them, or even sell them to me. He wasn't interested in the family history.'

'Wasn't?' Jess asked.

'He's dead,' Ethan said briefly.

'Oh, I'm sorry,' Jess said. 'Was it recent?'

'No,' Ethan replied. 'Not long after the house was sold.' His tone discouraged any further discussion. Even though it wasn't a recent loss, Jess got the message: Don't pry. Which was fair enough. She'd already asked more questions than it was probably polite to with a total stranger.

'We might be able to arrange something with the books,' she said delicately. 'If there are any that you'd like...' She let the sentence hang.

Ethan looked startled. He put the mug of coffee down with a snap. 'Are you serious?' he said. 'I mean...' Jess saw a tinge of colour on his cheek-bones. 'Thanks,' he said gruffly. 'I appreciate that very much.'

'No problem,' Jess said. 'I'd rather they went to a good home. You'll need to come in sometime during the week to have a look at them, though. Tavy wants it all sorted by next weekend.'

Ethan laughed. 'She's always in a hurry. But that's fine. Just let me know when suits you.' He looked at her. 'You're going to have your work cut out cataloguing all that in such a short time.'

'Plus, I need to do some research on the house's connection to Nell Gwyn as well,' Jess said, 'all whilst fulfilling whatever the housekeeper role is supposed to be.'

Ethan's brows shot up. 'Did you say Nell Gwyn? As in Charles II's mistress?' He rubbed the back of his neck. 'I've never heard that she had any connection to Beckett.'

'I think Tavy's programme researchers came up with the information,' Jess said. 'I'm not sure. I'll need to ask them, so I'll know where to go to do the research.'

'There's a history centre in the village,' Ethan said. 'They might have something. Plus, the library at Lambourn, since this was originally Berkshire. Sometimes the smaller centres have the local history that you don't find in the big museums and libraries, or a clue at least. But I expect you know that, being a librarian.' He smiled, his sudden rare smile. 'I'll see what other sources there might be,' he continued, 'in return for the favour you're doing me with the books.'

'That sounds fair,' Jess said, smiling back. 'There might even be something in the library here, although I'm not getting my hopes up. You know the place so well that I'm sure if Nell had been here, you would have heard about it.'

'Not necessarily,' Ethan replied. 'The land and property around here changed hands a lot during the mid-seventeenth century, with the Civil War and the Interregnum and then the Restoration of Charles II. Sometimes, people only held estates for a couple of years before they were sold or confiscated. So, it's not impossible.' He finished his coffee and stood up. 'This feels like a good cue to go and see the orangery.'

'Because Nell Gwyn was originally an orange seller?' Jess laughed.

'Weren't orangeries in country houses invented later than the seventeenth century, though?'

'Actually, the earliest orangeries date from the sixteenth century,' Ethan said, 'but that was mostly on the continent. So yes, the orangery here at Fortune Hall was a much later addition to the original Tudor house. It was built in the Victorian era.' He consulted the notebook in his hand. 'Eighteen seventy-four, to be precise, although it probably stands on the site of an earlier building and would have reused some of the original materials.'

'I don't even know where it is,' Jess admitted. 'Is it a free-standing building or connected to the main house?'

Ethan gestured towards the kitchen door. 'It's across the courtyard, attached to the stable block. It's more a glorified conservatory than a real orangery, to be honest.'

Zelda had raised her head when they stood up, looking from one to the other as though to weigh up if it was worth her getting up from the warm spot by the Aga. Clearly, she decided it wasn't as she put her head back down on her paws with a contented sigh and snuggled closer to the heat.

'Sensible dog,' Jess said.

She took the back door key from the set of hooks that Ed had pointed out the previous day and unlocked it. She hadn't been out into the courtyard yet and the first thing that struck her was how cold it felt out there. The shadows were deep and the pale spring sun had not yet made its way around to that side of the house.

Underfoot, the cobbled courtyard was crunchy with the accumulated dead leaves, twigs and dirt of many years. Moss grew on the low roof of what Jess assumed was the stables. The interior looked dark and unwelcoming, with rotted straw piled up and doors swinging on rusty hinges. The glass-roofed building tacked on to the end was in an even more dilapidated state. Half the panes were cracked or broken and others missing completely. Empty pots spilled dry earth over the red-tiled floor and bent and broken wire was the only remaining evidence of the supports that must once have held the espaliered fruit trees against the whitewashed walls.

'Oh dear,' Jess said involuntarily when she saw it. 'It looks so unloved.'

'Yeah.' Ethan's head was bent and he was scribbling in his notebook. Jess felt awkward, but really there was no denying the neglect.

She unlocked the door and tried to open it, but it was stuck fast. She gave it a shove. It flew open and the door frame snapped, the splintered end tumbling down towards her. Jess stumbled back and Ethan caught her and pulled her out of the way in a manner that suggested excellent reflexes. He let her go equally quickly.

'Are you okay?' His tone was perfectly expressionless.

'Yes, thank you.' There was a fizzing sensation below Jess's sternum, the buzz she was starting to recognise.

'I'll just shift that beam...' Ethan reached up and grabbed one of the rafters that was leaning at a dangerously drunken angle. Jess averted her eyes from the flex of his muscles beneath the jacket. She felt like a teenager with an unwelcome crush.

Ethan stepped over the debris into the middle of the floor and Jess followed carefully. There was nothing here to save, she thought.

'I don't think Ms Yates should have much trouble in getting this particular planning proposal through.' Ethan seemed to have read her mind. 'The orangery has little intrinsic historical value and wasn't part of the original buildings even though, as I say, it might have earlier features. Besides, turning it into a swimming pool and outdoor eating area would give it new life and purpose. I'll be recommending that the proposal goes through.'

'Really?' Jess couldn't hide her surprise. 'Tavy will be thrilled.'

'And suspicious.' A flicker of a smile touched Ethan's lips. 'She's not used to me agreeing with her.' He wrote a few more notes in the book. 'Despite what your sister thinks,' he added, 'I only object to inappropriate changes of use on a professional not a personal basis. Fortune Hall – or Beckett Manor, to give it it's real name – has been mucked about with for centuries. Most old houses have if they've been lived in. There's no point being precious about it.'

Jess appreciated his honesty. 'Tavy does like to get her own way,' she admitted.

'Comes with the territory of being a celebrity, I expect,' Ethan said. 'People generally tell them what they want to hear.'

Jess decided not to pursue that line of conversation. It felt disloyal to Tavy who had, at the very least, given her a roof over her head, and although she liked Ethan – and agreed with him – she wasn't going to gossip about her sister.

Ethan closed the notebook. 'I've seen all I need,' he said. 'Thanks. I won't disturb your Saturday any longer.'

Jess realised that she felt disappointed. She told herself that it was because she wasn't used to the quiet and didn't want to be on her own, but she knew that wasn't true; there was plenty for her to do. She could take the shopping trip she had promised herself for a start. No, she knew she was feeling disappointed because she had hoped to spend more time with Ethan, pure and simple. The realisation dismayed her. She needed to get over this quickly, whatever it was.

They went back out into the courtyard. There was no point in locking the orangery; she could see now that the door frame had rotted away completely at the bottom. She'd better let Ed know they needed to slap a warning notice on it.

Ethan paused for a second, looking at the jumble of roof levels, chimney pots and different types of stonework that made up the house. He smiled ruefully.

'It looks lived in,' Jess said. 'When you add an extension to your house, you're not thinking about how it will appear in three hundred years' time; you just want more space for the kids or the Georgian equivalent of a new utility room.'

Ethan laughed. 'That's it exactly. And this isn't a stately home. The Forsters were never an aristocratic family. They were farmers and country gentry who lived and worked here down the years. It wasn't a house designed for show.'

Jess nodded. 'Were they your ancestors?'

'On my mother's side,' Ethan said. 'My gran was a Forster.' He paused. 'I've always felt close to that part of my family history.'

Jess nodded. She could identify with the nostalgia of a happy childhood. In her memory, the time when her father had still been alive and her mother had been sober and Tavy was just her little sister seemed very simple and bright. No death, no crap relationships, no secrets and lies...

'Are you okay?' Ethan asked, and she realised that she had sniffed away a tear.

'I'm fine,' she said. 'Families are complicated, aren't they.'

'You said it,' Ethan agreed. He squared his shoulders. 'Listen, I expect you've got loads to do, but I've been thinking about the Nell Gwyn connection and there is at least one building on the site that dates directly from that period. Would you like to see it?'

Jess felt a flicker of excitement. 'Yes, please.'

'It's called the fishing house,' Ethan said. He looked down at her trainers. 'You might need boots, though – it's muddy down by the lake.'

'No problem.' Jess had brought her hiking boots with her. They hadn't had an outing for too long as Jared hadn't really been into the outdoors, not even London parks. She set off across the courtyard to the back door.

'There should be a key for the fishing house as well,' Ethan called after her.

'Okay.' Jess went to the key cupboard and checked along the row. There was nothing labelled 'fishing house', but there was a big iron key for something called the china house so she took that one, grabbed her boots and went back out. Zelda, snoring loudly from the kitchen, clearly had no intention of joining them on the walk. 'I'm not sure if this is the right one,' she said, showing Ethan the key, 'because it said china house, but it was the only thing that looked possible.'

'Yeah, the china house is the other name for it,' Ethan said. Seeing her puzzlement, he smiled. 'I'll explain when we get there. I take it you haven't had time yet to walk down to the lake?'

'No,' Jess said, 'I haven't explored the grounds. I was going to do it today as part of getting a feel of the place.'

Ethan nodded. 'We can go out of the side door,' he said, pointing to a battered wrought-iron gate in the courtyard wall. 'It leads to the shrubbery and the old kitchen garden.' He stood back to allow Jess to precede him under the narrow archway.

She ran her fingers over the worn brick of the wall as she walked through; it felt odd and slightly magical, as though she was stepping into a place that time had forgotten. And, indeed, the old vegetable beds looked deeply neglected, with spindly stakes that had once held runner beans and peas entangled with decades of dead stalks and old colourless leaves drooping in the cold. It was a striking contrast to the manicured lawns that surrounded the drive and the main approach to the house.

'This part of the garden hasn't been restored yet.' Ethan had read her thoughts. His tone was a little dry. 'It doesn't feature in the TV programme so there's no need to revamp it.'

'God forbid,' Jess said involuntarily. 'I can't see Tavy as a celebrity gardener. Too much dirt, and she always hated worms as a child.'

The path through the shrubbery was overgrown with weeds. Sharp spikes of holly and rampaging rhododendrons blocked the path and Ethan held a couple of wayward branches aside so that Jess could pass.

'Sorry,' he said. 'It's worse than I thought.'

'I like it,' Jess said. 'It's very *Secret Garden*-ish.'

A gravelled terrace opened up ahead of them with a flight of steps down to the lawn below, and Jess realised that they had come out on the south side of the building and her bedroom window was above them.

The morning was spring-bright now with the sun peeping through wispy light-grey clouds and the old house seemed to glitter a little, the weathered stone glinting as it had done when she'd arrived the previous day. It was a curiously arresting sight. From this angle, she could see exactly how higgledy-piggledy it was, with the bays, towers and turrets built at different times and in different styles. It should have looked a complete mess, but somehow there was a charm about it that she couldn't resist.

'I know what you're thinking.' Ethan sounded resigned. 'It's a hotchpotch of styles.' He sighed. 'A real dog's breakfast.'

'Only if you're a purist,' Jess said, smiling. 'And, actually, I was thinking that it's rather appealing. Far better that than a house with no character that looks as though it's been pickled in aspic – whatever that is – over time.'

'My grandmother used to make aspic jelly,' Ethan said, reminiscing. 'It was like a sort of solid consommé with bits of egg and vegetable in it. Gross.'

Jess laughed. 'Maybe that's not the right comparison, then. Whatever it looks like, I like it.' She'd spoken without thinking and when Ethan gave her a warm smile, she was taken aback. 'What?' she said.

'You really do like it, don't you,' he said. 'You're not very like your sister, are you, Jess Yates?'

'We were always very different,' Jess said. 'I'm the nerdy one and Tavy is the extrovert. There's no reason why siblings should be like each other, is there?'

'I suppose not,' Ethan conceded. 'My sister is a maths genius who loves working in accountancy, my younger brother is into sports, whilst I spend all my time looking at old buildings and buried in equally old manuscripts.'

By now, the path had led them down to the edge of the lake, which wrapped around the grounds in a half-moon shape. Pale sunlight shimmered on the water, shining through the shifting layers of mist that were rising from the surface. A wooden bridge spanned the spot where the lake narrowed. To the left of it was one of the most extraordinary and picturesque buildings Jess had ever seen, a little stone pavilion with a wide pyramid roof and deep eaves, set high above the water. Three sides of it had a door flanked by two mullioned windows and a metal rail ran around the edge, creating a terrace. She couldn't see the side that faced out across the water to the west.

'It's... perfect,' Jess said, stopping dead to stare. 'Quite magical.' She turned to Ethan, 'When was it built?'

'In dates from early to mid-seventeenth century,' Ethan said, 'so it fits the historical period you're interested in for Nell. Unfortunately, we've almost no records on who built it, although there is a local rumour it was designed by the famous architect Inigo Jones. But as for who owned the estate at the time and what this was for... Well, it's mostly guesswork. Its position high above the lake and with a terrace would make it a good spot for fishing, which is where it got its name from, but it's also known as the china house because, in the eighteenth century, the family china was displayed here and the ladies used to take tea by the water. Later, it was called the banqueting house. All a bit grand for what was essentially a working farm.'

'I can see why it would be the perfect spot for a picnic by the lake,' Jess said dreamily. 'I assume Tavy knows about it? I'm surprised she hasn't filmed here – it's so photogenic.'

'She hasn't walked this far,' Ethan said. There was a hint of mischief in his eyes. 'When she saw it was Grade I listed, meaning that she couldn't make any alterations to it, she wasn't interested. There are plenty of other bits of the house and grounds to work on, after all. Your mum loves it, though,' he added unexpectedly. 'I've met her down here occasionally when I've been working on-site.'

'Really?' Jess was surprised that her mother could be found wandering outside, but then, she thought, she'd had so little to do with her in the past few years that she could have developed any number of new interests Jess didn't know about.

'We chat sometimes.' Ethan shot her a sideways look. 'She's nice, your mum.'

Jess wondered if her mother had ever talked to Ethan about her, the other daughter, the one who wasn't famous. Then she thought about Jared and cringed. God forbid her mother had mentioned him. But she needed to remember what she already knew deep down, which was that most people were seldom as interested in you as you thought they were. It was more likely that Una Yates and Ethan had chatted about her mother's signature bacon sandwiches or Tavy's busy celebrity schedule.

Turning back to the china house, she gestured to the stone steps that led up to the parapet.

'Can we go up?' she asked. 'Is it structurally safe?'

'It should be okay,' Ethan said. 'It passed an assessment as part of the survey when your sister bought the estate.'

Jess went up the steps to the platform first, holding the rickety metal handrail on her left and gripping the key in her right hand. The door facing the top of the steps had peeling white paint, but the key fitted smoothly, suggesting that the lock had been oiled, and the door swung open easily and with none of the creaking hinges she had expected.

Inside, there was one room, empty but for drifts of dead leaves, swathed in cobwebs. There was a chill about the place that seemed to seep from the walls, which were white-painted and peeling, like the door. Some pretty, decorative plasterwork ran around the cornice, but it was crumbling, faded and patched with damp stains.

'It feels a bit sad now, but it's got a fabulous view,' Jess said, crossing to the window that looked out over the lake. A heron was dipping its beak in the shallows on the far bank. Beyond it was a wooden-fenced paddock, where she could see a couple of horses grazing in the dew-drenched grass. Within the room, there was no evidence of china display cases, fishing paraphernalia or banqueting. The room was swept bare and Jess thought it odd how its whole history could be brushed away, lost if there were no records to say who had built it or for whom. History was a very fragile thing.

'There's an amazing stained-glass panel at the top of the western window,' Ethan said. 'That has been dated to the second part of the seventeenth century, so it's later than the original build, but again we don't know who designed and made it.' He reached into his pocket and took out a slim torch. 'When the sun shines through at sunset, the colours are amazing.'

In the early morning, the window was in shadow. In fact, Jess hadn't even noticed the coloured panes when they had first come into the building, but now, with Ethan's torch playing across the cobweb-hung window, she saw a flash of vivid brightness.

She craned her neck to try to decipher the picture. She'd half-expected it to be religious in nature, but, of course, this wasn't a religious building and she could just make out the figures of two women, both with red hair, one in a gown of green and the other in one of blue. One woman was facing to the left and had what looked like a bouquet of ruby red roses in her hands. The other, facing right, held a basket of fruit.

'Wow,' she breathed. 'It's very pretty. I'd love to see it illuminated properly. Do you know who the figures are, or if there's any particular significance to the design?'

Ethan shook his head. 'I don't think I ever knew,' he said. 'Clara and I loved coming in here as kids and seeing the window light up as the sun creeps round to the west, but I was never able to find out anything about it.' He scrubbed a hand through his hair. 'It really needs to be restored properly – doesn't everything around here – but these things cost money and no one is willing to pay for it. So...' He gave a shrug.

'Red hair and a basket of oranges...' Jess said thoughtfully, staring at the faint outline of the panel. 'We're back to Nell Gwyn again.'

'That's pretty tenuous,' Ethan commented, 'but maybe.' He grinned at her. 'There's a danger here that you may be trying to make the evidence fit the facts you want.'

'I know.' Jess sighed.

Ethan walked over to the corner and pointed the torch upward, 'There's some initials as well… Can you see them – an E and an R?'

'E?' Jess said. 'I suppose E could be for Eleanor. Wasn't that her proper name? But what about the R?'

Ethan spread his hands. 'I don't know. R for roses? Those are roses in her hands.'

'Did Nell Gwyn have a sister called Rose?' Jess mused. 'I did find something in the library with the word ROSE spelled out on it. I'll show you later.'

'Rose Gwyn,' Ethan said. 'It doesn't ring any bells, but then…'

'Neither does Jess Yates,' Jess said with feeling. 'You don't hear much about the lesser-known relatives of celebrities, do you? In fact, you hardly hear about Nell's family at all in the narrative of her life, if I remember correctly. She's one of those historical figures who only ever seems to be defined in relation to Charles II.'

'Defined by a famous lover and little else apart from oranges and being an actress,' Ethan agreed. 'It would be interesting to dig into her history a bit. Alternatively, it might be nothing to do with Nell and the "ER" could be the royal initials "Elizabeth Regina", I suppose. The only problem with that is that the building is post-Tudor and it's too early to be Elizabeth II. We'd need an analysis of the glass to get a firm date.'

'It does look old,' Jess agreed. 'Some of the glass is cloudy and some looks sort of lumpy. The red of that rose, for example… That could almost be a gemstone rather than a piece of flat glass. It's fascinating. I wonder if Tavy would be prepared to pay for the frieze to be investigated?' She added. 'She might, I suppose, as she was interested in the Nell Gwyn connection.'

She thought Ethan didn't look keen and she wasn't surprised. Tavy could quite easily hijack the project and turn it into something else – hold a reality TV fishing contest on the lake, for example, or a celebrity banquet. Perhaps it would be better to keep quiet for now and try to make a few investigations herself.

'Can you smell roses?' Ethan asked suddenly.

Jess sniffed. 'No,' she said. 'Mud and dust and damp, but no roses.'

'Must be my imagination then,' Ethan said, 'or the auto-suggestion of seeing the roses in the window. Either that or I've got phantosmia. Hallucinating certain smells,' he added, seeing Jess's puzzlement. 'It's a side effect of some illnesses.'

Jess was thinking of the rose scent she had detected in the kitchen the night before. That had been very strong for a moment before it had drifted away and then vanished.

'I could ask Francesca,' she said, half-joking. 'She's supposed to be psychic, isn't she? If there's a phantom smell floating around, she should know where it's coming from.'

Ethan gave a snort of laughter. 'You know, it would be worth asking just to see what she would say. The first time I came here, she told me that she sensed I had some latent clairvoyant abilities and I should try to develop them.'

'What did you say?' Jess asked.

'I told her I felt fine as I was.' Ethan laughed. 'She seemed to think I lacked the courage to explore my shadow side.'

'Don't mock what you don't understand,' Jess said, smiling. 'I thought you were a friend of Finn and Lucy? You should know about the haunting at Gunpowder Cottage. Lots of people have seen ghosts there or had some sort of supernatural experience, Finn and Lucy included.'

'Yeah,' Ethan said, 'but that was different. I mean, I can't explain the supernatural nature of the things that happened there, but I trust Finn's judgement, and I know that he and Lucy wouldn't make stuff up. Whereas Francesca is a charlatan.'

'That's a little harsh,' Jess said. 'She may have a genuine gift. Although I hope not,' she added, 'as she seems to think I have a negative vibe or something.'

Ethan laughed again. 'Well, I don't think that's true.' He took a deep breath. 'All the stuff about there being a bad atmosphere here, and people dying...' He was waiting whilst Jess locked the door and preceded him down the outside staircase. 'The real truth is that Francesca doesn't like the countryside and from the start she was trying to persuade Tavy to pull out of the sale. When that failed, she started some rumours about paranormal activity—' He stopped abruptly.

'What is it?' Jess said, turning. Ethan was standing halfway down the steps, staring out across the little bridge to the shallows on the other side of the lake, where a huge tree spread its roots in the water.

'I thought I saw...' Ethan was screwing his eyes up against the glare of the sun off the water. Jess turned to see what he was looking at, but Ethan was already moving, taking the steps two at a time, sprinting across the wooden bridge.

Jess caught up with him by the tree, a broad-trunked weeping willow. Part of its gnarled and knotted roots were exposed by what looked like a recent landslip; the bank had broken away in great chunks of dark and sodden earth, revealing a cavity beneath.

'We had floods last winter,' Ethan said. 'The water must have undermined the bank quite badly. Damn it, now this tree will have to be felled and it's one of the oldest willows on the estate.' He dropped to his knees in the mud beside the water's edge, peering under the ledge, brushing away some of the soil. 'It's odd, but from the top of the china house steps I thought I saw...' He paused. 'Bones,' he finished.

Jess looked down and felt a rush of nausea. Ethan was holding a skull in his hand. Around it were scattered bleached-white bones and what looked like shreds of cloth and the glint of metal.

'What do you know?' Ethan looked up and his eyes met hers. 'It looks as though Francesca may have been right after all.'

8

ROSE – LONDON, JULY 1671

Just when I had given up hope, a messenger arrived from Nell. I knew nothing of it at first for he went directly to the governor with my pardon. It was only when the cell door clanged open and the gaoler appeared, smiling in a manner that was somehow more disturbing than her normal grim demeanour, that I stirred from my dark corner.

'Mistress Cassells, you are free to go,' she said, all obsequiousness. 'There is a gentleman waiting to escort you to your sister's house. He has a carriage.' She spoke as though this was some sort of magic, but perhaps it did appear a miracle to her that so filthy and wretched a creature as I was should be whisked away in a coach by a liveried servant.

A huge wave of relief broke over me to be free. The bright July sunshine struck across my eyes as I ducked beneath the lintel of the prison gate and I almost stumbled, dazzled after so long in the near-darkness.

'Take care,' the gaoler said, as though she were always solicitous of her prisoners' welfare. 'I'll hope not to see you again!' And she closed the gate with a cackle at her own joke.

The 'gentleman' Nell had sent to escort me was, I guessed, someone who acted for her as an agent and secretary. He was a thin-faced, pernickety sort of fellow, which I suppose was appropriate for a clerk, and he made no secret of his distaste for his errand. I could live with that, though, as he was springing me from gaol.

'This way, madam,' he said, gesturing to the bustling street outside the prison, where an equally disapproving-looking coachman was in attendance with a carriage and two high-spirited greys.

'Get a move on,' the coachman said to me, far less deferential, 'or the horses will bolt without you.'

It amused me that Nell had adopted the arms and colours of our noble Welsh ancestors, for her smart carriage was tricked out in the gold and grey livery of the Gwyn family. Even as a child, she had dressed up in a sack for a cloak and acted the part of a Welsh princess. Now she had the means to make her play-acting a reality, albeit the trappings of wealth might vanish in a puff of smoke if the King grew tired of her.

'I had not anticipated that my sister would send for me,' I said to the clerk, 'only that she would arrange my pardon. Are you sure she wishes me to accompany you back to Pall Mall?'

The clerk was looking at the dirt encrusted on my skirts and seemed as surprised as I was at the invitation. His nose wrinkled. He looked as though he was expecting a mouse to make a run for it from beneath my petticoats. 'Those were Madam Gwyn's precise instructions, mistress,' he said. He recited, 'See the governor, arrange for Mistress Cassells to be released and bring her directly to me.'

I thought about it for a moment. Despite the pardon, I had still intended to go into hiding when I came out of the Marshalsea, for I was suspicious that Thomas Blood would come after me. It seemed clear to me that he must have killed John in an argument over the stolen jewels, and if he thought I knew where they were, and heard I was free, he would be looking for me too. However, for the time being, I could find refuge with Nell. Perhaps she might even help me find a place to stay until my baby was born. It would mean that I would have to swallow all past resentments and show gratitude, but I could do that if I absolutely had to.

The clerk was still waiting for me to board the carriage.

'You may place a cloth on the seat if you wish to keep it clean,' I said, and he reddened and looked embarrassed.

'That will not be necessary, madam,' he said. He proffered a hand to help me up, then sat in the corner most distant from me, wiping his gloves on the seat.

The journey took a long time for it was mid-afternoon and the streets were clogged with people and animals and carts. The summer sun was bright and had brought out those who were intent on a gentle stroll as well as the street sellers and husbandmen driving their cattle to market. The noise was tremendous, as loud as the cacophony in the Marshalsea and just as ill-tempered, as the shouts of the coachmen mingled with the hammering of the blacksmiths and calls of the oyster sellers. Nell and I had sold oysters on the streets once upon a time; that was before the oranges paved her way to glory. I remembered the rancid scent of fish and the way it clutched at my throat and made the bile rise. I was not cut out for selling; I could not persuade a buyer that a rotten orange was still sweet the way that Nell could. She could sell anything and frequently had, including herself. I could not criticise, though; my way of scraping a living had been no more honourable than hers. Where survival was concerned, morality frequently went out of the window.

Even in a closed carriage the smell of dung and cesspits was overpowering in the heat, but I had no pomander to hold to my nose like a lady would, so I tried to ignore it. Instead, I gazed out at the sky where I could see it between the overhanging eaves of the houses. It was bright blue and full of fluffy white clouds, a proper summer day. An odd feeling filled my heart, almost a longing for something, though I knew not quite what; a need to be out of the city, perhaps, lying in a meadow of scented grass, church bells ringing in the distance. That, I realised, was another memory of my childhood. I was oddly nostalgic that day.

The streets widened and suddenly the houses were grand and elegant and the road was lined with elm trees. We had arrived. I clenched my fingers in my crumpled skirts. Though I had seen her recently on the stage, it was several years since I had spoken to Nell. What would she be like now? What should I say to her? I felt anxious. Meeting her, especially here where I was so out of my depth, was something I was completely unprepared for.

'This way, madam.' We were in a shady courtyard at the back of the house. Of course, I would not be invited to enter by the front door. The carriage had stopped by the stables, where I saw two servants standing beside a water pump. Barely had my feet touched the ground when the elder of the two, a woman of about five and fifty, lifted a bucket in her brawny arms and tipped water in a cascade over my head. She gave me no greeting, let alone a warning. I thought about screaming at the shock of the cold water, then realised it was rather pleasant on so hot a day.

'Another pail, Sylvia,' she snapped to the teenage girl who was gaping at her side, and the maid pumped vigorously to fill the bucket, which was once again emptied over me.

I emerged spluttering, with water streaming down my face and my filthy clothes sticking damply to me.

'Take off your gown,' the old harpy instructed me. 'It is fit for nothing but burning.'

'I am not stripping off my clothes in a courtyard,' I said.

She rolled her eyes. 'We've seen worse here.'

No doubt. But I was not my sister.

I wrapped my arms about myself and stood mutinously still. After a moment, she grabbed a horse blanket from the fence and placed it about my shoulders, hustling me inside the stables. They were clean and the flag-stoned floor was smooth beneath my bare feet. I waited while they filled a drinking trough with water and then, once the door was closed, I sullenly stripped off my gown, making certain to keep hold of my money bag with the ruby in it, and stood in my linen shift whilst the old woman scrubbed me with a brush which I suspected had most recently been used on one of my sister's carriage horses.

The shift ripped easily because it was old and thin, and the servant pulled it off me.

The brush was rough on my skin and when the other maid started to try to comb my hair and pulled the tangles, I protested again. They ignored me. I was like a parcel passed between the two of them, pummelled and poked until they were satisfied. At one point they tried to prise the purse from my hand but I clung on for grim death.

'It is all I have,' I said, and the old woman rolled her eyes.

'We're not going to rob you of your paltry pennies,' she said scornfully.

With a knock, the door opened and yet another maidservant appeared, her arms full of clean underclothes and a striped gown.

'Will these do, Mrs Renwick?' she asked.

The housekeeper – for I had gathered the fierce old woman was of some authority here – took one look and shook her head. 'There is no point trying to fit her into Madam Gwyn's cast-offs,' she said. 'She is far too big. Fetch something from Tall Doll's wardrobe instead.'

Ah yes, tiny Nell. I was always so very aware that I was tall for a woman and generously made whilst she was a little fairy creature, a sprite, a sylph.

It turned out that Tall Doll, whoever she was, was as amply proportioned as I, which was a relief. The bodice was not too tight and there was room in the skirts for me and the babe who, at four months, was starting to show. None of the maidservants had commented on my pregnancy, but then none of them had treated me as though I was in any way a real person. I was simply a task, someone to be made presentable enough to enter my sister's drawing room. Eventually, with my hair combed, arranged into a plain bun and covered with a matronly white cap, my feet in embroidered slippers and the russet gown, I was considered acceptable at last.

It was, in fact, a pleasure to be clean after the grime of the Marshalsea, which had felt engrained in my skin. The clothes were scented with lavender and I felt as though I was a lady now, or as close as I would ever be.

The house was quiet when we entered. I had never been in such an elegant mansion before, not even in my house-breaking days. It was a handsome building of three storeys with so much light pouring in. The floor was marble and the staircase both grand and graceful. The housekeeper beckoned me to follow her up to the first floor and my feet sank into the carpet, which felt almost too luxurious to be real. I wanted to take off the slippers and dig my toes into the softness of it.

We approached a door and I heard a murmured voice, my sister talking softly, then crooning a lullaby. The servant knocked and opened the door and there she was, Nell herself, pinned in a ray of light from the window, her gown a diaphanous white, her hair in masses of red curls that tumbled down her back. She was sitting on a daybed, singing to a sleeping child in a painted cradle. As we came in, she picked the baby up and handed him to the thin servant girl, Sylvia, who took him out, holding him in the crook of her arm with unexpected tenderness.

Nell stood up and I saw that like me, she was with child, another to join the King's expanding brood of bastards. Despite the fact that the hated Louise de Kérouaille had become King Charles' mistress the previous year, evidently he still visited Nell and had not tired of her yet. It was a miracle for a man who was so easily bored and distracted.

I had started to smile, for she looked as pretty as a picture standing there, lit by the afternoon sun, illuminated like a fallen angel. I could not help myself; no quarrels or strong words could come between us when I remembered the affection we had once had for one another. But then I realised she was not returning my smile; quite the contrary, in fact.

She marched up and planted herself directly in front of me, hands on hips. Fury sparked in her blue eyes. In a voice that could have been heard from the theatre gallery, she demanded, 'Where did John hide the jewels?'

I must have been gaping at her, for she repeated impatiently, 'Where are the jewels? Do you have them? Do you know where they are?'

'Softly, madam. You do not wish the whole of Pall Mall to hear you.' The housekeeper, Mrs Renwick, was at my back, blocking my way to the door, in case I chose to turn and run, which I had no intention of doing.

The words of thanks that I had intended to offer Nell for my freedom died on my lips. 'What are you talking about?' I said, 'Which jewels?'

Nell looked as though she wanted to shake me. 'Which jewels do you think?' She demanded. She lowered her voice to a hiss. 'The *Crown Jewels*, of course! The ones that were not recovered after the theft from the Tower of London.'

My jaw had dropped and I was staring at her like an owl. 'I do not have them,' I said. 'I do not know where they are. Why are you asking?' My voice was rising along with my suspicions. 'What has it got to do with *you*?'

I saw something in her face then, something that told me the answer even before she spoke. I knew Nell very well and I knew her expressions. I recognised guilt when I saw it. 'Nell,' I pressed, with increasing urgency, 'surely you were not involved in any way in the theft of the Crown Jewels?'

'Of course not!' Nell looked and sounded affronted. Her gaze slid away from mine. 'But... There is a problem... You see, I did do business with John occasionally.'

'What?' Incredulity filled me. 'Good God, Nell,' I said, 'why would you do that? *You* were the one who told *me* not to marry John! You said that he was unscrupulous and untrustworthy, a man with no morals or conscience, who was like a leech on the belly of the underworld. I remember your precise words! Why would you have anything to do with John when you thought so ill of him?'

Her eyes opened wide, as though I had asked a particularly stupid question. 'Sometimes a leech on the belly of the underworld is precisely the sort of man one needs,' she said. She gave a toss of her head. 'I would not have married him, obviously, but he was useful on occasion.'

'What sort of occasion?' I demanded. The thought that Nell had maintained a relationship with John, the very man she had warned me against, and yet had cut me from her life after our quarrel was dreadfully hurtful. So was the realisation that she cared not a toss whether or not I was free unless it could benefit her. She had not saved me because she was moved by my letter or cared about my fate – or my baby's. She needed my help.

'Of all the deceitful hypocrites!' I burst out.

'Hold your tongue!' Nell snapped, all signs of guilt vanishing, to be replaced with fury. 'You understand nothing!'

'Then explain it to me!' I spread my arms wide, as theatrical as her. 'Explain to me why you were in league with my husband!'

'I was *not* in league with him!' Nell shouted, incensed. 'I merely used him on occasion when I wanted some information, or a... a difficult job done.'

I shook my head. I knew the difficult sorts of jobs John had done and generally they were illegal.

'You don't understand,' Nell finished more plaintively.

'No, I do not,' I agreed. 'I do not understand at all. And to think that I was going to thank you for freeing me from the Marshalsea. I was abjectly grateful! And now I see that you did it only out of self-interest because you wanted something from me.'

Nell burst into tears, though I wasn't sure if they were real or merely for show. That was the problem with Nell – it felt as though she was acting even when she was not. She had been like this since she was a child.

Mrs Renwick made a clucking sound like a hen and gathered her into her arms. It was unexpected to see this stern woman act so tenderly. 'There, there, my sweeting,' she murmured, as she gently rubbed Nell's back. 'All will be well. Just you wait and see.'

I waited whilst Nell's sobs degenerated into a series of hiccups and heard her whisper, 'She cannot help me. Oh Rennie, I truly thought she might know.'

'I might be able to help you if I understood the nature of the problem,' I pointed out. I had calmed down a bit, for my temper often flared, then settled equally fast. I was also the more practical of the two of us, whilst Nell was away with her head in the clouds. 'Tell me what has happened and we shall see what we can do.'

Nell looked at the housekeeper, who nodded. 'I will fetch some tea,' she said. 'It will soothe you.'

'Thank you, Renwick,' Nell said meekly.

'Don't quarrel now,' the housekeeper said, looking from one of us to the other as though we were five years old. 'Sisters should watch each other's backs just like soldiers do.'

'We used to,' I said, and Nell took my hand and squeezed it. I was touched but tried not to believe she meant it. 'So, tea-drinking is something else you have borrowed from the Queen, then, along with her husband,' I said as Mrs Renwick went out, and Nell laughed. It broke the ice.

'The Queen has good taste,' she said. 'I like her.'

This surprised me, but then Nell tended to save her vitriol for her real rivals, for the King's former mistress Moll Davis, whom she had fed a laxative in a piece of cake, and for the new French harlot, Louise de Kérouaille, whom I had heard Nell called Squintabella. This hatred, I noted, did not stop Nell from arranging her hair in the French woman's style, and very well she looked too. Annoyingly, she was the sort of woman who could cry one minute and still look beautiful the next; her skin was pearly pale rather than the blotchy red that mine turned with emotion, and her eyes were bright blue, not rabbit-pink. She was blooming.

'How many months are you along?' I asked her. 'You look well on it.'

'Four,' she replied. She looked me up and down. 'You?'

'The same,' I said.

Nell gestured for me to sit on the sofa, which was rosewood and cream silk and which felt far too flimsy to bear my weight.

'I do want to thank you, Nell,' I said. 'I am genuinely grateful to you for persuading the King to free me, no matter the reason.'

Her gaze slid away from mine and she did not reply. But before I had time to think it odd, she was speaking again. 'I am sorry about John's death,' she said. 'I know you loved him.'

'I used to love him,' I corrected, 'but no more.'

She was looking at me thoughtfully. 'You once said that he was entertaining,' she reminded me, 'and funny and handsome and a good provider.'

'I thought he was all of those things at the beginning,' I agreed, 'before I realised that he was no more than a bully and a wastrel and a drunkard.'

There was a gleam of sympathy in Nell's eye. 'He was a terrible husband, wasn't he,' she agreed. 'He could never keep his prick in his trousers. I daresay Peg Cherry mourns him even if you do not.'

'She should do,' I said. 'All his money went to her, not to me.' I sat forward. 'Nell, tell me what happened. How did you come to be embroiled in this situation? What sort of work did John do for you?'

She hesitated, knitting her fingers together, avoiding my gaze. 'I bought things from him sometimes,' she said. 'Information, usually, for it was good to keep my ear to the ground and to find out what the common people thought about me, and about the King, and to know what was being said on the streets and in the alehouses.'

I nodded. That I could understand. John would have been a useful spy. He was a conduit directly to the mob, a means to gauge the mood of the populace and report back to Nell on everything from politics to public scandal. Nell always claimed that she did not meddle in politics, but she was a figurehead for those who opposed the French alliance and the influence wielded by Madame de Kérouaille. She swam in dangerous waters.

'All right,' I said, thinking how much it would have excited John to be in contact with Nell behind my back, to have that knowledge and that power, a link that I was denied myself. 'I can see the benefit to you of a connection to the world of the backstreets. But what about the jewels, Nell? How on earth did you get involved with that?'

Renwick came in bearing a tray. The tea was in a pot, with dishes and a sugar bowl – all of the most delicate porcelain. The sight of the chinaware made me feel big and clumsy. Tea was an outlandish drink in my opinion, bitter and dark, but I was prepared to take almost any refreshment I could lay my hands on.

Nell was looking at me thoughtfully; she sent Renwick off to fetch me a cold venison pie and some fruit and cheeses. 'You look half-starved,' she said, as she poured the tea for us. 'I would not wish your babe to die of hunger.'

'Thank you,' I said, hearing my stomach rumble. Not even the direst of disasters could make me lose my appetite.

I drank half my bowl of tea in one go and she filled it up again. Renwick reappeared with the pie and I fell on it with all the finesse of a starving cat, whilst Nell sat beside me and nobly forbore to comment on my terrible manners. Once I had set the plate aside, wiped the crumbs from my face and sighed with delight, I turned back to her.

'So,' I prompted, 'the jewels?'

Nell sighed. 'Yes,' she said. 'The jewels.' She pursed her lips. 'Occasionally, John would acquire objects for me – jewels, watches, gifts and trinkets, small items that I could collect for...' she hesitated. 'For my retirement.'

'Stolen gifts and trinkets.' I shook my head in disbelief. Whilst I could understand Nell's need for information, this was beyond my ken. Here she sat in her pretty little mansion and mixed with nobles and courtiers, and yet it seemed she still wanted to keep a foothold in the murky world of London crime. If I had escaped from that hellhole in the way that she had, I would never have looked back.

'I did not ask where he had got the items from,' she said loftily. 'I did not need to know. I paid him a fair price and we never spoke of their provenance.'

'No, of course not,' I said. 'Oh Nell!' I could not help myself. The words burst from me. 'Of all the foolish things to do! You must have known that one day John would betray you – or blackmail you – and everything would go wrong!'

She looked shamefaced. 'I knew I could not trust him, of course,' she admitted, 'but I thought that as long as our association was mutually beneficial...' Her voice trailed away.

'Why?' I asked for what felt like the umpteenth time. 'How could it possibly be worth it for a few trinkets and jewels?'

A shiver went through Nell. The room was warm, yet she looked pinched and cold. She wrapped her arms about her waist and hugged herself close.

'I'll tell you why,' she said in a harsh whisper. 'It is because I am afraid. I have climbed so high, but my grip is precarious. I may fall. And if I do, I will have nothing. Again.' She put one cold hand over mine and gripped tightly. 'I need to feel safe, Rose. Just as you do.' Her eyes filled with tears again. Her lower lip trembled. 'I need money of my own, you see. A nest egg should the King tire of me and cast me out.'

'But...' I looked at her. Surely her pregnancy was proof that the King was far from bored with her. Yet even as I was about to say precisely that, she spoke again.

'It all started last year when his sister Henrietta brought that bitch with her from France. I knew at once that Charles was smitten in a way that he has never been with me. I could feel him slipping away. It is almost as if...' She took a breath. 'Well, you know how fond Charles was of Henrietta – Minette, as he called her. It was as though some of that love was transferred to Louise, as though when Minette died, Louise was a way of keeping her alive, of remembering her, and keeping her close.'

'Louise is the King's mistress not his sister,' I said firmly. 'There have always been other women, Nell. You know that. There always have been and probably always will be.'

'Not like this,' Nell said stubbornly. 'This is different. And, of course, the French are cock-a-hoop and send her many, many gifts in the hope she will influence Charles in their favour. Why, the King of France sends more priceless jewels to her than he does to the Queen! She could sleep on a bed of diamonds should she wish it.'

'That sounds highly uncomfortable,' I said.

Nell gave a snort of laughter despite herself. 'The point I was trying to make,' she said, 'is that the entire French court supports Louise and would like to see me fall from favour. Aye, and some of the English courtiers as well. She is so clever, but she hides it well behind that babyish face! I am sure the King is taken in.'

'That is nonsense,' I said. 'King Charles is too shrewd to have his policy dictated by the French, even if it is wrapped up in so tempting a parcel. And you say she is clever, but she is nowhere near as quick or witty as you. Besides, the English people adore you, Nell, and that is what counts here. You are in no danger.'

She did not smile this time and it seemed my words could not reach her. I had never seen behind Nell's mask before to glimpse the insecurities beneath and it shocked me.

'It was the reason why I went back to the stage last year,' she said softly. 'Not merely because I miss the theatre, but to show Charles that I did not need him, that I could make my own way. And it worked, too. He came scuttling back to me like a chastised schoolboy.'

'You were magnificent,' I said truthfully. 'No one can take away your talent, Nell. You will always have that.'

She turned on me fiercely. 'But can you imagine the pity, were I to be forced back to the theatre for my livelihood?' she demanded. 'It is different when it is my choice. But to go from this—' her furious gesture encompassed the luxurious room '—back to the stage, getting older and older, a raddled crone, until the crowd laughs *at* me rather than with me?' A sob caught in her throat. 'I would rather die. I would cast myself in the Thames!'

'Dear lord,' I said, 'there is no need for such drama. That has not yet happened, nor will it.'

I squeezed her hand. For all my bracing words, I did understand how she felt, for was she not dealing with the same fears that I was? Growing up as we had in such abject poverty, where we never knew when we would next eat or whether our mother would drink or our father gamble the last few coins away, we had always grasped after any money we could lay our hands on. Now that Nell had so much, I could see that, contrarily, she felt even less secure than she did before. She had so much more to lose.

'I hate being beholden to the King for everything,' she burst out. 'He is my dearest friend – I love him! Yet...' A tear dropped onto her gauze skirts,

'I have to ask for everything. He could give my boy a title like his other brats, but he does not, because I am not highborn. I am only a lodger in this house – I have no claim to the property, or income. I have nothing that I own outright! And so, I nag him, which I hate to do, and he hates it even more.' She drooped artfully like a cut flower and I thought, perhaps unkindly, that were the King to see her now, she looked so seductive that he would simply sweep her off to his bed and the whole merry-go-round of love, passion and insecurity would begin again.

'So, what happened this time?' I asked. 'How did you get involved with John's ridiculous plot? Did you think to offer the King a special gift of his own Crown Jewels?'

She shot me a reproachful look. 'There is no cause for sarcasm. It was not as though I was buying the Crown of England, was I?' She sounded defensive. 'I was hardly intending to parade around with the orb and sceptre! John told me that a few of the smaller jewels were for sale. He offered them to me for a good price and I knew they would increase in value over time. I planned to hide them until the fuss had died down; I know a man who could cut them for me so that no one would recognise them.'

I wondered then whether Nell had coveted the jewels because she could never have the Crown. It might have given her a secret thrill to own a tiny part of King Charles' inheritance.

'So, what happened after John offered you the jewels?' I asked. 'Did you pay him in advance?'

She looked tragic, wringing her hands together. 'This is the rub,' she said. 'I had no coin, so I gave him as surety a gold locket studied with pearls. It was only until I could borrow sufficient funds from Lord Craven to cover the cost. John promised to return the locket to me as soon as I had the money. But...' She stopped and I finished the sentence for her.

'But John was murdered before he gave you the jewels. And not only that, but he had your gold and pearl necklace as well, so you are doubly out of pocket.' I thought of the ruby cabochon that I had kept for myself. Should I offer it to Nell in recompense for the loss of the other jewels? I decided against it. The ruby was my insurance, mine and my baby's. 'I am sorry, Nell,' I said. 'I do not know where the jewels are. I think you are going to have to write off this loss and forget it.' I gave her a sympathetic smile.

'That is far better, surely, than becoming involved in such a foolish and dangerous theft. In fact—' I seized on another thought to cheer her '—you could see it as a lucky escape! If the King had found out what you had done, I doubt he would be amused. He may have pardoned Thomas Blood for whatever quixotic reason, but to discover that his mistress had been conspiring with her criminal brother-in-law would leave a bad taste.'

'That is precisely my problem, Rose,' Nell explained. 'The locket was a gift from the King. His portrait is in it and our initials entwined. If it is discovered with the lost jewels, it will implicate me and many questions will be asked, particularly by my enemies, who will seize on it to be rid of me.'

'Madame de Kérouaille again,' I remarked.

'And the Duchess of Cleveland and the Duke of Buckingham, and scores of others,' Nell said. 'You do not understand, Rose! With no family to protect me and no political allies, I am entirely dependent on the King's charity.'

'What a pity, then, that you chose to bargain with a locket that bears the image of the King,' I said with exasperation. 'Really, Nell, what were you thinking? What a downright stupid thing to do!'

'I know it!' Nell snapped. 'I knew it even before I was sent this!' She got up and crossed to the pretty rosewood escritoire that matched the rest of the furniture in the room. Unlocking the top drawer, she rummaged around amongst gloves, brooches, scarves and stockings and, from beneath them, extracted a letter.

'No one would think to look there for anything of a secret nature,' I said, and she shot me another sharp look.

'You are not helping, Rose,' she complained. 'Here I am in a pickle, and it is all John's fault for dying when he did.'

'It is not *all* John's fault,' I corrected. 'Only a half of it.'

'Read it!' Nell instructed, brandishing the letter at me.

'I cannot read,' I said. 'You know that.'

She gave a huff, threw open the door and called for Mrs Renwick, who came so quickly I wondered whether she had been standing with her ear pressed to the panels.

'Read this to my sister, if you please,' Nell ordered her.

The housekeeper took the letter delicately between finger and thumb, as though it was contaminated. 'Madam Gwyn,' she read out, in a dry tone, 'we know what you did. You will pay, or the King will know of your perfidy.'

'That could refer to anything,' I said. 'It is no more than a lucky guess.'

'Someone knows,' Nell contradicted me, 'and they mean to blackmail me. Listen.'

'Send word to the Ram's Head by the Tower,' Renwick continued. 'Then we may meet to discuss terms.'

'What are we to do?' Nell said plaintively.

My head was starting to ache as I tried to unravel this knot. 'When did John offer the jewels to you?' I asked. 'Was it weeks ago, before he disappeared?'

'Six weeks ago,' Nell confirmed. 'Directly after the robbery at The Tower. I gave him the locket as surety, then I heard nothing from him. I was fretting over it, and then when I learnt he had been killed, I decided to try to find you to see if you could help.' She had the grace to look sheepish. 'I did not know you were in prison until I had your letter,' she said, 'but, of course, I would have saved you anyway, dearest Rose. You are my family.'

'Hmm,' I said. I knew she was lying – I did not need to tell her that I had heard she had denounced me in public. Yet still a smile tugged at the corner of my mouth, for we understood each other. How could we not? Many times in the past, it had been Nell and me against the world and, somehow, we had survived. 'My guess is that John hid the jewels after he first approached you.' I was trying to put myself in his situation and imagine what I might do. 'Either something happened to frighten him – perhaps Thomas Blood's men were after him, knowing he still had the jewels, or perhaps he simply wanted to make sure they were in safekeeping whilst you raised the money. He had your locket as well and I'm sure he'll have kept them all together. He must have gone somewhere to lie low whilst the authorities searched for him.'

'Somewhere in London?' Nell asked.

'No,' I said slowly. 'London is too dangerous. People think you can lose yourself here in the backstreets and rookeries, but the risk is too high. There would be people looking for him – soldiers, Thomas Blood's men, and those prepared to hand him over to the authorities for a reward. No, my guess is that John left London and only came back when he thought you would have had time to raise the money.' I was thinking of the missing key to the fishing house at Becote Manor. It would make sense if that had been where John had laid low.

'And when he came back, he was killed,' Nell said, 'and whoever did it stole the jewels, and my locket with them, and now they are trying to black-mail me.'

'No,' I said again. 'I do not think John had the jewels on him when he was killed. He would not have risked bringing them directly to you.'

'Then how do they know to blackmail me?' Nell objected. 'They must have the locket and know that it is mine.'

'Not necessarily,' I said. 'Someone might have seen John coming here and suspected what he was up to. Or he might have talked before he died of how he had planned to sell the jewels to you. But, whatever the case, I am certain the jewels are still hidden and your locket with them.'

'I don't see how you can know that,' Nell said. Once again, she wrung her hands together. It was a pretty little gesture. 'I am ruined!' she exclaimed. 'Either I pay the blackmailer or they will expose me.'

'You are getting ahead of yourself,' I said. 'The first thing to do is to discover who the blackmailer is, what they know and what they want.'

There was a sudden commotion below, the sound of raised voices, someone singing raucously and out of tune. Some china smashed, then there were faltering steps on the stairs.

'It is your mother!' Renwick shot Nell a sharp glance. 'I will go down and help her to bed, madam.'

Nell glanced at the clock, which showed the hour of four. 'She is drunk so early today.' Her mouth turned down at the corners. 'No matter what I do, I cannot seem to keep her away from the bottle. I even tried locking her up in her chambers, but she made so much noise, I was afraid she would raise the entire neighbourhood and damage the house beyond repair.'

'I had heard that you had invited our mother to live here with you. That is...' I paused. 'Very good of you.'

'Her health is failing,' Nell said. 'I thought I should take care of her.' She smiled wryly. 'I see very little of her, for she comes and goes as she pleases. She visits the Cock and Hen in Coal Yard Alley, drinks brandy, smokes her pipe, harangues the crowd about her famous daughter, and then she is carried back here dead drunk to sleep it off.'

I knew a little of this, for Old Ma Gwyn, as our mother was known, was as infamous now for her drunken exploits around London as she had been in the past for running the bawdy house where Nell and I had grown up. Unlike my more generous sister, though, I had cut my ties with her a number of years before. I had had enough to deal with coping with one drunkard in my life.

'Well at least it isn't the King,' I observed, as we listened to Renwick coaxing our mother up the stairs.

Nell looked rueful. 'The King is out of town, fortunately,' she said. 'He cannot know anything about the fix in which I find myself. That would be too terrible!'

Renwick came back in then, dusting her hands down her skirts. 'Madam Helen is abed,' she announced. 'I have left one of the servant girls to keep an eye on her and make sure she does not try to leave the house again.'

Nell visibly relaxed. 'Thank you, Renwick.'

I had been thinking hard over the previous few minutes. 'I have a plan to deal with your blackmailer, Nell,' I said. 'I will arrange to meet with them whilst you—' I looked at her hard '—will continue to behave as though nothing is out of the ordinary.'

Nell looked stricken. 'I am not sure I can do that. I am *riven* with anxiety.'

'You are a famous actress,' I said. 'Of course you can.'

'You are to go to Burford with the King for the races next week,' Renwick reminded her. 'And after that to Lord Craven's hunting lodge at Ashdown. There will be plenty to distract you.'

Nell looked even more miserable. 'What will Charles say if he discovers the locket is gone? He will expect me to wear it! And if someone were to tell him I bartered it for the Crown Jewels, I think I would die! Oh, what a fool I was!'

It was typical of Nell, I thought sourly, that when I had called her a fool earlier, she had denied it. Now, though, she was carried away by her own theatricality.

'I will cast myself at his feet and beg for forgiveness!' she announced.

I was starting to feel that I was in a play whose script I did not know. 'It is certainly an alternative plan,' I agreed. 'Confess all to the King and he will surely forgive you, for he loves you.'

'Yet I cannot,' she said tragically, changing her mind instantly, like the chameleon she was. 'I dare not take that risk!'

'Then if the King finds out, tell him you were buying the jewels so that you could give them back to him,' I suggested. 'People have believed more outrageous lies than that before now.'

'Calm yourself, madam.' Renwick took Nell's hands. 'This is not good for you or the baby. Your sister is a resourceful woman,' She looked at me with something approaching approval. 'She will deal with this. She will find your locket and the jewels and then we may all sleep soundly in our beds once more.'

'Oh Rose!' Nell said. 'It would be so *kind* of you to help me and, in return, I will, of course, provide a home for you and the baby when she arrives.' She gave me her dazzling smile as though the whole matter was already resolved and she need not worry any more. She even yawned. I thought her about to fall asleep.

My eyes met Renwick's. I recognised a kindred spirit in her, a woman who would very likely kill to protect those she loved. My sister was fortunate to have her loyalty, I thought.

'Very well,' I said. I knew it was in my interests as well as Nell's to settle this for good. I needed to know if it was Thomas Blood who was blackmailing her and whether he had the jewels in his possession. If so, there might be a way to come to terms, and at least that would mean he would not be coming after me to find them. I would be safe.

In any event, I could not abandon Nell to her fate. We had grown up together, each looking out for the other, and our lives were as entwined now as they had ever been.

'We shall draw out your blackmailer, Nell,' I said, 'and they will lead us to the jewels. We will send word to them to meet me at the Ram's Head by the Tower. It is always better to be the hunter than the prey.'

9

JESS – THE PRESENT

'It's old, I can tell you that,' Zoe Lovell said. She was a forensic archaeologist and the sister of a friend of Ethan's. The three of them were sitting in the kitchen at Fortune Hall drinking mugs of strong tea.

It wasn't a particularly scientific assessment of the skeleton in the lake, Jess thought, but it was a reassuring one in the sense that they didn't have a recently missing person or murder victim on their hands.

Zoe had arrived with the police and had spent the next hour examining the skeleton and the site where it had been found before it was taken away to the lab, and she had come up to the house to update them.

'How old is old?' Ethan was tucking into a slice of Jess's mother's lemon cake with enthusiasm. It was well past lunchtime; the past few hours had vanished in a haze of questions and activity. After they had discovered the bones, Ethan had called the police immediately, as well as the on-site security. He'd been cool, efficient and authoritative. Jess had found it disconcertingly attractive.

'My best guess would be seventeenth century,' Zoe said, smiling as Jess pushed the cake towards her, encouraging her to take another piece. 'Don't mind if I do, thanks. It's so delicious and we've all missed lunch.' She turned her attention back to Ethan. 'Maybe Civil War? There was a lot of action around here at that time, wasn't there? Or perhaps a bit later – the second half of the seventeenth century. I'll be able to tell you more when I've done a more thorough investigation. I'm fairly certain that it was a man, though, and probably not a young one. The clothing and artefacts we found with the body might help to ID him, but it's unlikely we'll be able to come up with a name.'

'What a fascinating job you have,' Jess remarked. 'Although I don't think I'd cope so well with the bones themselves.' She was still shuddering at the memory of the sightless skull in Ethan's hand, as though he were giving an impromptu performance of Hamlet.

'It's strange, we were just talking about the estate in the seventeenth century when I saw the landslip,' Ethan said. 'There's a legend that Nell Gwyn came here to Beckett Manor; that's why we were down at the fishing house. There's a stained-glass panel in there that may date from the same period. I wouldn't have seen the landslip from ground level,' he added thoughtfully. 'It was well-hidden by the trees on the bank.'

'It seems to have been very recent,' Zoe said, 'though, again, the police should be able to give you more information when we've had a chance to survey the ground more thoroughly.'

'The burial would have predated the trees if it was seventeenth century,' Ethan said thoughtfully. 'Those willows are only a couple of hundred years old.'

'And the landscape could have been quite different back then,' Jess acknowledged. 'If there are any old estate maps, they could be useful for determining that.'

Ethan nodded. 'That's a good point. I'll dig some out for you, Zo.'

'Thanks,' Zoe said. 'That would be awesome. I'm not sure yet that it was a burial,' she added. 'There was a wound on the back of his skull, but at first glance I wouldn't say it was enough to kill him. Perhaps he was stunned, and fell in the lake and drowned, and his body became trapped in the mud. Or he was thrown in. But, like I say, I'll be able to tell you more when I've done some work back at the lab.' She stood up. 'I guess I can't pretend it's my lunch hour any more, so I'd better get back to work. Thanks for the refreshments – much appreciated.'

Jess saw her out and then collected up the empty mugs and stacked them in the dishwasher. 'She seems nice,' she said to Ethan. 'You must need a strong stomach for that sort of work, though.'

'Oh, Zoe is as tough as they come,' Ethan remarked. 'She loves the job.' He gave her a searching look. 'Are you okay? It's not the nicest thing to discover a body, even if it's been dead hundreds of years.'

'I'm fine, thanks,' Jess said. 'Though I do seem to have lost my appetite. The cake's all yours.'

'It'll be interesting to hear more about it when Zoe's had chance to examine the skeleton further,' Ethan said, helping himself to another slice. Then, 'Sorry, did that sound too insensitive?'

Jess shut the dishwasher and turned back to face him. 'It sounded... detached, I suppose. Like he wasn't once a real person, with a home and family, and life and hopes, and all the things that we all have.' She gave a little shrug. 'No matter how long ago it was, he was still a human being, wasn't he? And I doubt we'll discover much about him.'

'You're right, of course,' Ethan acknowledged. 'I'm trained to look at history in a purely academic sense and sometimes that takes the humanity out of it.' He smiled at her. 'You're a very thoughtful person, you know. Thank you for the reality check.'

'Oh...' Jess could feel herself blushing. Thankfully, her phone beeped with a text at exactly that moment and she reached for it, grabbing the change of subject it offered. 'It's Ed,' she said. 'I thought I'd better let him know about the police investigation in case it interfered with the filming schedule next week.'

'Good plan.' Ethan stood up, picking up his jacket from the back of his chair. 'What does he say?'

'Everyone is very excited by the discovery of the body,' Jess said, scanning the text. 'The film company is asking if they can incorporate the police investigation into the programme, and take some shots of the lake and of the skeleton.'

'I'm guessing the answer to that will probably be no,' Ethan said dryly.

'Also, Tavy is wondering if there's any chance the body could be Nell Gwyn herself. Oh dear.' She gave a spontaneous giggle at the expression on Ethan's face. 'She doesn't really know her history very well.'

Credit to Ethan, she thought, that he simply shook his head in slight bewilderment. 'I guess, when I think about it, there are a lot of things your sister Tavy is knowledgeable about that I'm not,' he said. 'It's all a question of what you're interested in.'

'That's a very generous comment.' Jess's voice was still wavering slightly with amusement.

'I've got to go and write up the orangery report,' Ethan said, shrugging himself into his jacket. He looked at Jess. 'This hasn't been quite the introduction to Beckett that you might have been hoping for, I imagine. Are you going to be okay rattling around here on your own?' He stopped and scrubbed a hand through his hair. 'Sorry. Forget I said that. I know you can look after yourself. I think I'm just...' He paused. 'Concerned about you being on your own out here.'

'With a state of-the-art alarm system and twenty-four-hour security.' Jess smiled at him. 'Thanks, that's very considerate of you, but I'll be fine. I've downloaded a biography of Nell Gwyn to read so that will keep me company.'

'Well, if the excitement of that gets too much for you,' Ethan said, 'there's a local band playing at the pub tonight. I'll be there along with Ted and Zelda and some more of the neighbours, if you'd like to meet them. I can't guarantee the quality of the music, but the food's great.'

'Thanks,' Jess said. 'That's probably a good idea, rather than sitting around here on my own in the dark, imagining I can see the ghost of a cavalier rising from the lake.' She pulled a face. 'Finding a skeleton has certainly put me off any ideas of wild swimming in there.'

'Wild swimming?' Ethan cocked a brow. 'Is that another of your interests?'

'I used to go to the lido at London Fields,' Jess replied, 'and sometimes to Hampstead Heath. I thought I might give it a go here because the water looked so clear.'

'The lake is fed by chalk springs as well as the Ray Brook,' Ethan explained. 'It's freezing cold, but if you fancy it, don't let a few bones put you off. It's very invigorating.'

'You've tried it then?' Jess said.

Ethan laughed. 'Not since I was a child, but my brother, Tom, used to sneak in for illegal parties sometimes.'

'Wild partying, never mind wild swimming.' She looked at him. 'I suppose you were too busy poring over architectural designs to go wild?'

There was a sudden intensity in Ethan's eyes that almost made her drop the pile of plates she was stacking.

'Do you think?' he said, and she felt suddenly hot for such a cool day. 'I'll hope to see you later,' he added, after a beat. 'The pub is the Prince of Wales in Beckett High Street.'

He went out and Jess released the breath she had not been aware she was holding. It had been easy enough to ignore the buzz between her and Ethan when Zoe had been there and they had been talking about dead bodies; it was not so easy when it was just the two of them.

She went into the library, pushing back the heavy velvet drapes to let in as much light as she could. Dust fell in clouds from the pelmet, making her sneeze. In the daylight, the room no longer looked gothic and slightly sinister, only neglected and a bit sad like the rest of the house, with the tottering piles of books waiting to be sent away. There was a painting of a Victorian Forster ancestor complete with beard and side whiskers on the wall by the window. He looked sufficiently like Ethan with the high cheekbones, dark hair and green eyes that Jess felt an urge to stare at him.

The library was the only room on the ground floor where there was a view across to the fishing house as the slope of the hill blocked it out from the west. As Jess looked out, she had the same eerie sensation she had experienced on arriving at Fortune Hall; it was as though the landscape shifted slightly, the view blurred, and she was looking out on a different day in a different time. The fishing house was still there, its low roof sparkling in the sun, but the lake was a different shape and there was a stone bridge instead of the wooden one, and a little island in the middle of the water. Bullrushes grew high by the bank and, for a brief second, she thought she saw a woman with red hair, in a blue gown, walking by the water's edge. Then she blinked and the bright vision faded and all she could see was the orange incident tape wrapped around the trees and the forlorn policeman who'd been left to guard the place where the skeleton had been found.

* * *

On Monday morning, Jess woke up at eight o'clock, had a shower, got dressed and put some coffee on in anticipation of the arrival of Tavy and the film crew. Two days in and she was starting to feel more familiar with the old house. The renovations had not yet started on the servants' quarters and she recognised the groaning of the antiquated pipes in the heating system, the creak of the floorboards and the rattle of the windows when the spring gales blew from the west as they had on Sunday night.

After the discovery of the skeleton on Saturday, her weekend had run a rather more normal course. She'd gone out and bought a few things to make her room look more homely: a little wooden bedside table she'd seen on the pavement outside a junk shop which she planned to paint pale green, a stoneware lamp to sit on it and a rug for her bed that was made from the softest wool. She'd spent that evening down at the village pub with Ethan and a mixed group of his friends and neighbours, including Ted, the security guard, and Zelda the dog. The four of them had made a great team for the pub quiz; Jess had done well on the books and history rounds but was useless on the celebrity one, to the hilarity of the others. And she'd felt welcome. There were no snide remarks about her relationship with Tavy and no one here seemed to know about Jared and her past. The food had been great, just as Ethan had promised, and the band had played some cool jazz numbers. At the end of it, Ted and Zelda had walked her home before starting the night shift and she hadn't felt even a little bit lonely rattling around on her own in Fortune Hall.

On Sunday, she'd started her sort-out of the books in the library, which had been fascinating but had yielded nothing that related to the history of the house, the Forster family, Ethan's ancestors, or the seventeenth century, other than a couple of general histories. If, as Ethan had said, the house and family were not important enough to rank above the gentry, it was entirely possible that no one had ever written a history of them. Jess thought there would probably be a couple of paragraphs in county records and lists such as Burke's History of Landed Gentry or Commoners, as it was rather unflatteringly called, so that would be a place to start.

The biography of Nell Gwyn had been equally fascinating, but at a glance, there hadn't been anything that tied Nell to Beckett Manor. Oxford was one of the places that laid claim to being the city of her birth, but even that was not certain. She had had an elder sister, Rose, who was described in a number of books and articles as 'a notorious thief' who had married a highwayman. Rose, like Nell, had grown up in the bawdy house and been an orange seller, but none of the biographers seemed particularly interested in her. One noted that after her second marriage, she seemed to have disappeared into married respectability. The only thing that had caught Jess's eye was a note that Rose's second husband had been called Guy Forster.

Jess was keen to find out more, but she felt she should make an effort to appear in control of her housekeeping duties when everyone turned up. However, the clock struck nine and then half past and she began to wonder where they were, as the emailed schedule that Ed had sent had indicated a start time for 8.45 a.m.

At ten o'clock, he arrived in a taxi with Una, and at the same time, the film crew rolled up on the carriage sweep and the whole place sprang into life. The coffee was over-brewed, so Jess started afresh whilst her mother rustled up some toast and marmalade.

'Sorry we're so late,' Ed said, as he munched toast in the kitchen. He was in a very sharp suit that morning. 'It happens a lot. The schedule is only notional.' He rolled his eyes expressively. 'Tavy and Hunter had a busy weekend.'

'I saw,' Jess said. Her sister had been featured on a number of gossip sites that morning, having attended the birthday party of a minor royal in Dubai over the weekend. Tavy had made the best-dressed lists in a long red gown slit to the thigh, with what looked like a train of peacock feathers. Clearly, the news that a dead body had been found at Fortune Hall hadn't thrown her off her stride. In fact, Jess had seen it mentioned in a couple of the papers, with Tavy giving a 'no comment' on the police investigation, clearly hoping to encourage more speculation.

'Great marmalade, Mrs Y,' Ed said to Una. 'Is it homemade?'

'Not by me, hon,' Una replied, giving him a big smile, 'but when the orangery is rebuilt, maybe I could give it a try. Tavy's planning oranges in pots around the swimming pool, in honour of Nell Gwyn.'

'Awesome,' Ed said.

'Did you have a good weekend?' Jess asked him.

Ed looked startled, as though no one ever bothered to ask him that. Then he smiled ruefully. 'I was working,' he admitted. 'I often need the weekends to catch up, especially when something unexpected happens, like the discovery of a dead body.'

'Not an everyday occurrence, surely,' Jess observed.

'You'd be surprised,' Ed said darkly. 'I get all sorts to deal with.'

Jess wondered why he worked for Tavy when it didn't seem to be particularly rewarding, but she decided she didn't know him well enough yet to ask him.

He ate quietly for a moment, avoiding her gaze. Then he cleared his throat. 'I'd better go and talk to the camera crew,' he said. 'Hopefully, they can do some background shots until Tavy gets here. She's supposed to be doing the voiceover for the master bedroom and bathroom redesign today. Wonderful breakfast, thanks, Mrs Yates.' He waved to Una, who beamed back at him.

'He's such a lovely boy,' she said to Jess.

Jess had initially been anxious about being on her own with her mother, but it soon became apparent that she had nothing much to say to her. Just as Tavy hadn't wanted to talk about the debacle with Jared, Una buzzed about the kitchen tidying and cleaning, made herself a cup of tea and wandered off to chat to Tavy's make-up artist. Jess was left feeling slightly deflated. How could she reconnect with her mother when her mother didn't talk about anything beyond the superficial? Jared had always told her that she analysed everything too much, and perhaps it was true. He'd found it irritating that she didn't simply get on with life. But she had never been one to skate along the surface, although she could see that, in a lot of cases, it made for a much easier time.

Tavy finally arrived with Francesca at eleven-thirty in an open-topped sports car that she had apparently been given as a gift by a sponsor. She was in a great mood and spontaneously hugged Jess.

'I hear from Ed that you sweet-talked Ethan into agreeing to the plan for the swimming pool in the orangery,' she said.

'That's not how I put it!' Ed looked embarrassed as, weighed down with Tavy's tote bag, scarf, jacket and small Maltese dog, he tried to open the door for her.

'Whatever.' Tavy gave an airy wave of the hand. 'We're getting the swimming pool. That's all that matters.'

The news seemed to have revitalised her interest in the project, though Jess wondered how long for. Their mother had been insightful on that at least; Tavy was not remotely interested in the process of converting the house and would no doubt have been much happier if it could be transformed with the wave of a magic wand.

'It's not such great news about the dead body, mind,' Tavy said, stopping to check her appearance in one of the big cheval-glasses in the hall. 'We can't film down by the lake and we can't use the police investigation for publicity, and they've churned up the lawn with their vehicles. It sounds as though it isn't even going to be very interesting when they do discover who it was as it's some old guy dead hundreds of years.' She gave her reflection a final, approving nod, slipped her arm through Francesca's and sauntered off to talk to the camera crew.

'You need to be careful,' Jess heard Francesca tell her sister. 'I'm getting the sense that there could be a misstep along the way today.'

'Thanks, hon,' Tavy said. 'I'll watch out.'

'That's Francesca's prediction for the day,' Ed muttered under his breath. He put the Maltese down and it immediately peed on the rug. 'Oh, for God's sake,' Ed groaned. 'He's supposed to be house-trained. I'll have to call Tavy's dog whisperer.'

'I'll mop it up,' Jess said. 'That's the sort of thing a housekeeper does, isn't it?'

Ed looked blank. 'I don't know. Tavy never outlined a job description, but I think the rug's done the mopping for you. It's very absorbent. I'll have to get it cleaned. It's really expensive – 6,000 knots per square inch.'

Jess could see that, to all intents and purposes, Ed was already the housekeeper, along with everything else he did. She was just the house sitter, which was okay with her. She'd already started checking job sites online. There were a number of library vacancies that she was qualified to apply for and she had no ties; she could go anywhere in the country, or abroad if she wanted to. The idea did not fill her with joy, but she suspected that was simply because she was tired, physically and emotionally. She'd promised herself that her time here at Fortune Hall would be an opportunity to rest and think about what to do next, but that was before she'd been involved in the discovery of a centuries-old skeleton.

She grabbed Ed again as he was rushing past with the 6,000 knots per square inch rug bundled up under one arm to be sent for cleaning. 'I don't suppose you know who it was who first discovered the possible link between the house and Nell Gwyn, do you?' she asked. 'Was it one of the production team or a programme researcher? I'd like to check their sources to help me get started.'

'It was Francesca,' Ed said over his shoulder, as he lugged the rug and Tavy's other baggage down the corridor towards the set. 'She had a dream about it.'

'Oh, great.' Jess rolled her eyes. She felt embarrassed at having mentioned the story to Ethan now. She had assumed there was some sort of historical authenticity behind it, but it seemed that Tavy had taken a crackpot idea from Francesca and simply run with it.

'I saw her.' Francesca had evidently heard her name and popped out of the living room. Behind her, Jess could see the film crew adjusting lights and testing sound levels. It was complete mayhem. 'She was standing in the orangery, wearing a green gown. She told me her name was Nell and that she owned Becote.' She pronounced it 'Bee-coat'.

'I see,' Jess said politely. Francesca, in her black silk drapes and dramatic silver jewellery, seemed an unlikely conduit for Nell Gwyn to communicate with the twenty-first century, but who knew? She decided not to tell Francesca that the orangery hadn't been built in Nell's time. Evidently, the whole thing was part of Francesca's psychic schtick. Except the 'bee-coat' did give her pause, because that was the correct seventeenth-century name for Fortune Hall. Had Francesca looked that up to give her predictions more credibility? Jess wasn't sure.

Under the heavy kohl make-up, Francesca's eyes appeared tired and anxious and she looked older and worn around the edges. Jess suddenly saw her as another of Tavy's retinue who might be nervous for their job, rather than a complete fraud. It softened her feelings towards her. 'Well,' she said. 'I'll see what I can find out.'

There was a shriek from the living room: *'That bloody dog! I want it rehomed. Now!'* and Francesca gave an exclamation.

'I told her to be careful. I knew this would happen.'

Jess followed her down the passage to the living room, where the chaos had increased in intensity. Tavy, it seemed, had tripped over the Maltese and was claiming to have sprained her ankle.

'Who would have thought Francesca's prediction would have come true so quickly,' Ed whispered, as he speed-dialled Tavy's personal doctor.

Una scooped up the dog, which was yapping fiercely at anyone and everyone, and carried it off to the kitchen. The cameras were running, capturing every moment of the drama.

Jess went to join her mother in the kitchen. 'Is it always like this?' she asked.

'Oh yes,' she said happily. 'Always lots going on. Isn't it great? Cup of tea, pet?'

'I'm all right, thanks,' Jess said. She felt like an alien, an introvert trapped in an extrovert nightmare. How had she come to be the changeling in her family, the one who didn't like crowds and noise? She hadn't been too bad before all the problems with Jared, but now she shied away from it all.

'A bit much for you, is it?' Una said unexpectedly. 'You're like your dad, pet. He was a friendly enough chap, but he never wanted to be the life and soul of the party. Not his style at all, bless him, and there's nothing wrong in that.' She smiled at Jess. 'You're great as you are. No need to compare yourself to Tavy.' She stopped. 'No one's like Tavy, come to think of it, and a good thing too!'

A lump came into Jess's throat. 'Oh, Mum!' She hugged Una, breathing in the scent of her perfume. It smelled like a warm embrace and Jess suddenly had a rush of memory of childhood scraped knees and schoolgirl disappointments, and her mother's comforting arms. When she let go, she had tears in her eyes.

'Don't set me off, pet,' Una said, but she looked pleased all the same. They smiled at one another and Jess thought that perhaps reconnecting

with her family wasn't going to be about words at all, but was simpler than
that and was more to do with just being together. Then Una said, 'D'you
fancy taking Malcolm for a walk?' She gestured to the Maltese, who was
standing by the back door. 'Maybe you'd both like a bit of quiet time? He
doesn't like crowds either. He only pees on the floor because he's anxious.'

10

ROSE – LONDON, JULY 1671

I had been sitting for two hours in a dark corner of the Ram's Head alehouse, waiting for Nell's blackmailer to show his or her face. Customers had flowed in and out of the pub like the tide of the Thames: fishermen, dockyard workers, barrow boys and girls, all the flotsam and jetsam of life. This was not an inn that was patronised by the more affluent sort of guest. The walls were filthy with the smoke of old tallow candles and the floors deep in dirty rushes, but with money from Nell in my pocket, I could command a corner table, a plate of mutton chops and a pint of sack, and the landlord kept the riff-raff away from me.

I waited first with a sense of anticipation edged with nervousness, and after a while an increasing sense of irritation. I visited the jakes, making care that no one should knife me in the dark alley whilst I was occupied, and returned to my table to discover that I had a guest, Colonel Thomas Blood.

I was surprised to see him. Although I'd suspected he might be behind Nell's blackmail, I had expected him to send an underling to do his dirty work. Yet here he was, spreading out to take my place in the carver chair, smelling of stale beer and even staler tobacco, and looking dissatisfied as he viewed the remains of my plate of meat.

I took pleasure in offering him neither food nor drink, but slid into the seat opposite and fixed him with a gently enquiring gaze. 'I turn my back for one moment,' I said, 'and look what appears.'

He showed his teeth in an unfriendly smile. 'A lesson never to turn your back, then, madam,' he said.

'What may I do for you, Colonel?' I asked.

He paused a moment, considering me with a narrowed gaze. 'You are here on Madam Gwyn's business, I take it?'

'I am,' I replied. 'I assume you are too, Colonel? If so, let me save you time and tell you that there are no grounds under which you can blackmail my sister. I do not know what you imagine you hold against her, but you are mistaken.'

He laughed, but there was no humour in it. 'What about the locket that she so foolishly gave your late unlamented husband as surety to buy the Crown Jewels?'

I felt chilled to the bone. Either John had told him that Nell was interested in buying the jewels and had given her locket as a guarantee, or he had found it amongst John's possessions. Either way, he knew the truth. But blackmail was a game of daring and skill and this was only the first move. I took a deep breath.

'What of it?' I said coolly. 'Even if you *had* such a locket in your possession – and I am not at all certain you do – I doubt you could prove that Nell had given it to John under those circumstances.'

He was watching me like a cat with a mouse. 'There might be a witness to the transaction,' he said gently. 'Madam Gwyn should be more careful – there are some whom she trusts who might be prepared to sell her secrets for the price of a glass of wine.'

I wondered whether he meant our mother. Nell had said that she spent her time in the Cheapside alehouses and whilst I did not imagine she would betray Nell deliberately, she might easily divulge confidences when she was in her cups. Or perhaps it was Renwick who was the traitor. Nell trusted her, but she had admitted she was surrounded by spies and conspirators.

The truth was that it did not really matter. The only way I could convince Colonel Blood that he was wasting his time was to hold my nerve.

'Nell is mindful of her enemies,' I said, 'including your paymaster the

Duke of Buckingham. But I suggest that, in this case, it is merely your witness's word – should there be one – against hers, and we both know whom the King will believe.' I took a breath as I prepared to deliver a threat of my own. 'You might also consider this, Colonel. As my husband was murdered, it is probably unwise to draw attention to any contact you might have had with him around the time of his death, lest suspicion fall on you.'

There was a silence between us whilst the muted chatter of the alehouse continued. Then, 'You play a hard game, mistress,' he said. He sat back in his chair, took a long swallow of his beer and sighed. 'I did not kill your husband. It was in my interests for him to stay alive.'

I raised my brows. 'Indeed, Colonel? Because he had hidden the jewels and, despite your claims to the contrary, you do not know where they are?'

He gave me another of his lupine smiles. 'Had he been as sharp of wit as you, mistress, he might still be alive.'

'Perhaps.' I was growing tired of his company and made to rise. 'I do not think we have anything more to say to one another, Colonel—'

'You mistake.' His hand shot out and took my wrist in a tight grip, forcing me to resume my seat. I disliked it intensely.

'Release me,' I said, colder than ice, and he did, but he leaned closer, across the table and lowered his voice.

'It is true that I was not averse to taking a risk on blackmailing your sister,' he said. 'I heard about the locket from an informer and I saw my chance to make some money, but...' he shrugged, 'what I really wanted was you. It is my good fortune that Madam Gwyn freed you from prison and that in turn you repaid her by coming to meet with me.' He laughed. 'Sometimes I could even believe in divine providence – or perhaps it is the devil's own luck – for I could not approach you in either the Marshalsea or at the house in Pall Mall, yet here you are.'

I had not anticipated this at all and I felt a flicker of apprehension. I had assumed that the blackmail was Thomas Blood's prime motive for the meeting; it had also been an opportunity for me to discover whether he really had the lost jewels and Nell's locket. Now it seemed he had neither; in fact, he had nothing but an informer's gossip and his own arrogance. So why did he seem so remarkably pleased with himself and what did he mean that I was the one he really wanted? I felt confused, as though I had missed a step in the dark.

He drained his tankard and slapped it down on the table. 'Well, let us get down to the more important business of the meeting, Mistress Cassells,' he said. 'Cards on the table, eh? I'll admit that I have neither the locket nor the jewels. Neither, it seems, do you, for I doubt you would have stayed in London a moment longer than you needed, if you had.' He waited for me to confirm this, head cocked.

'Your assumption is correct,' I said. 'I have no idea where John hid the jewels.' This was not strictly true; I still suspected that John had gone to Becote Manor, given the evidence of the missing key, but I certainly wasn't going to tell Thomas Blood.

'So, your husband took the secret of their whereabouts to the grave,' Thomas Blood said. 'How inconsiderate of him.'

'You should have thought of that before you killed him,' I stated.

A flicker of irritation touched his eyes. 'I told you, that was no work of mine. There were plenty others who hated him.'

This was true.

'I am still not clear where this is leading,' I said.

His gaze did not waver from me at all. There was something disturbing about that single-minded and glassy stare. 'It leads to one point,' he said, 'which is that there is still a way for me to turn a nice profit from this evening.' He smiled, his self-satisfied, predator's smile. 'You do know that there is a price on your head, mistress? I would have been glad to ignore the fact, had you been able to provide a greater reward in the form of the jewels or a payment from Madam Gwyn. Lacking that, though, I will take what I can.'

'There is no price on my head,' I said coldly. 'Your information is out of date. I am a free woman. The King has pardoned me – just as he did you,' I added pointedly.

But Thomas Blood laughed. 'You are the one who has not heard the latest news,' he sneered. 'You may have been pardoned by the law, but there are still those who are willing to pay a ransom for you.'

I felt a bone-deep cold then. 'What do you mean?' I snapped.

'Sir Grey Cassells has offered one hundred pounds for you to be delivered safe and unharmed to him.' He cocked his head again as he took in my expression of shock. 'It is not a vast sum,' he mused, 'but still worth the effort in the absence of anything better. So—' he smiled as he took out a pistol '—you are coming with me, Mistress Cassells.'

There was no attempt to be covert or hide his purpose. The Ram's Head being a rough sort of inn, none of the patrons seemed surprised at this blatant public abduction. No one spoke or interfered; there was the briefest pause before conversation resumed around us.

'Come, Mistress Cassells.' Thomas Blood gestured impatiently with the gun. 'Let us go.'

'I am going nowhere with you, sir,' I said furiously. My heart was racing and my blood roared in my ears. How dare Sir Grey Cassells put a price on kidnapping me? He was as much a criminal as his son had been. First, he had tried to buy me from the governor of the Marshalsea and when that had failed, he had offered a reward for my abduction, and all to get his hands on my unborn child. Anger and protectiveness jetted up in me.

I upended the table, tipping my wine and the remains of the mutton chops into Thomas Blood's lap, splattering him with gravy. As I dived for the door, I heard the pistol go off and the crash as everyone leapt for cover. The landlord was shouting, there was a clatter of crockery and the thud of fists as a fight broke out. But I was already out in the alleyway and slipping silently around the side of the inn – when someone put an arm around my waist and a knife to my throat.

'Not so fast, mistress,' my assailant said. 'Colonel Blood wouldn't want you to leave without him.'

This was turning into a very bad evening indeed.

I drove my elbow hard into his ribs, whoever he was, and he let me go, doubling up and wheezing, 'You bitch!'

I would have run again, but the entrance to the alleyway was blocked by another man. As my assailant straightened up, the newcomer punched him hard and he went down again, this time without a word.

'Excellent work, Mistress Cassells,' Colonel Guy Forster said. 'Shall we go?'

* * *

'Number 79, Pall Mall,' I heard Colonel Forster tell the coachman as he handed me up into the carriage. He stowed his pistol in its holster, closed the door and we set off with the sounds of the alehouse fight still ringing in our ears.

The carriage was unlit, but nevertheless I was very aware of Guy Forster sitting opposite me. His presence seemed to fill the shadowed space and make the air sing. It sent shivers along my skin – not in the way that Thomas Blood's repellent nature had nauseated me, but in a different, wholly exciting way. This made me cross; I did not wish to be attracted to Colonel Forster. He was the man who had put me in gaol, and although his presence at the inn had been fortuitous on this occasion, I did not trust him an inch.

'What a talent you have for appearing at the most unexpected times, Colonel Forster,' I said. 'I confess I was almost glad to see you.'

I saw the gleam of his teeth in a smile. 'That makes a change from the last time we met.'

'You can scarce be surprised that I was not pleased to be arrested,' I remarked.

'Such a start can blight even the most promising relationship,' the colonel agreed.

'And you may call me suspicious,' I continued, ignoring the implication of his words, 'but I think it no coincidence that you are here tonight.'

'You are, as Thomas Blood rightly said, most acute, Mistress Cassells.'

'Are you following me?' I demanded.

'Not precisely.' Colonel Forster settled back in his seat. 'I am, like so many others, on the trail of the missing jewels. Therefore, Thomas Blood has always been of interest to me, as are the people he associates with.'

I felt suddenly deflated and at the same time even more annoyed with myself. It was perverse of me to want his interest in me to be of a more personal nature, and yet I did. 'Then he was the one you were following to the Ram's Head tonight,' I said.

'Indeed. I was sitting at the table next to you.'

I thought of the man I had barely noticed who had been slouched on the bench near us. All I could recall of him was a dark cloak, large hat and villainously smelly clay pipe.

'When he sought to coerce you to leave with him,' Colonel Forster continued, 'I slipped out so that I could be ready to follow you both. However, I am starting to know you, Mistress Cassells.' I could feel his gaze on me through the dark. 'I doubted you would agree to the Colonel's plan, and I was proved correct. I do not suppose that you needed my help, but it was satisfying, nonetheless.'

I was silent for a moment as I thought on his words. 'Did you overhear my conversation with the Colonel?' I asked.

He smiled at me. 'Every word.'

'Are you a spy?' I demanded.

Colonel Forster shrugged. 'My work may sometimes involve subterfuge.'

'You do not sound very trustworthy,' I declared.

'And yet I am on the side of the angels,' Colonel Forster replied.

'Huh.' I was no ingenue to be lured into believing him. He might well be working for the King, but if that were so, that was no good news for me – or for Nell. I decided to tackle that head on. Guy Forster seemed to be a man who appreciated straight talking. 'If you overheard the entire conversation,' I said, 'you will know that Colonel Blood was trying to blackmail my sister.'

'I did gather that,' Guy agreed. He said nothing else.

'He had misunderstood the situation,' I said, picking my words carefully. 'He has no hold over her.'

'Because he does not know the location of the jewels or Madam Gwyn's locket?'

I had meant to imply, of course, that Thomas Blood had been mistaken in claiming that Nell had agreed to buy the jewels from John. However, it was odd; under Colonel's Forster's intent gaze, I found I did not want to lie. 'Precisely,' I said, and saw him relax, as though I had answered some unspoken question that he had about me. 'Without any evidence, no one could prove anything.'

'I understand you, Mistress Cassells.' Guy Forster's tone was dry. 'Let me reassure you that neither Lord Craven nor I have any interest in seeing Madam Gwyn fall from the King's favour. That would be to no one's benefit.'

I breathed a little more easily. 'I am glad you think so too.'

'I cannot begin to imagine what might prompt her to get involved in such a scheme,' the colonel added, 'but no doubt she had a good reason.'

'She and I both live in fear of poverty,' I said. For a moment, I felt tempted to tell him of our lifelong scrabble to survive – dangerously tempted. I wanted him to *know*, to understand me. I wanted to spill all my secrets and to trust him. It was a shock to acknowledge it, even if it was only to myself. This man could get past all my defences.

I dug my nails into the palms of my hands and told myself not to be a fool. What was important here was that Colonel Forster had no interest in bringing Nell down.

The carriage drew up outside Nell's house. I made to open the door and descend, but he put his hand on my arm briefly.

'Stay,' he said softly. Adding, 'Please. There is something I wanted to ask you.'

I waited. Outside the carriage, the sounds of London at night were no more than a dim murmur.

'Thomas Blood wanted to abduct you to gain a reward from Sir Grey Cassells,' Guy stated.

'So, you heard that as well,' I said.

'I did. What does Cassells want from you?'

'He wants my child,' I replied. I rested my hand protectively on my bump. 'When she – or he – is born, Sir Grey plans to take the baby from me and raise it as his heir.'

I heard him catch his breath sharply. It was too dark to see his expression clearly, but I sensed that I had shocked him, and there was some other emotion there too, something like pain.

'Of course, she cannot inherit the title if she is a girl,' I added. 'Which she will be. I am sure of that already. But, either way, Sir Grey wants me within his control until the baby is born and he is not particularly scrupulous in how he achieves that.' I did not mention that my former father-in-law had already tried to buy me from the governor of the Marshalsea as though I were no more than a sack of coal. Nor did I say that hell would freeze over before I allowed Sir Grey to take any child of mine. I thought that was probably obvious.

'And what of you?' Guy's voice had an edge of cold, hard anger. 'Has Sir Grey offered you a settlement, a home?'

I laughed. 'A home at the bottom of the Thames, perhaps. Once he has the baby, I would not give much for my odds of survival. He wants no truck with me or my family. Vermin was the word he used to describe us.'

I waited for Guy to argue with me, to tell me that a gentleman such as Sir Grey Cassells would never behave so poorly, but he said nothing.

'Sir Grey has an old name and a high regard for his station,' I said, on a sigh.

'You are defending him?' Guy sounded outraged.

'Not at all. I am merely explaining his reasons.'

'No reasons are good enough to excuse such villainy,' Guy said, and there was such controlled fury in his voice that I felt oddly comforted, even though I knew his opinion should not matter to me and could make no difference.

'I have a place to go, a place of safety, until the baby is born,' I said, omitting the fact that I hoped Becote Manor would also prove to be the place where John had hidden the missing Crown Jewels. 'I shall leave London for a while. You need not concern yourself about me – if that was what you were doing.'

'And then what?' Guy demanded. 'Are you to be looking over your shoulder the rest of your life, trying to protect yourself and your child from whatever Sir Grey Cassells plans?'

'I had not thought that far ahead,' I admitted. 'For now, just to be safe would be enough.' It was only as I spoke that I realised how deeply I longed for that security, for a time when I might no longer need to always be on my guard, a time and place where I could sleep and rest.

I certainly could not have anticipated his reply.

'Then think about it a little now,' he said. 'Marry me.'

11

JESS – THE PRESENT

The church in Beckett village was a sturdy affair, foursquare with a squat tower. Jess let herself in and stood for a moment absorbing the smell of dust and lilies mingled with polish, and watched the light slant through the stained glass to speckle the stone floor. She was no expert on architecture – she needed Ethan for that – but it struck her that there was a lot going on in the building, with classical and gothic styles side by side, round arches, pointed arches, dark wood, ironwork, a strange mishmash that was quite charming. It reminded her of Fortune Hall in the way that higgledy-piggledy bits and pieces had come together.

The guidebook gave a succinct history of the building, originally twelfth century but extensively rebuilt in the seventeenth through the largesse of a Lord Craven, and it detailed the major monuments. Putting her pound coins in the box, Jess flipped the pages over and one line immediately caught her eye, quoted from Simon Jenkins' book of *England's Thousand Best Churches*: 'The first impression is that Inigo Jones paid a flying visit, told a local builder to try Tuscan, and then vanished again...'

Inigo Jones. There he was again. Jess could imagine the famous architect dropping in to give the locals some advice on everything from churches to fishing houses, scribbled on the seventeenth-century equivalent of the back of an envelope.

The Viscounts Benfleet had been the local aristocrats and patrons of the parish, and the church chancel was a shrine to the family, stretching back to the eighteenth century. Admirals, government ministers, philanthropists and soldiers were all commemorated in plaster and stone; the women of the family were, as always, far less prominent.

The Benfleets, Jess read, had lived at Benfleet Hall on the far side of the village from Beckett Manor, a vast Georgian edifice that was now a conference centre. They were clearly the first family of the neighbourhood. After some searching, Jess also found the gravestones and tombs of the Forsters, Ethan's family, a few inside the church but mostly out in the graveyard, as befitted the less-important dynasty in the village. Social hierarchy, she reflected, was nowhere more clear than in the local church. It was impossible to work out any sort of family tree from the gravestones as many were so weathered that the names and the dates were barely visible. She would need to wait for Ethan to send her the family tree he had promised. As for the mysterious benefactor, Lord Craven, he was nowhere to be seen.

In the meantime, the local history archive was just along the street in the village hall. Jess wandered down Church Walk, lined with lime trees, and out onto the high street, with its deli, pubs and craft shops. It was a bright and busy place – buses went to Oxford and Swindon every half-hour, there was a school and several cafés and, Jess was pleased to see, a telephone box library. You never knew what you might find in one of those.

'What can I get you?' the cheerful man behind the counter in the village hall tearooms asked, balancing a plate of scones in one hand and a china teapot in the other. He had on a stripy apron and a badge that announced he was Clive and was the curator. Evidently, there was some multitasking going on. From the next room came the sound of music and children playing; it was pre-school, according to the signs.

'A cup of tea and some carrot cake please,' Jess said. 'My mum recommended it,' she added, 'and she knows a thing or two about cake.'

'You must be Una's daughter,' Clive said. He put the scones down on the display counter. 'I thought you looked familiar.'

Jess waited for the inevitable comments about being Tavy Yates' sister, but none came.

'She pops in to the village quite a bit, your mum,' Clive continued. 'She's a live wire, isn't she?' He reached for a china teacup and poured for her. 'Milk, sugar?'

'No sugar, thanks,' Jess said. 'I didn't realise Mum had had the chance to come into Beckett,' she added. 'The filming schedule keeps everyone pretty busy.'

'She recommends the shops and local business on her YouTube channel,' Clive said. 'It's great for bringing in custom. She even said the history centre was worth a visit if you liked that sort of thing. Can't ask for better than that.'

'That's why I'm here,' Jess said, smothering a smile at Una's backhanded compliment. 'I thought I'd pop upstairs to the history centre after I've had my tea. I'm trying to find out about the seventeenth-century history of Beckett Manor and the Forster family.'

'There's very little information on the building of the original Becote Manor,' Clive said. 'There's even less on the building of the fishing house, if that's what you're after. The story about it being designed by Inigo Jones is pure speculation based on the style and approximate date.' He passed her the cup and saucer, and cut a generous slice of carrot cake. 'People always want to know about that, plus the tale that the Crown Jewels were hidden there. It's not proper history,' he added disapprovingly. 'Only myth.'

'The Crown Jewels?' Jess was startled. 'That's a Beckett legend I hadn't heard.' Tavy, she thought, would be beside herself if she knew. Forget Nell Gwyn; she'd have Jess out searching for lost treasure. 'When was this?' she asked. 'The English Civil War? Charles I's royal jewels were sold off, weren't they? Didn't someone find part of them in a field in Northamptonshire a few years ago?'

Clive nodded. 'That's the sort of discovery that encourages these daft theories,' he said morosely. 'But the Beckett story is later than that. It dates to the Restoration period, when Thomas Blood tried to steal the jewels from the Tower of London.'

A couple and a family came up to the counter and he excused himself to serve them whilst Jess took her tea and cake outside onto the terrace. It was pleasantly warm in the sun if she kept her jacket on, and there was a view across the quintessential village cricket pitch to the rows of houses beyond. The houses were new, but the setting felt timeless, the layers of history overlaid on one another stretching back to the time of Ethan's ancestors and beyond. Jess thought of the armies of the Civil War rampaging across this landscape and the other historical events that had shaped the nation's story but also touched local places like Beckett. Not everything had happened in London. It wasn't, she thought as she cut into the carrot cake, entirely impossible for all these legends to have their origins in truth.

Clive reappeared as she was refilling her teacup and she said as much to him.

'Well, the Crown Jewels aren't in the fishing house now, that's for sure,' he said. 'People have searched it time and again as a result of that daft legend.'

Jess wondered why Ethan hadn't mentioned it when they'd been discussing the history of Becote Manor. Perhaps he hadn't wanted Tavy going off on another pseudo-historical tangent or perhaps he knew it was plainly untrue.

'Why do people always want to believe fiction over fact?' Clive was musing now.

'It's usually more fun,' Jess said, smiling. 'Humans like storytelling.'

'Well, that's true,' Clive said. He took off the apron. 'There's already plenty of stories going round about the body they found in the lake. I don't suppose you know anything about that?' He looked hopeful.

'Sorry,' Jess said. 'There's no news on it yet other than it wasn't recent, fortunately.'

'Rum business.' Clive was shaking his head. 'Well, I'll nip up and set up the computer for you. All our records are online, but there are books and files as well, of course. Come up when you're ready.'

'Thank you,' Jess said. She would try to hunt down the story of the Crown Jewels as well as the more historically attested records of Becote Manor.

When she'd finished the last crumbs of cake and drained her tea, she went up the spiral stone staircase to the first floor, where the history centre was signposted opposite the parish council rooms. It was up in the attics, a long room with a sloping, beamed roof, lined with metal shelves, but it was brightly lit and the computer was by the window with a view out over the playing fields.

Clive had helpfully called up a list of articles from the archives and put a small pile of books and files on the table next to the computer. The first item was a document about the different building phases at Becote with the information that in the Tudor era it had belonged to a courtier called Sir William Essex, who had been a major landowner in Berkshire at the time. There were no drawings or pictures from that period, though it was conjectured to have been a long, low L-shaped building with a dovecote to the west. Jess could see that the east wing of the present house was newer, as was the second storey in some places. A later pencil sketch, again undated, showed the same house but with the addition of the fishing house and – she felt a chill down her neck when she saw it – a small stone bridge over the lake, just like the one she had imagined she'd seen when she had looked out on Saturday morning...

She turned her attention to the fishing house itself. Here, there were various records, ranging from the formal Grade I listing on the Heritage Register to a delightful extract from *A Book of English Gardens* by M. R. Gloag, dating to the early twentieth century. This had no hesitation in attributing the fishing house to Inigo Jones and gave a wonderful description of the flower gardens and arboretum into the bargain. *'The house is approached by a long terrace walk of grass, along which runs a railing covered with trailing roses... It bears the seal of its master – the princely Inigo Jones,'* the paragraph concluded. Jess wondered whether there had once been an actual architect's signature of some sort or if this was just hyperbole on the part of the author. The bit that amused her the most was a disapproving postscript: *'There is a stained-glass window in rather naïve style on the west side of the building. This was added later in the seventeenth century and is most definitely not the work of Jones.'*

On impulse, she looked up Inigo Jones in the Dictionary of British Architects, but there was nothing there about the fishing house, nor did it seem likely that his work would have taken him to Becote. It was only a small house and Jones was surely too important to work for anyone below the rank of a duke or, at a pinch, an earl. It was always possible that someone had copied his style, however, and whilst they were about it, maybe they had advised on the rebuilding of the church in the seventeenth century as well. A pupil of Jones had visited the area in the 1650s and Jess's money was on him.

Going back to the records of the manor held at Berkshire Records Office, she noted that Sir William Essex had sold the estate in the early 1600s to Oxford University and that only a few years later it had been purchased by a Dr Edmund Gwyn, Canon of Christ Church, Oxford. Jess was so shocked that she knocked her pen and notebook off the desk.

'All right?' Clive popped up beside her. 'You look as though you've seen a ghost.'

'I think I might have done,' Jess said. 'I've been looking for a connection between Becote Manor and Nell Gwyn and I think I may have found it.'

She went to the search box and typed in Dr Edmund Gwyn. There was very little about him other than that he had been a clergyman who had died in 1624. Then she found a comprehensive article by a genealogist which suggested that Edmund was the father of Nell Gwyn's father Thomas, and another son. A number of historians had rejected this lineage as the clergyman had apparently been forbidden from marrying.

'That seems a little naïve of them,' Jess observed to Clive, who was reading the article over her shoulder. 'So, do you think the Becote estate passed from Edmund to Thomas Gwyn and from Thomas to Nell?' she added, but Clive was shaking his head.

'I doubt it,' he said. 'There was too much upheaval and change during the mid-seventeenth century for the estate to have been passed down that smoothly. There's documentation to show that Becote belonged to a parliamentary supporter for a while after the Civil War.' He extracted one of the books from the pile. 'Here it is. In 1650, Becote was the property of Henry Marten. He was one of the regicides of Charles I – he signed his death warrant.'

Jess remembered the biography of Nell that had stated that her father had been a Royalist soldier. 'I expect Thomas' estate was confiscated because he supported the wrong side,' she said. 'Plus, he apparently died in prison, probably for debt; he might have sold it.'

'You'd need to check the National Archives to see if the estate was awarded to Nell Gwyn by Charles II after the Restoration,' Clive opined. 'It's possible. He tried to push some poor bishop out of his house in Winchester so Nell could stay there in the 1680s, so you can imagine him granting Becote to her. Maybe she was the one who sold it to the Forsters. They came along soon after, but again, any official documentation seems to have been lost.'

'All these gaps in the historical record.' Jess rubbed her eyes, which were starting to feel a bit sore from staring at the screen. She stood up; stretched. The clock was showing ten to four. 'I know you close in a few minutes,' Jess said, 'but might I borrow the book about the Civil War? I promise to bring it back. And I don't suppose you have anything about the theft of the Crown Jewels, do you?'

'No,' Clive admitted, 'but Lambourn Library could get one for you. They've got a good local history section as well. And there's plenty of stuff about it online.'

'One last question,' Jess said. 'Who was Lord Craven? The one who rebuilt the church here in the seventeenth century?'

Clive laughed. 'You've hit on another bit of contested history there. Whilst the church gives Craven the credit for the rebuild, based on a number of historical sources, there's plenty of people around here say he had nothing to do with Becote. What is a fact is that he was a friend of King Charles II. He owned the big house over Lambourn way that belongs to the National Trust now, Ashdown.'

'He was a friend of King Charles II?' Jess said. She gathered up the books and slipped them into her bag. 'That sounds promising. I'll add it to my list of things to investigate.'

'Give my best to your mum,' Clive said, as he ushered her to the door. He smoothed his hair in a gesture Jess found endearingly self-conscious.

'Will do,' she replied, smiling. 'If you're passing Fortune Hall any time, why not drop in for a cup of tea? I'm sure Mum would be thrilled to see you.'

Clive blushed. 'I couldn't do that – don't want to get in the way of the TV folk and celebrities.'

'Trust me,' Jess said, 'Mum would be really happy if you did.'

She walked back along the high street in the sunshine, admiring the cottage gardens with their bright splashes of daffodils, and crossed the road when the big stone wall around the Beckett estate came into view. Tavy's security firm had added metal railings to the top, which made Jess wince, as they looked both ugly and anachronistic as well as downright unwelcoming. There was an old, ivy-clad arched gateway in the wall that would have been reminiscent of something out of *The Secret Garden* if it hadn't been for the keypad and security cameras. Ed had given her the code, so she keyed it in and went through into the arboretum.

When she'd walked into the village earlier, she'd gone round by the road to the church, but this route was quicker, Ed had said, as long as she didn't mind the muddy paths. Jess thought it was well worth it. There was a vast avenue of beech trees leading down to the lake. Their bronze buds were already starting to unfurl into spring green, framing the view of the house on the other side of the water.

As she came down the path to the lake, the fishing house came into view, and the wooden bridge beside. She realised that approaching from this side, the path was still fenced off by the police incident tape. She was going to need to duck under it to cross, but the way was guarded by a constable in a high-vis jacket. Somewhat to Jess's surprise, she saw that he was chatting to the unlikely combination of Una and Francesca, or at least Una was chatting. Francesca was standing slightly to one side, smoking.

'...I'm a widow myself,' Jess could hear her mother saying, 'but I wouldn't rule out remarrying if I found the right person.' She patted the policeman on the arm. 'You're quite right to be wary of making a commitment though, Jack. It's a very serious thing, marriage.' She looked up at the sound of Jess's footsteps. 'Hello, pet! We just popped out to bring Jack a cup of tea. It's boring being stuck out here on your own.'

'I don't mind,' Jack said. 'I've got Panda Pop on my phone. D'you want to come through?' he added to Jess. 'Mind you don't slip into the lake.'

So much for not contaminating the scene of an investigation, Jess thought. She stepped gingerly over the edge of the bank and Una gave her a surprisingly strong pull onto the lawn.

Francesca threw away her cigarette butt and came to join them. 'Any news on when the investigation will be finished?' she asked Jack. 'Or who the body might be?'

Jess assumed this was why Francesca had come outside, other than to have a quick smoke. Her black stiletto boots weren't designed for the grass and usually she didn't venture further than the terrace, but if she could pick up a few clues about the police investigation, she might be able to parlay them into another premonition or two.

'Nothing new,' Jack confirmed. 'You got any tips for us? We sometimes have psychics helping with investigations.'

Francesca looked vague. 'He wanted revenge,' she said after a moment. 'He was consumed by it.'

'Right-o.' Jack drained his mug and passed it back to Una with a word of thanks. 'Let us know if you get any more insights,' he added to Francesca and Jess was fairly certain he meant it.

The three of them walked back towards the house together.

'Clive at the history centre says hello,' Jess said to her mother. 'You really do know everyone, don't you, Mum?'

'People are interesting,' Una said. 'I like chatting to them.' She fixed Jess with her disconcertingly intent blue gaze. 'You mustn't let that one bad experience with Jared make you hide away, pet. There are lovely people out there. For a start, there's Ethan—'

'Mum,' Jess warned. 'I'm not ready to move on yet.'

'Jared Carter will come to a bad end soon,' Francesca put in unexpectedly. 'When the stars align.'

'Crikey,' Jess said. 'I almost feel sorry for him.' She was genuinely taken aback. Francesca's gnomic sayings could be very disconcerting when they arrived like that, out of the blue.

'You should trust her.' Una gave Francesca a little smile and a pat on the arm. 'She was right about Tavy having a slip-up today. Francesca sees things the rest of us don't.'

Jess wondered whether Francesca had encouraged Malcolm to trip Tavy up, then reminded herself that she was trying to be more charitable to her sister's psychic. After all, Francesca had apparently seen Nell Gwyn in the orangery and now it seemed there *was* a Gwyn connection to Beckett Manor.

'Do you know why Tavy chose to rename Beckett Manor as Fortune Hall for the TV series?' she asked.

'I expect she was hoping it would make her another fortune,' her mother cackled.

Francesca smiled thinly and Jess remembered Ethan saying that Francesca had tried to put her sister off the project with her comments about hauntings and negative vibes. 'There was a fortune lost and found here,' Francesca murmured. She stopped for a moment to release one booted heel from the gravel path. 'Sadness and joy, happiness and grief.'

Once again, Jess had to bite her tongue to stop herself from pointing out that that was the case with most houses – the sadness and joy bit, if not the fortune lost and found.

And then, as if on cue, a private ambulance swept round the bend in the drive and came to a halt outside the main door of Fortune Hall. Several people ran to open the doors – Ed, two paramedics and someone carrying three bouquets of flowers.

'From the hospital staff and fans, I expect,' Una said. 'Did you see the pictures of the nurses posing with Tavy on Instagram?'

'I didn't even know she'd been taken to hospital,' Jess said.

A second car arrived and a camera operator hopped out, positioning himself at the best point to capture Tavy's descent from the ambulance. The lens swept around to show Jess, Una and Francesca standing nearby.

'Great,' Jess said, under her breath. 'Now we look like a reception committee.'

Tavy appeared in the doorway. She was leaning on crutches and also leaning heavily on a good-looking paramedic. Her left ankle was in plaster, but she was smiling at the camera and looked radiant.

'Livestream,' Una grabbed her phone and went directly to Tavy's Instagram feed.

'I'm home!' Tavy was saying. 'Back at my lovely Fortune Hall! Thank you all so much for your kind and caring messages. My fans are the best! So are the wonderful staff at the Great Western Hospital in Swindon.' She blew them a kiss.

To Jess, watching simultaneously live and on Una's screen, it felt surreal. But then she stopped hearing Tavy's words and stopped focusing on her on the screen, because in the tiny background to the shot of her sister, she could see the fishing house and the lake, and there was a woman in a blue gown walking over a stone bridge that was most definitely not there...

Then the camera swung around again and the woman and the fishing house vanished from view.

12

ROSE – LONDON, JULY 1671

'Have your wits gone begging?' I asked Guy Forster. 'We have met only three times. The first time you had a sword at my throat, the second time you arrested me and the third you propose marriage! I barely know you!'

He shrugged easily. He seemed amused. 'What you see is what you get, Mistress Cassells. I am thirty-two years old, I served in the army under Lord Craven's command and now I am his agent. I am the younger son of a family with a little land, less money and no title; I earn enough to support a wife and child and would be honoured if you were to accept my suit.'

He could have added that he was handsome and honourable and would never raise a hand against a woman the way that John had to me or force his attentions on an unwilling wife. These things I was sure of from instinct and observation. But that did not mean that I was prepared to trust him with me and my baby on so little acquaintance.

That said, I was flattered once I had recovered from my shock. I had never received a formal offer of marriage like this, so I did take a moment to appreciate it before I rejected it.

'Colonel Forster,' I said, 'I am very aware of the honour you do me in asking me to marry you, but—'

'The honour would be all mine, I assure you, Mistress Cassells,' the colonel put in gravely.

'I cannot believe it!' I said. 'I am the pregnant widow of a criminal. I am a convicted criminal myself!' I held out my wrist where the thief's mark was invisible in the dark but felt to me as though it glowed like the original brand. 'I have lived by my wits since I was a child. I lie, I steal and I put my own survival and that of my child above all else. I would kill for her! Do you understand that, Colonel Forster? Do you understand the sort of woman I am?'

There was a moment when the silence in the coach seemed very loud, then Colonel Forster said, 'You are also clever, brave and loyal, Mistress Cassells, and—' a hint of amusement came into his voice '—men can be strange, quixotic creatures. We know what we want, and I want you. I have done since the moment I first saw you in that alleyway fending off those foolish lads, with your wit and your little knife and your gallant spirit. So, yes, I do understand the sort of woman you are.'

Almost every part of what he said took my breath away. And then he took my hand, the one with the thief's mark, and brushed his lips against my wrist. The skin had always been tender there after the branding, but now it felt sensitive in a different way, alight to his touch. I could not have spoken had I tried. I was as tongue-tied as a girl with her first suitor.

'Think about my proposal,' he said persuasively. 'I shall not seek to press you for a decision, but please consider the benefits for yourself, but more particularly for your unborn child. And meanwhile...' He opened the carriage door and sprang down to help me alight. It was ridiculous to feel cherished with such a small gesture, and yet I did. 'Please allow me to escort you to wherever you will be staying in the country,' he finished. 'I would like to see you safe.'

This snapped me out of my romantic preoccupations. It was not in my interests for Guy Forster to escort me to Becote as my main task there was to discover if John had hidden the jewels and to recover Nell's locket. All my suspicions came rushing back. Did he still suspect me of knowing the hiding place of the missing jewels? Was his proposal all a sham to trick me into confiding?

'I do not think so—' I began, but he held up a hand.

'Please, Rose. I need to know all will be well with you.'

I closed my mouth in a tight, mutinous line.

He seemed to take my silence for agreement, albeit reluctant agreement, for he added, 'I would like to come in and speak with both you and Madam Gwyn about the arrangements for our journey.'

'I do not suppose I can stop you, Colonel,' I said grumpily. 'You seem like a man who makes his own decisions.'

'Forgive me.' He shot me a smile that was pure charm. 'In the military, we are accustomed to acting swiftly and decisively.'

He rapped on the door, and when the porter answered, a very brief conversation took place before we were both ushered upstairs by Renwick. She cast me one sharp, suspicious look but remained tight-lipped.

It was clear that Nell already knew Colonel Forster and she greeted him with every appearance of delight. I felt a twinge of jealousy that she made her liking for him so clear, but Nell always bathed every attractive man she met in the warmth of her smile and the colonel was undeniably attractive.

He was also extremely proper, bowing to her and showing her every respect, refusing her tacit invitation to flirt. This pleased me, although I did not care to admit it to myself.

'Thank you for receiving me at such a late hour, Madam Gwyn,' he said. 'I met your sister Mistress Cassells at the Ram's Head by the Tower this evening and escorted her home after we ran into a small amount of trouble with Colonel Thomas Blood.'

'It was nothing that I could not deal with,' I countered, but Nell, ever the actress, had thrown her arms around me and exclaimed in feigned horror.

'Rose! I *knew* that horrible man was the cause of *all* our problems...' She broke off, realising she was about to incriminate herself in front of Guy Forster, but he simply smiled.

'You may speak freely before me, madam. I only want what is best for Mistress Cassells – and indeed for you too, of course.'

Nell gave him a ravishing smile. 'You are so very kind, Colonel Forster. We *do* indeed need a strong protector—'

I deliberately trod on her foot and sent her a look that told her very plainly to hold her tongue. For once, she did as she was told.

'Colonel Forster is here to discuss my plan to remove to the country until the baby is born,' I said as blandly as I could. 'He has some noble design to escort me.' I glared at Guy. 'But, of course,' I finished, 'there is no need for that, no need at all. I can manage quite well on my own.'

'On the contrary,' Guy said, smooth as silk, 'as I hope to be your affianced husband, I would claim the right to protect you both.'

'You are not my—' I began, but Nell could not help herself from emitting a little squeal.

'A wedding! How romantic! Rose, you sly creature, I did not even know you were acquainted with Colonel Forster!'

'I met him when he arrested me,' I said crossly, 'and we are not betrothed.'

'I have proposed,' Guy said, 'and very much hope that Mistress Cassells will accept.'

Nell shot me a look that suggested I was the veriest fool for hesitating even a moment to grab this opportunity. I glowered back at her.

'We must have wine to celebrate!' she exclaimed, clapping her hands. 'Renwick, please fetch a bottle of the white malmsey!' She drew Guy confidingly over to the fireside and gestured him to a seat. 'You should know, Colonel,' she said, 'that my sister has a reluctance to form an attachment to any man after her unhappy marriage.'

'I had observed it,' Guy commented, flashing me a smile. His tone hardened. 'Given the nature of her late husband, it is scarce surprising, but I hope to persuade her that I am cut from a different cloth.'

'No one doubts that, sir,' Nell said warmly. 'But I pray you be patient with Rose. She has yet to discover the pleasure of the marriage bed, having experienced nothing but misery in it previously.'

'Nell!' By now, I was bright red and furious. 'Cease this conversation at once! And you, sir,' I turned to Guy Forster, whose eyes were full of mirth and something else brighter and hotter, meant for me alone. 'Pay no heed,' I said. 'I am grateful to you for your concern, but it is misplaced. I need no escort – even *less* do I need a husband – and I shall be perfectly safe at Becote—' I stopped, realising that in my mortification my tongue had run away with me and I had inadvertently revealed where I was planning to stay.

'Becote?' Guy raised his brows. 'Is that Becote House, the manor in Berkshire that is near Lord Craven's hunting lodge at Ashdown? How very convenient, for I am bound for Ashdown on the morrow to prepare for the visit next week of the King and—' he bowed to my sister '—Madam Gwyn.'

Nell beamed. 'It has all fallen out so well,' she said. 'It must be preordained.'

'Indeed, it has,' I agreed, through gritted teeth. So now I would be obliged to accept the colonel's escort as far as Berkshire, but at least if he was obliged to fit Ashdown out for the King's visit, he would not be around to see what I was doing at Becote Manor. Perhaps all was not lost.

Renwick came in with a tray and four glasses and a bottle of wine. 'The King is on his way, madam,' she said to Nell. 'He will be here any moment.'

'Damnation! Not now!' Nell jumped to her feet, smoothing down the white gown and fluffing up her ringlets. She grabbed my arm tightly, bending close by my ear. 'Whatever you do,' she hissed, 'do *not* mention the pardon or thank him for his intervention in your case!'

I stared at her in blank incomprehension for a moment before remembering that it was the King who had freed me from prison only two days before. 'Oh, but surely I should—' I began, thinking it would be base ingratitude not to thank him.

But Nell dug her nails into my arm most painfully. 'Not a word about anything!' she said. 'Speak only when spoken to.'

It was too late to discuss the matter further. Already, there was a masculine tread on the floorboards outside and the door was flung open again.

'Your Majesty!' Nell was all radiant smiles now.

I stared. I had seen the King before, at the theatre and when Nell and I had been a part of the immense crowd that had greeted him from his return from exile over ten years earlier. Close up was a different matter. He brought a sense of energy and action into the room, for he was still a vigorous figure of a man at one and forty. Tall, impeccably dressed, very dark, and with a shrewd gaze that seemed to take in everything in a moment, he halted when he saw that Nell was not alone.

'It seems I intrude,' he said, with a smile that indicated he was well aware that he could intrude anywhere at any time, as much as he wished, since he was the King. His gaze lingered thoughtfully on Guy. 'Forster.' He nodded to him. 'What do you do here at this hour?'

Guy bowed. 'Your Majesty,' he said.

'Colonel Forster and my sister Rose—' Nell drew me forward, poking me hard in the ribs to remind me to curtsey '—called by to acquaint me of their betrothal...' She gestured to the tray of wine glasses and smiled winningly. 'We were about to toast their future when you arrived, Your Majesty.'

'How delightful.' The King turned to me before I could elbow Nell in turn to prevent her from perpetuating the fiction of my betrothal. 'You are to be congratulated, Mistress. Forster is a fine man.'

'Thank you, Your Majesty.' I found my tongue at last. 'I think so too.'

The King's eyes crinkled with merriment. There was a charm about him that was palpable. I could feel myself relaxing. 'I am glad that you agree with me,' he said. 'And you, Forster—' he clapped Guy on the shoulder '— you are a lucky man.' He poured the wine himself and passed it to us. 'A toast to your betrothal – and to the wittiest and prettiest women in London.' He smiled at Nell, who preened like a peahen, although I thought the King could have been talking about anyone.

However, we raised our glasses and the King downed his wine in one gulp and placed his glass back on the tray with a rather decisive click.

'Forgive me,' he said, 'There is much I wish to... discuss... with Madam Gwyn, having been out of town this week past. I am sure you understand.'

He slid an arm about Nell's waist and I did not imagine for one moment that it was talking he had on his mind.

'Of course, Your Majesty.' Guy bowed again. He seemed neither surprised nor discomposed by the King's haste and extracted me from the room with minimum fuss, Nell embracing me fondly on the way out.

'You could do a lot worse than Colonel Forster,' she whispered in my ear as she hugged me close. 'Try not to be too much of a fool by refusing him.'

Downstairs in the hall, Guy took my hand in his. His was warm and slightly rough, his skin calloused from soldiering. 'So, you think I am a fine man, do you?' he asked, a glint in his dark eyes. 'I am touched by your regard.'

'Do not let it go to your head,' I said, trying to ignore the racing of my pulse. 'I did not wish to disagree with the King, that is all.'

'Of course,' Guy said smoothly, 'and I imagine that it would take more than the congratulations of the King of England to persuade you to marry me. Yet I would ask you to consider it. For my sake, because I wish it. And for yours, because I think there is also a part of you that would wish it too.' He leaned forward and kissed me.

I had not been kissed in a very long time, not a proper kiss that was not merely a quick prelude to or an unwelcome part of sexual congress. I was aware of the featherlight brush of Guy's lips across mine, the warmth of them, his gentleness. I found myself leaning in to test the sensation a little further and his mouth slid and opened against mine, and his tongue brushed mine. My head spun and I grabbed his coat with both hands to steady myself, and his hand was in my hair and he kissed me as though I was made of glass and yet as though he wanted to ravish me, all at the same time.

When he released me, we both had to take a moment to catch our breath.

'I will collect you on the morrow for our journey into Berkshire,' he said. 'But before I leave, I have something of yours to return.' He opened the door of his coach and took out a rectangular object. 'I have been keeping this safe for you.'

'My tin!' I said, as I ran my hands over the familiar dented lid. 'I thought it lost!' I remembered how I had been holding it when he arrested me.

'I am grateful,' I said sincerely, wondering if he had opened the box whilst it had been in his possession. Thank God I had not left the ruby cabochon inside. 'There is nothing of great value in it, but it matters to me.'

'I imagined it did,' Guy said. 'That was why I kept it. Goodnight, Rose.' He touched my cheek gently and then he was gone, leaving me as starry-eyed as a young girl.

As I went up the stairs I thought of our kiss, of his gentleness and passion, and of what it might lead to, and I shivered. I was so wrapped up in it that, at first, I did not see the figure standing in the shadows of the landing beside my bedchamber. I jumped and almost dropped my candle, but then a door opened further down the corridor and a maid rushed out, rubbing the sleep from her eyes.

'Helena! There you are. Let me take you back to your bed.'

It was my mother. The grotesque shadow against the wall resolved into an unkempt woman swathed in draperies whose hair was a knotted nest and whose eyes were blank and without recognition. Something in me prompted me to take her hand.

'Mama,' I said. 'It is me – Rose.'

But there was no spark of life in her eyes, there was very little at all.

The maid gave me an apologetic look and, taking her arm, steered her away and closed the door of her chamber very firmly behind them.

It was only as I got into bed that I realised that something was troubling me. It nagged at the back of my mind but had been overlaid and forgotten momentarily because I had kissed Guy and was dangerously besotted. But now, on the edge of sleep, I remembered.

If the King had been out of town for the past week, as he had claimed, how had he been able to sign my release from the Marshalsea gaol?

13

JESS – THE PRESENT

'How is it going?' Lucy asked. It was Tuesday morning and she and Jess were sitting in the window of the deli café in Beckett High Street. There was a splendid view of everything going on. Jess had already seen her mother going to the history centre, Hunter drive through in his Porsche (everyone had seen that because he had made as much noise as possible) and Ethan popping into the post office. He'd looked across the street and waved, mouthing 'see you later,' to Jess, which had made her feel ridiculously fizzy inside.

'It's madness,' Jess said, spooning the cream and marshmallows off the top of her hot chocolate. 'Utter chaos. I had no idea that people lived like Tavy do. It's been a complete eye-opener to me. It's unreal.'

Lucy nodded. 'Unreal as in starry or as in disorganised?'

'Both,' Jess said. 'Ed, Tavy's PA, is incredibly organised as well as a really sweet person, but he's run off his feet just trying to keep her diary straight. There are always people asking her to do something – open a club, go to an event – so she drops all the plans to do something else, and then Hunter turns up and demands everyone do what *he* wants.'

Lucy wrinkled up her nose. 'Entitled git. I've never liked him. Not that I've met him. He just seems that way when you see him on TV.'

'His TV persona is pretty much the real Hunter,' Jess said. 'But it's easy enough to avoid all the chaos. I just go and hide in the library or go out for a walk. No one notices I'm not there. Tavy only needs me as house-sitter when she's not around. I've already started applying for other jobs.' She tapped the copy of the *Guardian* lying on the table next to her.

'Anything good?' Lucy worked part-time at a musical charity foundation in Swindon and part-time at the historic gardens that she and Finn had set up in the next village. She'd given herself a morning off to catch up with Jess, though. 'I thought it would be nicer just the two of us,' she'd said on the phone when she'd set it up. 'We've got friends round for dinner later in the week and you're very welcome to join us, but I didn't want to over-whelm you from the start.'

And it *was* nice, Jess thought, just sitting here, the two of them in the sunshine with the buzz of conversation around them and the busy village life passing by. A bus stopped in front of the doctor's surgery opposite, disgorged a woman with a pushchair, a man with a small dog and various other passengers, then pulled out again.

'There are a couple of things,' Jess said. 'A librarian post at Bath Uni and a school librarian job in Manchester. I don't know though...' She frowned a little. 'I feel as though I'm going over old ground in a way. It would be safe to pick up where I left off, but I want to do something different. I just don't know what yet.'

Lucy nodded. 'You don't need to make any quick decisions, do you? Keep looking around for something that appeals to you.'

'Well, I haven't any money,' Jess said, 'or not much anyway, and although I'm living rent free for a while, it's not going to carry on for long.' Then when Lucy raised her brows enquiringly, Jess added, 'Tavy is already bored with the project. I think she'll abandon it soon and just sell the place. Or try to.'

Lucy pursed her lips in a soundless whistle. 'All that work for nothing! Wow!'

Jess grimaced. 'Tavy has a short attention span. She always did. She'll move on.'

'Speaking of which,' Lucy said, 'have you heard from Jared?'

'No!' Jess was horrified. 'I told him I don't ever want to hear from him again.'

'I hope he respects that.' Lucy drained her coffee cup. 'I'm so sorry, Jess. He's a total creep. Did you see in the paper that he's apparently writing a book about his experiences?' She looked so concerned that Jess felt a rush of affection for her, realising that Lucy had only brought up Jared's name because she wanted to make sure she knew and was okay.

She nodded. 'It was online this morning.' She'd only read the headlines: '*Sleazy fraudster ex-brother-in-law of TV Influencer quids in with book deal.*' 'Tavy will be furious to be dragged into it all over again,' she said gloomily. 'Not that he'll manage to write a book without help and even if he does, all the profits will have to go to paying off his debts.'

'Would you like another hot chocolate?' Lucy asked. 'It might help. Or an almond croissant? I usually eat my way out of a crisis, though I shouldn't recommend it as therapy, I know.'

'I will have one of those delicious cherry Bakewell slices,' Jess agreed, 'and a cup of tea.' She gave a little sigh. 'This is so nice, Luce. I can't wait to come over to Knightstone and see you and Finn – and the Gunpowder Cottage gardens, of course. You've worked amazingly hard to make them such a success.'

They chatted for a while longer about the garden and Finn's latest project for the Chelsea Flower show, then Lucy grabbed her bags and stood up. 'I must dash,' she said. 'I'm back at work this afternoon, but it was lovely to catch up and please do come over on Thursday. It's just a few friends – Lizzie who I work with, and her husband, and my sister Cleo, and Ethan. Six-thirty?' She bent to kiss Jess's cheek. 'See you soon. Nothing personal, Ethan,' she added, over Jess's shoulder, 'but I've got to go.'

Jess swung round and saw that Ethan had just come into the café and was heading over to the counter. 'Then your seat's free,' he said with a smile. 'If that's all right with you, Jess.'

'Oh, of course...' Jess glared at Lucy and mouthed the words '*you are so obvious*' at her, but her friend just waved as she went out.

Ethan put in his order and came over to take Lucy's vacated seat. He looked good, Jess thought. He was in a suit and it fitted well, the formality of it contrasting with his hint of stubble. He rubbed his chin self-consciously when he saw her looking. 'No time to shave,' he said ruefully, and Jess repressed the urge to tell him not to bother, that she thought he looked great. 'It's nice to see you again. Sorry I haven't been in touch. Work's been pretty intense.' He shrugged it off. 'I was on my way to the Hall when I saw you and Lucy in here. I've finally got around to printing this off.'

'This' was a family tree which Ethan extracted from the cardboard poster tube he had under his arm and unrolled on the table, securing one end with the salt pot and the other with a plate. Jess could see Ethan, his brother and sister at the bottom of the tree and at the top Sir George Forster of Aldermaston in Berkshire, 1470–1533.

'I put it together from family records and *Burke's Landed Gentry and Commoners*,' Ethan said. 'You can see we're a rather minor branch.'

'Don't knock it,' Jess said, smiling. 'Most "commoners" don't even get into *Burke's*.' She traced a finger down the tree. Many of the Forster heirs had been knighted and had served as sheriffs of Berkshire. In the early seventeenth century, the tree split with no fewer than five sons. The second-youngest, Guy, was the ancestor of Ethan's line. 'Sir Guy Forster, knight,' Jess read out, 'in the service of William, Earl of Craven.' She looked up. 'I've seen that name already in my research. Clive, in the history centre, told me that William Craven owned Ashdown House, a few miles away and was a mate of Charles II.'

Ethan nodded. 'That's right. Guy Forster was Craven's land agent for a while and the first of our family to live at Beckett. I've tried to find out who he bought it from because that would have been around the right time for Nell Gwyn, the 1670s. I can't find any records, though. It could have been Craven himself; he owned most of Berkshire around that time.'

'And that line continued at Beckett right up until your grandmother's day.' Jess felt slightly awed to see the long line of descendants unfurling down the centuries. Then she realised how tactless this might sound. 'Sorry,' she added, touching his hand. 'I didn't mean to be insensitive.'

Ethan smiled. 'Things change,' he said. 'We had a good run.' For a long moment, he left his hand under hers and Jess was acutely aware of the warmth of his skin and the tingle of pleasure it gave her, then she forced herself to draw back.

'Some of the names of the wives are missing,' she said, a little randomly. 'Guy's wife is only referred to as Rose.'

'I'm working on it,' Ethan said. 'It was a man's world, as you know. Or at least they thought it was. The antiquarians who put the family trees together often omitted the wives' names completely unless they were heiresses.'

'I'm almost certain she was Rose Gwyn,' Jess said. 'I've found the connection between Becote and the Gwyn family now, and the biography of Nell I'm reading also mentioned in passing that Rose married a Guy Forster as her second husband. There's so little about her in the historical record, though.'

'Then it sounds as though she may be the Rose from that manuscript you found in the library,' Ethan said. 'There aren't any other women with that name in the family tree. It's tantalising, isn't it.' He smiled at her. 'So many little clues that we need to join up somehow.'

'And so many pieces of the jigsaw still missing,' Jess acknowledged. 'I'm going to Oxford to follow all of this up.'

Ethan's espresso and piece of carrot cake arrived.

'What a treat this place is,' Jess sighed. 'They have some amazing bread I'm going to take back for my sandwiches this week.'

'How are you finding it after the cameras have stopped rolling?' Ethan asked, cutting into his cake. 'I'm assuming it's mayhem whilst the crew are around, but is it weirdly quiet the rest of the time?'

'I like it,' Jess said. 'I don't feel lonely.' She wasn't going to admit to him that sometimes when it was quiet, she thought she saw the place take on a different shape and form, as though she'd had passed through time. She hadn't told anyone about that, or the strange moment watching Tavy's livestream when she'd seen the figure by the lake. 'There was something I wanted to ask you. Clive mentioned that there's a local legend that some of the Crown Jewels that were lost in the attempted robbery at the Tower of London in 1671 were hidden at Becote. Do you know that story?'

Ethan laughed. 'Sure, I've heard it. But there's also a rumour that a woman who lived near here in the eighteenth century was a shapeshifter who would turn into a hare at night, and another one that Boudica is buried somewhere up on the Ridgeway.' He spread his hands. 'When it's so unlikely, where do you start?'

'Fair enough,' Jess said. 'I went to Lambourn library yesterday and took out a book about the theft of the Crown Jewels. Some of them were lost in the attempted robbery, but I must admit it doesn't mention that they ended up here. It was a strange business, though. Anyone with the slightest bit of common sense should have realised that it would never work, for so many reasons. Yet the rather gruesomely named Captain Blood seemed to think it was a brilliant plan.'

'It was an odd episode,' Ethan agreed. 'Didn't he get away with it? I vaguely remember that he was pardoned or even rewarded. And did they ever find the lost jewels?'

'Not according to the accounts I've read.' Jess drained her teacup and stacked it neatly with her plate. 'By the way, has there been any word from Zoe yet on the skeleton?'

Ethan's phone rang. 'You must be psychic,' he said. 'Like Francesca.' He smiled. 'That's Zoe now. Do you mind if I take the call?'

'Of course not, but don't put her on speaker,' Jess said. 'Her descriptions might put people off their cake.'

Ethan grimaced and pressed answer. 'Zoe, hi,' he said. 'Yes...' He looked at Jess. 'She's here now. Right, okay...' He took out a pencil and scribbled a few notes on the back of the family tree as Zoe talked. His writing was illegible to Jess, especially upside down. 'Thanks, Zoe,' he said at the end of the call. 'See you.' He was frowning a little as he put his phone away. 'Well, that's all very curious.' He took a mouthful of his coffee and sat back. 'Zoe says to pass on that the police have ended the investigation. Access is restored to the lakeside, fishing house and grounds. They've let your sister know.'

'Great,' Jess said. 'Tavy will be pleased that the outdoor shots won't be ruined with incident tape.'

'As for the skeleton,' Ethan continued, 'it was a man aged between thirty-five and fifty-five, who died sometime in the second half of the seventeenth century.' He scanned his notes. 'As Zoe had previously thought, he had had a blow to the head, but it was insufficient to kill him. There were no other signs of violence on the body and no grave cut to suggest that he had been deliberately buried. Zoe thinks he may have died by accident, falling in the water and drowning, perhaps, and his body trapped beneath the bank as it gradually silted up over the years.'

'Poor guy. What a horrible accident to happen. Was there anything to identify him?'

Ethan shook his head. 'They don't have a name, but there were some items found with him that might help the identification process. Apparently, he hadn't been robbed – another reason Zoe thought his death might have been an accident rather than a deliberate act. They found some shreds of leather, a belt buckle, some coins and a sword in the mud beneath the body. Quite a haul.'

'Wow.' Jess raised her brows. 'A sword? But date-wise too late to be a fatality from the English Civil War?'

'Probably,' Ethan said, 'although there's always a bit of leeway when you're dating bones that old.'

'So, if it was later, that would place it around the time Sir Guy Forster owned Becote, or thereabouts,' Jess said. 'We need to know when and how he died. And the sword – any engravings on it, coat of arms or initials?'

'It's badly corroded, but Zoe is going to ask a historic weapons expert to take a look anyway,' Ethan said. 'It's all unofficial as the case is closed. She wondered if we'd like to be there when he comes over.' He laughed at Jess's eager look. 'I thought you probably would. She's going to let us know the time and date.'

'Thanks,' Jess said. 'This is all fascinating. Or it would be if he weren't a real person whose body has been lost for centuries. Will he get a proper burial now?'

Ethan smiled at her. 'That would be a thoughtful gesture. I don't know, but we could find out if you like, and organise something, even if it is only a prayer at the graveside or a bouquet of flowers.'

'I think that would be nice,' Jess agreed. Her phone buzzed with a text. 'It's Mum,' she said, reading the screen. 'Tavy needs her housekeeper, apparently. I expect she's just found out about Jared's latest bid for attention.' Then, when Ethan looked blank, 'Sorry, that's my ex. It's all very messy but...' She could feel her face turn a fiery red. 'He's in jail for fraud. It was a high-profile case and every time he's in the news, Tavy gets mentioned because she's a celebrity.'

'That's par for the course, I suppose.' Ethan, eating his cake, didn't sound very sympathetic. 'What about you, though?' He was looking at her closely. 'Are *you* okay? It can't be very nice for you having it raked over in the paper.'

Jess was simultaneously touched that he was concerned for her and mortified that he evidently knew all about the case. 'I hate it.' She found the words bursting out of her with more force than she had intended. 'Every time I feel as though I'm starting to move on, something else happens to derail me. I try not to let it get to me but...' she stopped. 'I should have realised. I should have known what he was like.' Embarrassed, she started to get up, only for Ethan to cover her hand with his.

'Don't go yet,' he said quietly.

'Tavy needs me...' Jess objected.

'She can wait,' Ethan said. 'Listen, Jess, you can tell me to mind my own business if you like, but you don't have to take responsibility for any of this. You shouldn't have to.' He sounded suddenly fierce. 'So, your ex is a crook. That's his issue, not yours. None of this is your fault.'

Jess gulped. 'Right,' she said. Then, 'Wow. Thank you. I do know that, but it isn't always easy to remember it.'

Ethan's hand tightened over hers and she lost the thread of her thoughts. The sounds of the café and the people around them faded and then he released her and sat back with a self-deprecating smile.

'Sorry,' he said. 'It is none of my damned business. I just felt...' He thrust a hand through his hair. 'Sorry,' he repeated.

'Please stop apologising.' Jess felt suddenly reckless, light-headed. She leaned across the table and pressed a quick kiss on his lips. 'Thank you' she whispered.

Ethan looked poleaxed. Jess felt her emotions swing back towards embarrassment to have indulged in what was evidently an unwelcome public display of affection, but then she saw the heat in his eyes. 'You're welcome,' he said, picking up his coffee cup with great deliberation. 'Perhaps we can discuss it some more when I come over to check out the books? Will tomorrow evening be convenient?'

'Sure.' Jess cleared her throat. 'Would you like to come for dinner? Nothing fancy, just a meal.'

'Thank you,' Ethan said simply. 'I'd like that.' He smiled again and she stood up, almost knocking over her mug in the process.

'Right,' she said, 'I'll... um... see you then.'

Ethan nodded. He looked... The word was satisfied, she thought, as though she had answered a question that they had both been ignoring since they had met. And she had, she realised. The buzz between them, the sense of recognition; he felt it too.

14

ROSE – JULY 1671

I sat opposite Colonel Forster in Lord Craven's coach as we made painfully slow time on the rutted road out of London. I felt grateful that my pregnancy was not more advanced or I might have delivered the baby there and then with all the shaking around. Coach travel was said to be dangerous for pregnant women, but then so was most of life. I felt in good health that morning, leaning back on the sumptuously appointed velvet cushions and looking out on the rest of the world as they toiled whilst I rested. It was a novel experience.

Across from me, Guy looked relaxed and as though he too was enjoying the trip. The coach was laden with goods destined for Ashdown House, as was another cart that followed behind us. My meagre bags, containing clothing and necessaries provided by Nell, took only the smallest corner of space amongst such a huge pile of provisions. Servants swarmed around us at every stop, but only Guy and I had the privilege of travelling in the coach. I suspected that had I not been with him, Guy would have ridden. I am sure it would have suited him better, but he made no comment, merely sitting watching me and enjoying my pleasure in the journey.

For someone who seldom lacked confidence, I felt strangely tongue-tied in his company and as the miles passed in continued silence, I also started to feel awkward. It was not as though I had imagined he would take this opportunity to force unwanted attentions on me, but I had wondered whether he would choose to press the case for our marriage. When he did not, I was not sure if I was glad or sorry.

Rather than travelling via Oxford, we were taking the Great Road to Bristol, for both Ashdown Park and Becote were in the most northern part of the county of Berkshire. When the coach had passed the villages of Hounslow and Colnbrook, Guy turned to me with a smile.

'Are we to remain silent for the entire journey?' he enquired. 'Some observation about the state of the roads or the clement weather might help to pass the time.'

'The weather is fine and the road is bumpy,' I said. 'Now what?'

He sighed. 'You are as prickly as your namesake this morning.'

'I am not accustomed to going from pregnant widow to affianced bride in the shake of a lamb's tail,' I pointed out. 'Nor do I recall agreeing to it.'

'Ah,' he sat back with a smile. 'You are shy.'

'Of all the things I am,' I snapped, 'shy is not one of them.' Then, seeing he was teasing me, I turned my shoulder and gazed out of the window.

'My dear Rose,' Guy said easily, 'think nothing of it. Until you agree to marry me, we are not affianced, no matter how much I desire it, and should you decide you do not wish to wed me, that is an end to it.'

Perversely, I was now cross that he was being so affable about it. 'You must allow,' I said, 'that it is difficult for me to think kindly of a man who arrested me.'

'I thought that might be the main reason for your displeasure,' he said.

'You are perceptive,' I sniffed.

He smiled. 'I apologise. I thought you had committed a crime.'

I could not in truth deny that. 'I spent six weeks in gaol because of you. It cannot therefore be a surprise that I do not wish to engage with you in conversation. Or anything else,' I added, untruthfully.

There was a silence. 'It was difficult for me too,' he said, after a moment.

That infuriated me. 'I can only imagine, Colonel,' I replied coldly, 'how hard it must be for you to uphold the law.'

'I have never been tempted to *break* the law before I met you, Rose,' Guy said, looking me straight in the eye. 'I knew you were guilty, but the urge to let you go – the need to protect you – was very strong.' His voice was rough.

There was passion in it now and the ring of truth. 'I almost betrayed everything I believed in to allow you to go free.'

My throat closed. Unexpected tears prickled my eyes. I knew he would
have hated himself had he given in to that temptation. And if he had done
so, he would not have been the man I so admired. The awareness of this
shook me to the core. It was too much and far too soon.

'I am glad you did not, damn you.' I glared at him. 'Yet I am still not
happy about it. Make of that what you will, for I cannot understand my
own feelings.'

The light flared in his eyes and for a moment I thought he might kiss
me there and then in the carriage, but after he took a deep breath, the
tension went out of him.

'I hear that the Marshalsea is very rough,' he said. 'I am sorry you had
to experience that.'

'It would scarce be a deterrent were it not,' I said. 'The Marshalsea is, I
understand, quite pleasant if you have the cash to make your stay more
tolerable. Which few people do, of course, it being in the main a debtor's
prison.'

His steady dark gaze rested on me. There was something about him that
seemed to draw out confidences from me, which was extraordinary, given
my lack of trust. Still, I found myself telling him things I had never told
anyone else.

'A few years after the King returned,' I said, 'when I was about sixteen
years old and Nell was twelve, we were imprisoned for debt. I never forgot
the careless cruelty, the sickness and the squalor. And I had Nell to protect,
of course, just as now I have this one.' I patted my bump.

Guy looked pained. 'I am sorry,' he said. 'You both suffered too much,
too young.'

'Nell and I are not unusual,' I replied. 'Our father had already died in
Oxford Gaol, arraigned for debt. We have never had any money. When war
is over, heroes are often forgotten.'

Guy's mouth twisted. 'That is sadly true,' he agreed, 'though I hope that
if your father had lived to see the King's Restoration, much might have been
different.'

'Perhaps.' I shrugged. I had little faith that matters would have been different at all, for the King had no money with which to reward his father's faithful followers even had he wanted to do so. Most of all, I suspected he wanted to forget the whole bloody business of the wars, and put the past behind him. If that meant that old soldiers starved in the streets and their families died in the slums, so be it. I smoothed the cotton of my skirts. 'In the event, Nell and I were fortunate. I was able to call in a favour from Harry Killigrew – in return for the favours I had been doing him, you understand.'

Harry Killigrew had been my first lover and the only other man I had slept with apart from John, my husband. His father had been a member of the King's household and Harry had persuaded him to plead for my release on the grounds that my father had served in the Civil Wars. It was an early lesson for me on how power and influence could mean the difference between life and death.

Guy's mouth twitched into a smile. 'I do understand you,' he said. 'You are trying to shock me by telling me that you were Harry Killigrew's mistress before your marriage.'

'I would hardly claim to have been his mistress,' I said judiciously. 'We were but boy and girl together and barely knew what we were doing. And no, I am not trying to shock you, Colonel Forster. I cannot believe that you are a virgin either.'

He threw back his head and laughed aloud at that. 'You would be correct in that, Mistress Cassells. But indulge my curiosity for a moment so that I may be spared any more potential shocks in the future. What happened after you were freed? Your sister became an actress, but what became of you?'

'I became a thief,' I replied. I saw his gaze go to the brand on my wrist. His head was bent so I could not read his expression. 'It was a year later,' I said. 'We were still poor, our mother was still a drunk, sometimes we went hungry. I was caught taking a loaf of bread. I could have hanged for it, but I lied about my age and the judge was feeling generous that day.'

Guy rubbed his thumb gently over the branding mark. 'And after that?' he said.

I swallowed hard, distracted by the gentleness of his touch. As always, it felt like weakness and I fought against it. 'After that I was careful not to get caught again, for I knew there would be no second chances.'

Our eyes met and I knew we were both thinking that he had arrested me for another, far more audacious theft than a loaf of bread. I did not want to talk about that.

'I had not Nell's talent for acting,' I hurried on, 'nor for charming the gentlemen the way she has – and I had no stomach to be a whore.' I shuddered at the thought. 'For some, it is a path out of poverty, but I had served drinks to the customers in Madam Ross's bawdy house ever since we had come to London as children. I saw too much, too young. Too much lust and depravity and—' I winced '—the calculating transaction of money for sex. I have seen my mother begging in the streets and prostituting herself for a few coins. Selling oysters and oranges to theatre-goers was little better. Everyone tried to touch me, begging for kisses and favours.'

Guy's hand tightened over mine. 'And nothing you experienced inside or outside of marriage persuaded you that it might be different,' he said. 'I am sorry for that.'

I withdrew my hand gently from his. 'As I said, Harry Killigrew was a mere boy, and John, my husband...' I stopped and swallowed hard. 'He beat me and he raped me,' I said bluntly. 'And I am glad he is dead, because I had promised myself that if he hit me again, I would kill him and then they would have hanged me for it.'

The tightening of Guy's jaw, the blaze of fury in his eyes, spoke more clearly than any words. 'Rose,' he began, and I shook my head quickly, because I could not let him speak, I was not ready.

'If you still wish to wed me,' I said. 'It is best you understand.'

He nodded. 'My offer still stands, as protection for you and your child. I would ask nothing of you that you were not willing to give.'

'Thank you.' I believed him. 'Now, let us speak of less melancholy things. Can you explain to me, Colonel Forster, why so many former soldiers take to the stage? John Lacy, who took Nell under his tutelage at the King's Theatre, was a blunt Yorkshireman, who had served in our father's regiment and yet there he was, cavorting around at the theatre. Have you ever been drawn to become an actor, sir?'

Guy laughed. 'Not I,' he said, 'but until you mentioned it, I had not seen the connection. You are right; I could name half a dozen men who once served and are now pounding the boards. Perhaps it is the drama of it – without the excitement of war in their lives, they need to make some up.'

'That would not surprise me,' I said. 'I have long observed that if men have no real reason to fight, they will invent one.'

He winced. 'You have a low opinion of my sex, Rose.'

'Not entirely. But I think men generally believe they are the superior sex. Men think that just because they have experienced war that makes them stronger than women. Well, I have to tell you that in most cases the wars are unnecessary and the hardships overcome by women are greater by far.'

He gave a nod. 'I believe you, on the latter at least. Sadly, wars are sometimes necessary, although the ones that tore this kingdom apart might have been avoided.'

'Have your family always been Royalists?' I asked, curious to know what his childhood had been like growing up under the shadow of the Commonwealth.

'My father, Sir William, was a great supporter of the King,' Guy said, 'despite being a distant cousin of Oliver Cromwell. He walked the political tightrope well, as does my older brother Humphrey. I have no time for such games, which was why I became a soldier.' He laughed. 'As a younger son who showed some signs of scholarship, I was destined for the Church. However, that would never have suited me.'

'I can imagine.' I thought he was too vital, too active a man, to flourish in the confines of the Church or academia.

The rest of the morning passed in pleasant conversation about Guy's childhood at Aldermaston Park and his exploits at university. Only when I pressed him on his military career did he show some hesitation. He had served in the first Anglo-Dutch War and with the Spanish against the Commonwealth, and had found a place at the court in exile of the Winter Queen of Bohemia, which was where he had met his patron Lord Craven.

'Soldiering is no fit topic to discuss with a lady,' he objected, when I asked, which made me laugh as I would scarcely have considered myself thus.

'I am curious,' I said. 'I have seen so little of the world – and cannot read more about it. I want to know.'

'You would enjoy travelling.' His gaze dwelt on me thoughtfully. 'You have an appetite for learning.' There was warmth in his eyes that made me feel admired and cherished. It was very disconcerting.

'I have scarcely had time to learn,' I said. 'I have been too busy surviving.' I spoke brusquely to cover my feelings, but he was not fooled. The smile deepened in his eyes and I felt an unfamiliar sensation in my stomach, which I suspected was happiness.

We stopped for a meal at Langley, where I unpacked the basket that Nell's housekeeper had sent with us. There were all sorts of delicacies: lamb pie, cheeses, bread rolls with rich butter, chicken and summer fruits. Truly, I was starting to feel like a princess.

In the afternoon, I dozed, the movement of the carriage, the fullness of my stomach and a sense of wellbeing luring me to sleep. The weather was fair and the pretty countryside passing by reminded me of my childhood in Oxford and the rare times we had visited Becote. It was about this that Guy spoke when, finally, I woke as we were approaching Theale, where we were to lodge for the night.

'Tell me about Becote Manor,' he said, 'and how it came to be in your family.'

'That, I do not know for certain,' I said. 'I believe it belonged to my grandfather, Canon Gwyn of Oxford, who left it to my father. But even when I was a child, I remember it was in disrepair and he never had the money to restore it. I loved it though...' I thought of the lake and the little fishing house and the old trees and the sweet scent of the long green grass. 'It was a magical place to visit as a child.'

'I heard that it was taken by a parliamentarian during the Commonwealth, but that the King restored it to Madam Gwyn,' Guy said. 'Should it not have been yours? After all, you are the elder, and if it was not entailed...'

I was not going to admit that this had been a sore point. 'I am glad that it is back in the family,' I said, then, seeing his raised brows, I added honestly, 'I would not have had the means to repair it anyway. And although Nell has no interest in the place, at least she keeps a caretaker there.'

Nell had in fact told me that whilst I was staying at Becote, I had a free hand to consider myself the tenant and do whatever I wished to the house. This was generous of her, but there was no money forthcoming from her to change or improve things, so I suspected that I would simply have to make do. Nell had also sent ahead of our journey to warn the caretaker of our coming, and had asked him to engage a housekeeper and some servants from the village. I was taking one of her own servants as maid on her insistence; I had no real need for such indulgences and did not feel comfortable with other women prodding and poking me about to dress me and arrange my hair.

I had not, however, forgotten my reason for going there, and had there been the slightest chance I would, Nell had pulled me to one side as we were leaving and hissed in my ear, 'I will expect the locket and jewels found when we arrive at Ashdown in a se'ennight.'

'You can expect whatever you like,' I had hissed back. 'I shall do the best I can, but beyond that I can promise nothing.'

Naturally, I hoped that I would be able to find Nell's locket, and quickly. I knew that her harshness sprang from fear and I could understand that. Beyond that, though, I did not yet know what I was going to do. I was certain John had hidden his loot there, and so I refused to make plans for any alternative outcome. There was no need, not yet. I would take one step at a time.

Talking to Guy about Becote had made me nostalgic for those long-lost days of childhood summer and I thought how wonderful it would be for my baby to grow up there. I think I saw it as some sort of magical refuge from Sir Grey Cassells, but I suspected that he could find me easily enough if he chose. That led me inexorably to thinking of Guy's proposal, for he was right that to marry him would give protection to both me and my child, his name and his strength guarding us from danger. It was such an unfamiliar feeling to know that someone was prepared to do that for me, that it brought a lump to my throat.

I sat across from him, watching the play of afternoon sun across his face as though learning his features by heart. Simply looking at him gave me a fizzy feeling inside, which made me laugh at myself. I was infatuated. I knew it and I was also old enough to know that infatuation could flee quickly enough on marriage. It bore little resemblance to reality. Marriage was a business arrangement and, in this case, the price was high, tying myself to another man so soon into my widowhood, and one whom I did not really know, for all the spark and attraction that there was between us. I felt as though I were on the edge of a precipice and did not dare to jump.

* * *

We reached Theale as the evening light was dying from the sky. The inn was comfortable, far superior to the types of establishments I had known in London. With a quaint thatched roof and leaded windows open to the breeze, it felt fresh and clean. There was a delicious smell of roasting meat coming from the kitchens. The lamb pie suddenly seemed a long time ago.

We ate in the parlour, just the two of us, with Guy waiting on me once the inn servants had brought in the food. The landlord was obsequious to Guy both because of Lord Craven's name but also, I thought, because of his air of natural authority. He was more equivocal of me, his gaze speculative as it dwelled on me. He would offer no direct insult, but I knew what he was thinking. Guy had told them I was his widowed cousin whom he was escorting to her country house, but I knew the entire inn saw that for the fiction it was.

It was full night by the time we had lingered over our meal and though I had been enjoying Guy's company and did not want the evening to end, I was also exhausted and, with the prospect of more travelling on the morrow, knew I needed to sleep. He escorted me gravely up the stairs and we stopped outside the door of my chamber, where he stood, looking at me with an unreadable expression.

'What is wrong?' I asked him. 'You are acting quite oddly.'

'I disliked the way the landlord looked at you,' he said, after a moment. 'He thinks you are my pregnant mistress and we are pretending to a family relationship to appear more respectable.'

'Oh...' I felt some of my tension subside. 'Well, of course.'

He flattened his hand against the wall beside me. 'Is that all you have to say, Rose?'

I shrugged a little, confused. 'Everyone is going to believe that. What else would they think? It is the way of the world.'

'I do not care for it,' he said, through gritted teeth. 'It demeans us both.'

I shook my head slightly. 'You make too much of it. It is not important.'

This, however, did not appease him. Now he was drumming his fingers against the wall, a quick, staccato beat that indicated irritation.

'There is something you should know,' he said.

I sighed. 'Then tell me,' I said. 'You are making me feel nervous.'

He did not speak. Instead, he gently turned my face up to his and very softly touched his lips to mine. It was a question as much as a kiss. Even though we had kissed the night before, he was not taking anything for granted.

As with the previous night, I felt a sensation I had forgotten, a rush of helpless desire that almost carried me away. I had not felt this way since the first heady days of John's courtship, if it could be dignified with such a description. I had been younger then and not so careful to protect myself. I had given him everything, all of myself, and had regretted it ever after.

The memory made me hesitate, draw back a little, and immediately Guy let me go. Not so much like John then, who would not even have noticed and would have cared less.

'I apologise,' he said. His voice was rough. 'That was wrong of me. This is neither the time nor the place, but the truth is that I can barely look at you without wanting to kiss you – more than just kiss you. But you know this already. I have made my feelings plain.'

The warmth still suffused my whole body. I put my hands against his chest and stood on tiptoe so that I could kiss him again. Immediately, his arms went around me, his hands resting lightly on my back. I could feel his heat through the thin material of my gown. A shiver of pleasure rippled through me.

He opened the door of my chamber, spun us over the threshold and closed the door with a decisive click behind us.

'Are you sure you want this?' His lips were an inch from mine. 'I have not forgotten that you took no pleasure in the marriage bed before now. I want to court you, Rose, not to rush matters between us.'

'I cannot be sure what will happen,' I said, 'but I think that with you it might be different.' I was certainly willing to find out. I pressed closer to him, and his arms tightened and we kissed again, a proper kiss this time.

After a long time, he let me go. 'Much as I am enjoying this,' he said, 'I have no intention of living down to everyone's opinion of us.'

'You are a gentleman,' I observed. 'That must make life very difficult at times.'

He gave a short laugh. 'It has certainly been more of a challenge since I met you, but I will not accept anything less than marriage.'

Damn him for being such an honourable man. He was not going to blackmail me with my own desires. I needed to make this decision in cold blood, not hot.

'Then I will not add to your difficulties any further,' I said. 'Goodnight, sir.'

When he had gone, I pressed my back to the cold wall and closed my eyes. Every part of me felt alive with sensation. It would be easy to forget any fears and scruples I had in the rush of desire that swept me away in Guy's arms. But for the first time in my life, I felt guilty, for I was deceiving him, hiding from him the truth that part of the reason I was going to Becote was to search for the jewels. He would neither understand nor condone my deceit. It would hurt him, and I could not bear to do that.

And then the devil of mistrust that lived inside me whispered in my ear that perhaps he knew already and that he was merely playing along with me to find the jewels and arrest me all over again... How those voices taunted me, telling me that Guy's regard for me was nothing but a pretence to get what he wanted, and if he got me into bed at the same time, so much the better.

I put my hands over my ears as if to block them out, and told myself that whilst I was a thief and a deceiver, I could still recognise integrity when I saw it. Guy was a man of principle, which made him the worst possible match for me. If I were to marry him, sooner or later I would disappoint him.

15

JESS – THE PRESENT

'Have you found Nell Gwyn yet?' Tavy accosted Jess unceremoniously as she hopped into the house on crutches on the Wednesday morning for the second day of filming in a row. 'The producers are asking,' she added, as Ed staggered in behind her, weighed down with even more stuff than usual, having to juggle Tavy's medications bag in addition to everything else. Her sister pulled Jess into the parlour. 'The TV company want to get one of the telly historians involved,' she said. 'One of the glamorous ones, not the crusty old ones, but I'd rather they didn't.'

'I'm working on it,' Jess said. She realised Tavy didn't want to share the spotlight with another celebrity presenter, but she didn't feel ready to tell her sister what she had found out so far. Although it was exciting to her, she knew Tavy would want more than just a vague suggestion that Nell's grandfather had owned the house, and that her sister had possibly lived there. Jess realised she had started to feel protective of Rose. She'd spent the previous evening chasing down the few references to her that she could find in the historical records and had gone to sleep, only to dream of a woman with red hair and hazel eyes whose presence seemed to wrap around her like the scent of roses.

Tavy's mouth turned down at the corners and Jess remembered their mother talking about how her sister always wanted instant gratification. That wasn't generally the way that historical research worked.

'If you need quicker results, why not hire a professional researcher?' Jess suggested. 'I'm just following my nose, really. I'm not trained in this stuff.'

But Tavy was shaking her head. 'No, it's not worth it. I'm likely going to throw it all in soon, anyway. I'm talking to my agent about getting out of the contract, but it's complicated.'

'Make-up in ten, Tavy,' Ed said, opening the door after a brief knock. 'And your flowers are here.'

'Cool,' Tavy said, as a man staggered down the hall beneath a huge bouquet of pink roses. 'Get Denise to arrange them around the bathroom. Strew them – is that the word? Sort of romantically.'

'Where's Malcolm today?' Jess asked, as they went back out into the hall. The Maltese was nowhere to be seen, which was probably a blessing given his talent for getting underfoot.

'I've left him with Mum,' Tavy said. 'She thought it would look bad if I rehomed him after I'd done that dog rescue programme.'

'Well, she's right about that,' Jess said.

Una, it turned out, had apparently decided to spend the day in Oxford, which was one reason why Tavy was cross. 'I need her in the show today,' she groused. 'Someone has to join me for champagne in the new whirlpool bath, though I'm going to look stupid with my leg hanging over the side.'

'It's a shame Hunter isn't around,' Jess said. She'd seen her sister's boyfriend briefly the previous day when she'd got back from the village. As usual, Hunter didn't appear to remember who she was, which didn't particularly bother Jess. He and Tavy had been filming a romantic picnic in the grounds of the Hall, or pretending to do so. The minute the cameras were turned off so were the smiles and Hunter had disappeared shortly after.

'Hey, perhaps you could do the scene with me!' Tavy turned her full-wattage smile on Jess. 'Have you got a swimming costume with you? Never mind.' She made a quick gesture of dismissal. 'We'll find something for you. Your stuff probably wouldn't look right anyway. I'll get wardrobe to come and kit you out—'

'No,' Jess interrupted. 'Thank you,' she added quickly.

Tavy looked astonished. It was so comical, Jess almost laughed.

'I told you, it's not my thing,' she said gently.

To Tavy's credit, she didn't try to argue. 'Fine. It'll have to be Francesca, then, though she doesn't like water. She says she was a cat in a previous life.'

She hopped off down the corridor towards the kitchen and Ed shot Jess an apologetic look. It was his default mode where Tavy was concerned.

'Sorry,' he said. 'She's in a lot of pain from her ankle.'

Jess privately thought Tavy was managing to share the pain around pretty well, but she didn't say anything to Ed, merely giving him a sympathetic smile as Tavy bellowed at him from the kitchen.

'We won't be here from Thursday to next Monday,' Ed said, as he hurried away. 'Tavy's going to the US to film a chat show.'

Of course she was, Jess thought.

'You'll be all right on your own, won't you?' Ed looked worried.

'Yes,' Jess said. 'No problem. I'm seeing friends a couple of times and I've got the library to finish sorting before Friday, and my research...' She felt a little thrill of excitement to have the house all to herself for four days with no film crew milling around and plenty of opportunity to explore. By the time they all came back the following week – assuming they were coming back and Tavy hadn't thrown in the towel – she hoped she'd have plenty of news.

* * *

There was an oddly subdued air about the filming that day, as though the crew knew that Tavy was trying to get out of the show and felt it wasn't really worth it. Or perhaps it was simply that everyone was walking on eggshells around her. Without Una there to smooth things over and make tea and sandwiches, Jess felt as though things were getting rather frayed at the edges. She did her best to fill in for her mother in the kitchen, which seemed to be appreciated.

Francesca floated in at one point to get a coffee.

'How are you doing?' Jess asked her, as she put a pod into the machine.

She found it hard to talk to Francesca, who never asked anyone anything about themselves and seemed to exist on a different plane.

'I'm tired.' Francesca perched on one of the bar stools looking as insubstantial as a wraith. She was tapping her fingers impatiently as the coffee machine worked its way through its program, but Jess suspected that was because she wanted to go outside for a cigarette rather than anything else.

'Do you travel everywhere with Tavy?' Jess asked. 'I can imagine that's quite hectic.'

Francesca turned her big dark eyes on Jess's face. It was disconcerting. 'She needs me with her,' she said. 'I might have a message for her at any time.'

'Does our father ever send a message for her?' Jess asked, thinking of the homely man she remembered from their shared childhood twenty years before. What would he have made of Tavy's success? She wished suddenly that she could hug him again, press her face against the rough wool of his V-necked jumper and feel his warmth.

'I'm a psychic, not a medium. I don't get messages from people who have passed over. I use my intuition and receive guidance through dreams and visions.'

'I see,' Jess said. She passed Francesca the mug of coffee.

'Thanks,' Francesca said. She took it in one hand and patted her jacket pocket with the other, taking out a battered packet of cigarettes. 'If anyone wants me, I'll be in the courtyard. Oh, and Jess…' She turned her headlight gaze back again. 'You'll find Rose in the fishing house.'

Jess stood for a moment, resting both hands on the worktop. How had Francesca known she was interested in someone called Rose? Had she seen the parchment in the library? And what had she meant that she'd find Rose in the fishing house? Was she *buried* there?

Jess felt a cold shiver tiptoe down her spine. She could see Francesca out in the courtyard now, in front of the orangery, the smoke from her cigarette spiralling up into the sky. She was studying her phone intently and, yet again, Jess wondered whether Francesca's gift was totally bogus. If it was, she was a hell of an actress.

With another violent shiver, she shoved all the dirty coffee cups into the dishwasher and turned it on, anything to break a silence that felt suddenly sinister.

* * *

Jess was deep into the account of the theft of the Crown Jewels in 1671 when she heard Ethan's car on the gravel outside. She put the book down on the kitchen worktop and went to let him in. He had texted earlier to say he would be a bit late – some sort of crisis with his younger brother, Tom – and she thought he looked tired when he came in. She repressed the urge to hug him – they weren't really on those sorts of terms, despite the impromptu kiss earlier. She felt a rush of heat remembering the touch of his lips against hers.

'Thank you for inviting me,' Ethan said formally when she opened the door. He was holding a small posy of the palest lemon-coloured roses, the buds on the edge of unfurling. 'I thought they were appropriate,' he commented, with a crooked smile, as he held them out to her, 'given your interest in Rose.'

'That's so kind, thank you.' Jess felt touched by his thoughtfulness. 'There's a cute little posy vase in the kitchen that will be perfect for them.'

'Sorry I'm so late,' Ethan said as he took off his coat. There were raindrops in his dark hair. 'Tom was talking about dropping out of uni so I had a long chat with him. Now that the euphoria of the first couple of terms is over, he's suddenly realised he has to work and he isn't sure he's up to it. But he's agreed to wait until he gets back for the Easter holiday next week and we can discuss it properly.'

'I imagine it's a tough gig being a surrogate parent,' Jess said. 'Do you need a drink? We've got non-alcoholic stuff as well as wine,' she added quickly, in case it sounded as though she was inviting him to stay over. God, she was out of practice at this relationship thing. She always felt awkward around Ethan and they weren't even *having* a relationship.

'I'll have a beer, thanks,' Ethan said. Watching her peer uncertainly into the fridge he added, 'Ghost Ship is very low alcohol. I'll have that, thanks. You've got enough drink here for an all-night party.'

'I think that's the idea,' Jess passed him the bottle and a glass. 'The kitchen is kept fully stocked in case any of Tavy's friends rock up unexpectedly.'

'And do they?' Ethan asked.

'Never,' Jess said, 'but then she's barely here, so it's not surprising.'

'The word in the village is that she's going to sell up,' Ethan said. 'Or try to. It might be even more difficult to sell the hall now it's half redesigned to Tavy's very personal specification.'

'Or it might be easier to sell as a celebrity has lived here,' Jess replied. 'You can be sure the estate agents will make that point. Dinner will be about twenty minutes,' she added. 'Would you like to look at the books first?'

'It smells great.' Ethan looked appreciative as he followed her out into the hall. 'My cooking is strictly functional. I learned as a student and developed a basic repertoire to suit a teenage boy and I've never really advanced from that point.'

Jess laughed. 'Well, my repertoire is small but with a few signature dishes. We used to eat out a lot in London.' She stopped. She didn't want to talk about Jared again. 'Tonight, it's moussaka,' she said, as she opened the door of the library, 'with a salad.'

'Perfect,' Ethan said. He looked round the room as she snapped on the gothic-style wall lights. 'God, it's gloomy in here, isn't it. I remember being slightly scared of this room when my grandmother lived here. It always seemed a bit creepy, even though some of my favourite books were in here.'

'Well, hopefully you can give them a new home now,' Jess said. 'I finished sorting them all out earlier and I'm taking the more unusual ones to a bookseller in Oxford tomorrow.' She gestured to the neat piles on the battered mahogany table. 'I've categorised them as rare, modern classics, history/biography/military, fiction, children's and, the useful catch-all, miscellaneous.'

Ethan laughed. 'Spoken like a true professional. Thank you.'

'I'll leave you to sort through them,' Jess said, 'and give you a shout when dinner's ready.' She didn't want to inhibit him by standing over him as he sifted through a part of his past life. It felt too personal.

Back in the kitchen, she took the salad ingredients from the fridge and whisked up a simple vinaigrette dressing. Ethan reappeared just as the oven timer went off and she was taking the plates out. He had a modest selection of half a dozen books under his arm.

'That was emotional and a bit weird,' he commented, with a lopsided grin. 'I hope it's okay to have these? Everything from *Where the Wild Things Are* and *The Very Hungry Caterpillar* to the biography of Alan Turing.'

'Is that all you want?'

'It's all I need,' Ethan said with emphasis. 'Sometimes you've got to move on.' He took a seat at the table as Jess put the dish of moussaka on the hot pad in front of him.

'Help yourself.' She passed him the serving spoon. 'Speaking of moving on...' Jess ladled some salad onto her plate. 'Lucy said you were thinking of travelling now that Tom is settled at uni. If he is,' she added quickly. 'Where had you thought of going?'

'It's no more than an idea at the moment,' Ethan replied, taking the salad bowl from her, 'but yeah, I'd thought about a gap year. It's only about ten years after everyone else did it.'

'I went to Europe for mine,' Jess reflected. 'All my friends were visiting Asia or Australasia and thought I was very boring, but I loved it. So many art galleries and museums.'

'You've got to do your own thing,' Ethan acknowledged. 'I fancy New Zealand – I've always thought the scenery looked amazing. Maybe in the autumn...' He looked pensive.

'You've spent a large part of your time prioritising other people,' Jess said. 'I hope you get what you want as well.'

'Thanks,' Ethan gave her his warm smile. 'I feel a bit of a fraud sometimes, though. I mean, people make out I'm some sort of hero for devoting ten years of my life to bringing up Tom, but I've enjoyed living around here and I've had a job I've loved most of that time. Plus, Tom's a good kid and we just muddled along, really. Clara's done her bit too; Tom talks to her a lot, which takes the pressure off me sometimes.'

'How old was Clara when your dad died?' Jess asked. 'You're the eldest, right?'

'Yes. I'm thirty-two,' Ethan said. 'Clara's two years behind, so she was at Durham University when Dad died. Tom was only twelve. He'd been an afterthought, a baby to patch up Mum and Dad's marriage. Needless to say, it didn't work, and Mum left when I was fifteen and Clara twelve and Tom nearly five.'

'God,' Jess said. 'That must have been hard. I'm sorry.'

'Your mum told me that you lost your father about ten years ago too,' Ethan said. 'She was very honest; she said she self-medicated with alcohol and it was Tavy who finally helped her get sober again.'

'I'm surprised you didn't see the TV programme about it.' Jess tried hard not to sound sarcastic. 'Tavy knows no other way than to live her life in public and Mum doesn't seem to mind. Dad and I...' She sighed. 'We are – in his case, were – totally different to them. Bookworms, introverts, very private people really...' She shrugged. 'I suppose with my parents, opposites attracted, but it always felt to me that I was born in the wrong nest somehow.'

'Complicated stuff, family dynamics.' Ethan cleared his plate. 'I was seeing someone for a few months who told me that I'd sacrificed my twenties to bring up Tom and was prematurely aged. I thought that was a harsh judgement.'

'Ouch.' Jess wasn't sure whether to laugh or wince. 'I don't suppose that relationship lasted long.'

Ethan shook his head. 'Strangely, it didn't.' He looked hopefully at the moussaka dish. 'May I have a bit more?'

'Sure.' Jess smiled. 'I'm keeping a bit for Ted to microwave for his supper later. He's on the night shift tonight. But the rest is all yours.'

'Thanks.' Ethan reached for the dish. 'How's the Nell Gwyn biography going?' he added, seeing it on the worktop alongside the book on Thomas Blood and the Crown Jewels. 'Anything useful?'

'She had a fascinating life,' Jess said. 'I'm riveted. Did you know three different places claim she was born there – Hereford, London and Oxford. She's an icon – everyone wants a piece of her. And because there aren't many written records relating directly to her, so much of the so-called history is hearsay and rumour.'

'That feels appropriate,' Ethan said, 'for someone who's such a legend.'

'Absolutely,' Jess agreed, 'but it doesn't help when you're trying to trace things like land grants. There's even less information on her sister, Rose, although I did pick up a few more details: the highwayman Rose married as her first husband was called John Cassells. I couldn't find anything more about him but I did read a couple of references to the fact that Rose was allegedly an infamous thief and had been in jail several times. She was supposedly quick, cunning and courageous, according to one record.'

Ethan was smiling at her enthusiasm. 'I imagine you would need to be all those things to survive in the backstreets of London in that era,' he said. 'She sounds a hell of a woman. As gutsy as Nell in her own way.'

'I think so,' Jess said. 'I really like what I know of her. Oh, and both Rose and Nell were illiterate, or at least they were never taught to read and write as children.'

'That makes the parchment you found in the library even more interesting,' Ethan commented. 'Perhaps she was learning to write.'

Jess scooped the last of the salad onto her plate and lavished dressing on it. 'That's what I was thinking,' she said. 'I've got the papers here – I'll show you in a moment. I know all of this is speculation,' she added, 'and no historian worth their salt would give it the time of day without proof, but I'm finding it so interesting.' She paused. 'Francesca said something about Rose earlier,' she said. 'She told me that I'd find her in the fishing house. What on earth do you think she meant by that?'

'She's messing with your head,' Ethan said. 'Honestly, that woman has cold reading to a fine art.'

'Well, maybe,' Jess conceded, 'but it is odd. I mean, there definitely was a Rose here, although I'll admit there's no proof at all that it was Rose Gwyn. But Francesca didn't even know I was searching for a Rose. She thought I was looking for Nell. So...'

'So, it's still bullshit,' Ethan said tersely. 'Sorry,' he added. 'That was out of order. I don't mind Francesca taking advantage of Tavy's gullibility, but I feel differently about her misleading you. You've had enough crap to deal with already. And I know it's nothing to do with me, but that's how I feel.'

Tension hummed between them, then Jess broke it, hastily collecting up the plates and shoving them to one side. Her heart was beating light and fast.

'Let me show you the old parchments I think Rose was using for writing,' she said, reaching for the folder she'd propped up by the toaster. 'Here...' She passed the papers over to Ethan, along with the copy of the poetry book with the poem by Sir Walter Raleigh that had the same letters underlined. She watched him as he read through them carefully, head bent, a pair of ridiculously sexy black-framed spectacles on his nose. 'I didn't know you wore glasses,' she remarked.

'Reading glasses,' Ethan said absently. He looked up and gave her a flashing smile. 'Age is catching up with me already.'

'More likely it's the result of poring over old documents and tiny print.' Jess released her breath as the tension in the room eased. She moved the used dishes to the worktop so that they could spread out the pages on the table.

'It definitely looks as though someone was practising their writing,' Ethan said, looking from the carefully formed ROSE to the letters under-lined in the book. 'What a beautiful poem,' he added, reading aloud:

> *'But true love is a durable fire,*
> *In the mind ever burning,*
> *Never sick, never old, never dead,*
> *From itself never turning.'*

He finished and looked directly at Jess. Instantly, the tension returned, hotter this time.

'And the other sheet,' she said hastily, to break the moment, 'that has the same writing and the careful formation of letters.'

'*My love for you is ever true,*' Ethan read. 'There's a bit of a theme here. Do you think Rose was writing love letters to Guy? Or someone else? Did you find any more like this?'

'No.' Jess found she was almost whispering. 'I checked all the other books when I sorted them.' She cleared her throat. *Damn*, she thought. *I need to get away from this topic and fast*, but her mind was blank, apart from the love poetry that very unhelpfully kept repeating through her mind.

Ethan stood up and came around the table towards her and she stood up too. He took both her hands in a very simple gesture. 'Can I ask you something?' he said. His voice sounded rough. 'Do you have a strange sense that we already know each other very well despite only meeting...' He paused to count. 'Five days ago? Or is it just me?'

Jess hesitated. 'You might just be under the influence of Sir Walter Raleigh,' she said. 'He does write powerful stuff.'

'It's not Sir Walter,' Ethan said steadily. 'It's you.'

Jess gave up any pretence. 'I do know what you mean,' she said. 'It's... very odd, isn't it? As though I've known you for ages.' She stopped. When Ethan didn't follow up, she added, backtracking slightly, 'I suppose there are people you feel an immediate affinity with when you meet but—'

'Not often people you feel as though you've known in a past life,' Ethan said.

Jess felt a bit shaky. 'Like your emotional compass has gone haywire,' she whispered, 'and is misleading you by telling you that you can trust someone with your life when you barely know them.'

Ethan took a step closer. 'Emotional compass,' he said thoughtfully. 'I like that. Although I'd say it feels as though mine is pointing me to true north rather than misleading me.'

He cupped his hand around Jess's chin and gently tilted her face up to his. The butterflies that had been chasing each other madly around her sternum went positively wild now. He paused just long enough for her to pull back if she wanted to, but Jess wasn't going to do that. She leaned in a little and when he skimmed his lips softly against hers, she pressed closer and slid her arms around his neck. She forgot everything that wasn't Ethan, the warmth and the taste of him, the deep sense of recognition and rightness.

She broke away at last and he released her at once.

'Wow.' Jess pressed her fingers against her mouth. 'Oh my God.'

'Sorry,' Ethan said. He looked as shocked as she felt.

'No.' Jess put her hand on his arm. 'I didn't mean it like that. That was quite some kiss.'

She saw him relax a little and a gleam of satisfaction came into his eyes. 'It was,' he agreed.

'So, what do we do now?' Jess asked. She grabbed the back of her chair, still feeling a little shaky.

'You don't sound happy,' Ethan said. 'Not quite the reaction I'd hoped for.'

Jess laughed. 'I'm not unhappy,' she said, 'but you've got to admit it's strange, Ethan, and whatever we feel, we don't really know each other very well. I've just come out of a toxic relationship and I don't want to make another awful mistake.' She stopped. 'Sorry, that came out wrong. I know you're nothing like Jared, but—'

'I'll overlook it,' Ethan said. She could hear the laughter in his voice. 'And as for what we do about it – we don't need to do anything, do we? It's out there, which is a relief, and we can be honest about it, but we don't need to actively do anything. Just hang out together if we want to and see where it leads?'

'But you're planning on going travelling,' Jess objected, 'and I'm applying for jobs...'

Ethan took her face between his hands and kissed her again. 'Maybe we can travel in the same direction,' he murmured.

That took her breath away. 'You make it sound very easy,' Jess said.

'It is, isn't it?' Ethan asked. 'Easier than swiping right on Tinder, anyway.'

Jess gave a snort of laughter. 'I'll take your word for it. I've never been on Tinder.'

'Me neither,' Ethan said. He checked the clock. 'I'd better go. Ted will be round to collect his moussaka soon, won't he?'

'They come on duty at ten,' Jess agreed. She was starting to feel a little more normal now and Ethan's suggestion that they take things slowly and see where they led had taken away the panic that she'd felt at the speed things had changed between them. 'Will you be at Lucy and Finn's tomorrow?' she asked. 'She mentioned something about having a few friends over.'

'Oh, yeah,' Ethan said. 'Lizzie Kingdom and Arthur and a few others.'

'Lizzie Kingdom as in the pop star?' Jess looked at him horrified. 'I'll kill Lucy for this! She said it was Lizzie, her boss from work!'

'Which is technically correct,' Ethan said, shrugging on his coat. 'Lucy works for Lizzie's charity. Finn is godfather to Lizzie and Arthur's son.' He laughed at her expression. 'I really didn't expect you to be starstruck, Tavy Yates's sister.'

'I'm an introvert, remember?' Jess said. 'Well, I suppose I'll see you then.'

'Have a good day in Oxford,' Ethan said. He touched her cheek very gently. 'See you tomorrow.'

As she tidied away the sheets with the writing on them, Jess lingered over the carefully formed letters, tracing her finger gently over the R for Rose. Had Rose been thinking of Guy when she wrote them? She could almost imagine the two of them in the library, he leaning over her shoulder to show her how to hold the quill, Rose concentrating as she formed the words *'my love for you...'*

Jess smiled. She was getting sentimental; imagining things, too. The house felt warmer, full of a soft happiness she couldn't pin down but which seemed to embrace her. And on the kitchen worktop the yellow roses glowed.

16

ROSE – SUMMER 1671

There was no sign the following morning of how desperately matters were to change by the end of that day. We broke our fast early, as the sun was rising over the fields, turning them to a hazy pink and gold. The birds were singing. As Guy handed me up into the coach for the second stage of our journey to Becote, I felt more tired than I would have expected after such a comfortable night's sleep. My eyes were heavy and there was the beginning of an ache at the back of my head.

'Are we to talk about what happened between us last night?' Guy said, as the coach picked up pace along road.

'It was only a kiss,' I said.

'And that does not warrant a discussion?' He raised his brows.

'It was a very nice kiss,' I said, 'but not sufficient to persuade me into marriage.'

He smiled, settling back against the cushion squabs. 'Then I shall have to try harder.'

I did not feel like flirting that morning. My headache increased and the bright sunshine made my eyes water. I rested my head against the back of the seat and tried to sleep, but the motion of the carriage made me feel sick and I had to concentrate to ensure that I kept my breakfast down. By the time we stopped to change horses, I had no desire to eat or drink anything and only wished to be left alone. We set off again and immediately I felt worse, hot and nauseous.

Guy, observant as always, leaned forward and touched my arm. 'Are you quite well, Rose? You are looking very pale.'

I was aware of the sweat springing along my forehead and my gown clinging to me in the heat. 'I believe I may have a touch of fever,' I said.

'We are almost at Lambourn, and from there it is but a short distance to Becote.' Guy was frowning. I could see the concern in his eyes and, behind that, something else. He tapped on the roof of the coach and it ground to a halt.

'Send one of the lads to Newbury to fetch a doctor to Becote,' I heard him say. 'Then spring the horses. Hurry, man.'

Whatever followed was a blur as I slid further into the fever. Each jolt on the road seemed agony, sending shooting pains through my limbs. I gritted my teeth to prevent myself from crying out. I felt cold and yet hot at the same time and my head was so heavy, I thought I could not hold it up. Time seemed endless, running on the longest thread, and yet spinning in short, sharp jolts that made me shiver violently.

I was dimly aware that Guy was cradling me in his arms, smoothing the damp hair back from my hot forehead with the gentlest movements, murmuring words of comfort I could barely hear through the harsh buzzing in my ears.

'It is the marsh fever,' I gasped. 'I had it before as a child.'

'We are at Becote now,' Guy said. 'The doctor is on his way. All will be well, Rose.'

I remembered nothing after that. My world became a tangle of pain and heat and then the sharp smell of blood. I heard voices, but they made no sense to me. I felt hands on me and the coolness of water. Then I heard someone cry out. Perhaps it was me, for I knew then in my deepest being what was happening; that the fever was stealing my child away from me. I was dreaming now, shreds of nightmares where my baby was slipping from my arms and no matter how hard I tried, I could not hold her. And I knew, even though I was barely conscious, that in the quickest and most brutal way possible, death was taking her from me, taking the only thing that I truly cared about, my daughter, the one thing that had mattered above all else. I felt her spirit leave me and then there was nothing – no purpose, no future, nothing to live for. I could have screamed at the pain of it, but I was too weak and the darkness that swallowed me was a blessed relief.

* * *

When I woke up, I felt it was true before I knew it. I felt the loss and the emptiness like an unbearable void, and I simply turned my face into the pillow and wept.

Someone was sitting beside me and she moved when she realised that I was awake. To my shock, I realised that it was Nell. I recognised her scent and the warmth of her touch against my cheek.

She spoke to someone, 'Mama, she is awake! What can we do?'

But, in truth, there was nothing anyone could do. I wanted no one. I cried as though my heart had broken – which it had – and then I closed my eyes and feigned sleep and a moment later I was unconscious again with exhaustion and grief and that made me glad because I could not face life any more.

* * *

'Guy was with you the whole time until we arrived,' Nell said. She sat by my bed, holding my hand, talking to me, though she seldom received any response. 'He never left your side. He refused to let the doctor bleed you, which was very wise since it would certainly have killed you. And he...' Her voice faltered. 'He spoke to the priest and arranged a baptism for the baby. He told us you had named her Harriet.' Her voice broke. 'Oh, Rose...'

'We must bury her,' I said, finding my voice at last. 'I must be there.'

Nell looked shocked. Her hand quivered in mine at the hard tone of my voice.

In the shadows, another figure stirred, our mother, a permanent presence in the rocking chair beside the window. Nell frequently asked her advice and she never replied. I was not sure if she could. But she looked at me with her faded blue eyes – eyes that had seen so much suffering like mine and more – and she nodded gently.

'You are not strong enough,' Nell objected.

'I will be,' I said. 'It is over a week now, or so you tell me. The fever is fading. Tomorrow I shall get out of bed.'

I do not think that Nell, always so expressive, understood that I had locked down all my emotions so tightly because I was afraid that if I let them out, they would destroy me. It was true that the fever had died down now, leaving me with nothing but aching exhaustion. I knew I would recover from that in time, but whether I would ever be myself again was a different matter. I felt lost, with no interest in life at all. I wanted to die and yet whatever strength had driven me on from the day I was born refused to leave me. It prompted me to get up and to move forward, even though I would be an empty shell, and that angered me. Why could I not simply drift away as Harriet had done? Why had I lived when she had died? The thought hurt me so much, it made me scream inside.

'Guy wants to see you,' Nell said, but I shook my head, for I could not even begin to think about how that would be. I imagined Guy would stand by his proposal to me, because he was an honourable man. I found the thought intolerable. With my baby dead, I had no need of his protection from Sir Grey Cassells. I didn't need Guy any more. Yet neither did I want to hurt him.

Let me bury my child first, I thought, *and then...* But there was no after. There was nothing. I could not see a future when my grief was so huge that it was all I could feel.

* * *

'I must be gone,' Nell said. 'The King has spared me for an entire fortnight whilst he had the races at Burford to distract him, but now I am to join him at Ashdown Park. If I leave it any longer, he will find another woman to amuse him and that will be the end of us all.'

We were sitting in the parlour at Becote. It was August now and the summer sun was flooding into the dark-panelled room and filling it with light. Nell was in a gown of pale yellow and looked fragrant and beautiful, as well as blooming with her pregnancy. It hurt me to see her and that made me feel doubly unhappy, for it was not her fault that I had lost my

baby whilst she was still carrying a healthy child. A return of the dreaded
marsh fever that had been prevalent in London that summer had been the
cause of my miscarriage; the doctor told me I was fortunate it had not taken
me as well. I did not feel fortunate.

By the time another month had passed, my physical strength was
returning but my mind was empty of thought and feeling. It was better
that way. I would drift through the days, flitting through the rooms at
Becote like a ghost, noting the beautiful roses in the gardens, wandering
through the trees, yet feeling unmoved by the summer beauty all around
me The servants that Nell had installed there kept the place looking well,
although it was a sadly old-fashioned house. She was always deploring the
lack of comfort. That did not matter to me. Becote wrapped me around
with a sense of home that I remembered from my childhood, and
although nothing could touch me in those early weeks, the familiarity
helped me.

Sometimes I sat beside Harriet's grave in the churchyard for hours at a
time. Guy had arranged for a local mason to carve a little headstone for her
– another of the many kindnesses for which I had not yet thanked him –
and sometimes I would trace the sharply cut marks on the stone with the
tip of my finger. I knew what the letters and numbers spelt out. It was her
name and the date. But below that was another word. Nell had told me it
was 'Rosebud' to acknowledge that she was my child. There was a carving
of a Rose beside it.

The household at Becote watched over me to make sure I did not throw
myself in the lake; Mrs Lambert the housekeeper, Millicent my maid and
Ned the steward with his old, smelly dog Eliza. Nell had told me that Lord
Craven had made Guy the agent for all his Berkshire estates – 'so that he
may be near you,' she said, but I did not want him near me. I did not want
to see him. I wanted no one.

Before she left to rejoin the King, Nell had mentioned that she had
searched the whole house, looking for the jewels and her locket, but that
she had found nothing, and that Mrs Lambert had told her that no one had
come by over the past few months. Nell had pressed my hands in an orgy of
anxiety. 'What will happen now, Rose?' She had said. 'You must stay here
for as long as you wish, of course...' She had looked momentarily guilty.

'But what will happen to *me*? What if Thomas Blood renews his threat of blackmail? I shall not be safe until the locket is found.'

I must confess that it was weeks before I found I could care a jot about Nell, or the jewels, or her locket. Nothing mattered to me but the loss of Harriet.

They could lock me up in the Tower of London again for all I cared. It was of no significance whether I lived or died. Thus I drifted through time like a wraith.

Then, finally, a tiny sliver of emotion cut through the numbness that surrounded me. We were at dinner one evening, my mother and I, in the small parlour where Mrs Lambert had lit a cheerful fire that did not fit my mood and made a bowl of broth to tempt me back to eating. There was silence but for the chink of spoon against china, for my mother seldom spoke and often had a vague look in her eyes as though she were far away. Then suddenly, she looked directly at me and said, 'Eat your soup, Rose, it will make you strong,' and I was transported back twenty years to the same room and the same words, and I was a child of four, kicking the leg of my chair in impatience to escape from the tyranny of mealtimes to play outside in the gardens. Something awoke in me then, a connection to the past, although I wanted to ignore it, and I felt a wave of love for my mother and for Nell. They had nursed me through my sickness. Nell was giving me a home here. She deserved my help if I could grant it.

Perhaps I was starting to wake up. Perhaps I was starting to think and feel again.

I did not want to. I did not want to feel alive, to question, to think, with all pain that would bring, but it was too late. I thought back to the moment in London when I had found the key to the fishing house missing from my precious tin box. It would be a place to start.

After dinner, I went up to my chamber and took the box from the chest, where it had been tidied away with the clothes I had brought with me to the country. I opened it and studied the things I had collected as a child, keepsakes that had no intrinsic value but which I might one day have given to my own child: My father's knife, the toy soldiers, the buttons, the thimble, the horoscope that Mr Ashmole had made for me, and the blue ribbon I had stolen from baby Nell to adorn my own red curls. These things, like my memories, belonged to what felt like my previous life. I took the tin and placed it carefully in a cupboard behind the panelling of my bedroom and locked it away.

The clothes did not interest me. They were all too big now on my gaunt frame, but there was no need to dress to impress anyone, least of all Guy. I still did not want to see him. I had turned away his messages and his gifts – a small bunch of flowers now and then, a basket of apples, even a pair of gloves made from the softest leather. It was better this way. There was nothing to bind us together now and although I knew I owed him my thanks for taking me safely to Becote, that 'before time' felt like nothing more than a dream.

The late summer night was not yet dark and so I went out into the gardens, where the scent of wild honeysuckle and rambling rose hung elusive on the air. Down on the lake, a moorhen gave a shrill call. The rippling water reflected the deep blue of the sky and the shape of the evening clouds sailing lazily overhead. It was a night for romance but I felt nothing. The gravel path to the fishing house crunched beneath the thin soles of my slippers. Nell had told me that whilst she had repaired the house as much as was necessary for it to be habitable, she had done nothing with the grounds or the outbuildings.

'They are as tumbledown as they were at the end of late wars,' she had said cheerfully, 'for I cannot afford to improve them. The King thought he was doing me a favour giving Becote to me, but with no income, it is a mill-stone around my neck.'

The long grass brushed my skirts as I walked. It seemed to me that the Becote estate might turn a good profit if it were managed well, but I knew Nell was not interested in it, so it would continue to crumble. Certainly, the steps up to the door of the fishing lodge were broken almost into dust.

I hung on to the iron railing as I climbed, at one point losing my footing in a tumble of stones and hanging over the edge as the world swung sicken-ingly around me. At the top, I had to stop to regain my breath, so weak had I become from the fever and the miscarriage.

No one had been here in a long time. It was evident from the stiffness of the door and the way I had to rattle the handle to encourage it to yield. And yet were those not footprints in the dust? Was there not a paler patch of board in the corner where someone had perhaps knelt to conceal something beneath the floor? Despite myself, my pulse started to beat a little quicker as I imagined John here, stowing away the missing Crown Jewels and Nell's locket with them.

But no. There was nothing beneath the floorboards except dust, old leaves and a dead bat. I sat back on my heels, feeling frustrated, certain that I had been right that John would come here. Perhaps he had done, and then he had come back to collect his booty before returning to London and meeting his end in the Fleet ditch. The jewels could be anywhere and Nell's locket lost, a threat hanging over her forever...

The scrambling of a bird in the chimney made me jump and simultaneously realise how foolish I had been. The footprints led to the corner where the boards were loose, but they also led to the right-hand side of the fireplace. Had I not used this same trick myself in London to hide my valuables?

A chimneypiece, and halfway up inside it a ledge... My searching fingers touched something and clung to softness – a bag of velvet that dropped into my other outstretched hand. I searched around some more, but there was nothing else on the ledge, so I withdrew into the room and moved over to the window to catch the last of the light.

The drawstring gave way to my tug and a necklace fell into my hands, a delicate gold chain and a heart-shaped pendant depicting the head of the King. I gave a gasp. There were no loose jewels here then, but Nell's locket was found.

I sat for a long time holding it whilst the last light died from the sky and a new moon rose over the lake and the sounds of the birds quieted to silence. And then I rose stiffly and, shivering a little, made my careful way back to the house through the dark because there was something I had to do to make matters right.

The next day, I sent for Guy Forster.

* * *

'I need to thank you,' I said. 'For all that you have done for me – and for Harriet.'

We were sitting outside, on a rug on the lawn, surrounded by the wild-flowers, with the buzz of the bees loud as they moved from plant to plant. The sun was warm and it felt good, although it could not reach into my heart. I had not been able to see Guy inside; the rooms felt too airless and dark, my feelings crushing me.

Guy looked older, thinner, more worn. There was grief in his face and with a little leap of the heart, I realised it was for me and for the loss of my daughter. This was the man who had offered us both his name and his protection and now he had lost us. I wanted to reach out to him – either to take comfort or to give it – but the effort was too great.

'It was my honour to help you,' he said, 'although I wish—' He stopped. 'I wish matters could have been different.' There was a fierceness in his tone that made me shiver. 'I am sorry, Rose,' he added. 'So very sorry.'

I nodded, unable to speak. There was too much to say and it was too soon. It was better to concentrate on the practical. I had no wish to cry in front of him and my chest already felt tight with tears. 'I asked you to come...' I cleared my throat. 'I have a favour to beg of you. Another one, I fear.' I tried to make light of it. 'It seems I shall always be in your debt.'

'Never think that,' he said. 'What may I do for you?'

I took the little velvet bag that was lying on the rug beside me and held it out to him. 'I would like you to return this locket to my sister,' I said. 'She will be most grateful – and even more so if the King is unaware that it was ever out of her possession.'

He took the necklace from the bag and looked at it thoughtfully. It sparkled in the sunlight. 'You found it then,' he said. 'I am glad.'

'Yes,' I said. 'I was not entirely honest with you, Colonel Forster. Not at the beginning. When I told you that I was coming to Becote as a place of safety for me and for Harriet...' My voice wavered but I got it under control. 'That was true, but there was another reason. I suspected that my late husband John had brought both Nell's locket and the missing jewels and hidden them here. I wanted to find them.'

Guy was silent for a moment. 'I suspected as much,' he said at last. He looked up from the glitter of the locket in his palm and smiled at me. 'You will remember that I overheard your conversation in the inn with Thomas Blood. It was obvious to me that your sister had been involved in the theft of the jewels in some way and that you were bluffing when you denied it. But I thought you would tell me in your own good time. Which you have done.'

'I see,' I said. I felt mildly astonished, both by his perspicacity and his faith in me where I had none. 'So, you thought the jewels might be here too?'

'I wondered,' Guy said. 'But if so, they were safe. And I am a patient man. I was prepared to wait to see what happened.'

We sat in silence for a little. It felt quite restful. 'You must be wondering why Nell ever involved herself in so foolish a plot,' I said.

'I knew that she did some business with your late husband,' Guy said. Then, at my look of surprise, 'I was a spy, if you recall.'

'Of course,' I said. 'You would make it your concern to know such things.'

'I far prefer being a land agent,' Guy replied, settling back on the rug. 'It is less complicated. But I do understand that you and Madam Gwyn have often had to fight to survive. So...' He shrugged. 'I can see the appeal of shiny, valuable things to her.'

I smiled. 'And you will return her property and ask no further questions?'

'Certainly,' he agreed stowing the necklace inside his jacket. 'As I say, I am a land agent now, not a spy for the Crown.'

'Thank you,' I said. I settled back on the rug too and let the drowsiness of the day soothe me. 'There is one other small thing I should tell you,' I added, and felt rather than saw him laugh as he lay beside me. For a moment, I felt happy, a fleeting sensation, quickly lost as soon as I remembered Harriet. 'The jewels are not here. At least, I could not find them.'

'Ah,' he said. 'And if you had?'

'The question does not arise,' I said, 'since I did not.'

I turned my head and saw he was smiling. 'That sounds more like the Rose I know,' he said. 'If they are not here, then where could they be?'

'I have no notion,' I said, 'and I do not want to know. It is over, all at an end.'

We were quiet again then, amongst the call of the birds and the scent of the roses.

'What will you do now?' he asked, after a while. 'Will you stay here?'

With anyone else, I might have bitten their head off when they asked me about a future I could not see and did not want to plan, but something had changed in me when I saw Guy again, something small, as yet only a spark, but still it was something.

'I shall stay into autumn,' I said cautiously, 'and then I will decide. It may be that by then I will miss city life. I do not know. At present, there is very little I want to do.'

'That is understandable,' he said. 'You are grieving. You must give yourself time.'

I looked at him. 'However, there is one thing I would like to learn this summer,' I said, 'and I would like you to teach me.'

He was quite still, his face impassive. 'Name it.'

I thought of Harriet's gravestone and the carved letters I had traced with my fingers to decipher them. 'I want to learn to read and write,' I said.

17

JESS – THE PRESENT

Oxford was exactly as Jess remembered it from her days working at the Bodleian: busy with tourists, noisy with buses and dangerously populated with bicycles, yet when she cut down a narrow street away from the main thoroughfares, it was as though the past and present had fused in a world of high walls, old windows and tumbled roofs.

The booksellers in St Philip's had a small yard where she was able to park and unload. Sue, who owned the shop and had been recommended to Jess by an old colleague at the Bod, was profusely grateful, exclaiming over the first editions of Agatha Christie and Ian Fleming, and getting engrossed in the *Memoirs of Madame Pilsudski* from the 1940s as soon as she had plucked it off the top of a pile in the first box.

'I mustn't read anything until I've catalogued them all,' Sue said, reluctantly putting the memoirs aside as she helped Jess empty the car. 'Thank you so much – I'll be in touch to give you a price for the collection once I've sorted through it.'

Jess had told her that the house needed to be emptied quickly – without explaining that this was so that Tavy could install glass shelves and white bookcases for her TV show – and had given her complete freedom to keep or get rid of the stock as required. When Sue had offered to pay for the books, she had at first refused, but the bookseller had insisted, so in the end

Jess had suggested the money be given to a local charity. Tavy didn't need payment and if it came out, she thought rather cynically that her sister would appreciate the publicity.

'Give my best to Phil,' Sue said as she waved her off, and Jess bumped away over the cobbles to find a parking space in St Giles and go for lunch with a few of her former colleagues in the Weston Library. She'd booked a time in the library's manuscripts collections in the afternoon to look at the papers of Canon Edmund Gwyn.

When she'd been at Oxford, Jess had worked in the Old Bodleian library, amongst the arched Gothic magnificence of all the medieval buildings, but the papers she wanted to consult were in the special collections in the Weston. The building was new, but some of the traditions persisted; the librarian who showed her to her desk and brought out the documents for her was wearing his academic gown and looked more like an undertaker than a curator. Talking in the library, eating, drinking and various other pursuits were firmly discouraged.

Opening the ancient leather-bound volumes gave Jess a thrill, though, as did turning over the pages of thin, seventeenth-century parchment which were covered in spidery writing, most of which she couldn't decipher. Her Latin had been neglected in the past few years and she peered in vain at several formal-looking decrees. Then she struck lucky; the contents list told her there was a grant of sale between Sir William Essex of Lambourn and Canon Edmund Gwyn, dated 1610. Amongst the dry legal terms, she could see the phrase 'Becote Manor and all appurtenances'.

She sat back in the uncomfortable chair feeling a rush of excitement. Here, then, was the proof of a Gwyn link to Beckett, and if, as was suggested, the less than virtuous Canon Gwyn had fathered two children out of wedlock, he could well have left Becote to one of them – Nell's father Thomas.

A further search of the papers did not turn up a convenient document proving this, but there was an entry in the accounts paying for the board and education of two boys, the 'wards' of Canon Gwyn. Jess thought that looked a little suspicious, the churchman perhaps passing off his bastard sons under the guise that he was no more than their guardian.

As she was putting the big ledgers back on the trolley, a text came through from the National Archives at Kew, whom she had contacted to check whether King Charles II had ever made a grant of land to Nell Gwyn at Becote in Berkshire. There was a land grant referred to in the patent rolls dated 1669, the archivist reported. They would send her the full details. Jess was so excited that she could have punched the air, but she was sure that would also be on the list of forbidden library activities.

It was getting towards four o'clock, so she thanked the Bodleian staff and headed out into Broad Street. She was due at Lucy's for dinner at seven.

Her phone buzzed again as she passed Balliol College on Broad Street.

'Jess? It's Sue from the bookshop.' There was a barely repressed note of excitement in Sue's voice and Jess's heart rate picked up on hearing it. 'Are you still in Oxford?' she asked. 'There's something I think you should see.'

* * *

Sue was waiting in the parking lot when Jess pulled in. She beckoned her inside the shop. 'I found it in one of the books,' she said, without preamble. 'It's a document and I think it might be old. And important.'

'I thought I'd checked through all the books.' Jess followed her inside. She'd enjoyed finding bookmarks, postcards and various scraps of paper amongst the pages, but there had been nothing old or valuable – or so she'd thought.

'It was folded up inside a map and tied with a ribbon,' Sue said. 'You probably missed it if you didn't open up the whole map. I only looked because it was a plan of Civil War Oxford, which is always popular with the customers.'

She led Jess into her office, where the document was spread out on the table, a faded piece of square parchment with squiggles, letters and random odd symbols that were so pale as to be almost illegible. Beside it was the book – a walking tour of Civil War Oxford published in the 1950s – and a piece of frayed ribbon that looked as though it might once have been blue but was now a pale grey.

'The document was tied with the ribbon,' Sue explained. 'I probably shouldn't have touched it without gloves, but I wanted to see what was inside.'

'I'd have done the same,' Jess said, smiling. She touched a finger to the fabric. It felt fragile, insubstantial enough to fray into dust. 'The book must be a lot newer than the document seems to be.'

'Oh yes,' Sue said. 'The document has come from somewhere else originally.' She picked it up gingerly and showed Jess the other side. 'I think it's been reused. It even has a shopping list on the back.'

'Two pints of milk, half a dozen eggs...' Jess read the neat list, written in blue biro. 'Oh my God, someone used an old piece of parchment for their weekly shop!'

Sue turned the paper face up again. Once again, Jess could feel the excitement that gripped her. 'It's not just any old piece of parchment, Jess,' Sue said urgently. 'I think it could be really old and really interesting.'

'Well, yes...' Jess looked again at the numbers and symbols. 'But what is it? I've never seen anything like it.'

'I have,' Sue said. 'Just once. There's a document in the Ashmolean Museum that's almost identical to this.'

Jess felt a shiver down her spine.

'The one in the Ashmolean is Nell Gwyn's horoscope,' Sue said.

* * *

Jess texted a picture of both sides of the paper to Ethan and he called her back on the hands-free as she was driving home. She'd left the document with Sue to take to the Ashmolean the following day to show to one of the seventeenth-century specialists.

'The shopping list is in my grandmother's writing,' Ethan said. 'I recognise the loopy "g" she used to write. But I've never seen the paper before. What is it?'

'Sue thinks it might be a seventeenth-century horoscope,' Jess said, 'but we won't know until tomorrow.' She summarised what Sue had told her. 'So, it can't be Nell's,' she finished, 'unless it's a copy. But it's obviously something special. It was tied up with a piece of old blue ribbon, but I'm not sure that was original to it. I've got it in my bag. I suppose I should have left it with the parchment for the historians to take a look at. I didn't think.'

Anyway, we can sort that all out when we know if it's genuinely old and important but...' She ran out of breath.

'You sound excited,' Ethan said, amused. 'I'm glad. Did you find out anything else at the Bodleian?'

'I found Canon Gwyn and his two wards,' Jess said, 'who I am assuming were his sons. And I heard from the National Archives that Charles II granted Becote Manor to Nell in 1669, so we're making good progress.'

'Tavy's producers should be pleased,' Ethan remarked.

'I expect they are hoping for something a bit more dramatic,' Jess said. 'Maybe a play Nell performed in a private show for Charles at Becote, or something like that. Somehow, I don't think a couple of old legal documents is going to cut it with them.'

'Have you got a photo of the ribbon you mentioned?' Ethan asked suddenly. 'It rings a bell with me, something to do with my grandmother and a tin I found in one of the bedrooms when I was a kid... I'm trying to remember why it feels familiar.'

'No,' Jess said, 'but I can show it to you later. Like I said, I've got it in my bag.' The sign for Beckett appeared and she switched on her indicator. 'I'm nearly home. See you at Lucy's?'

'Sure,' Ethan said. 'I'm looking forward to it.' And he rang off, leaving her wondering if he had meant the dinner, seeing her again or both.

* * *

The meal at Lucy and Finn's, which Jess had secretly rather been dreading, turned out to be pleasantly relaxed. There was only six of them, and Lizzie Kingdom, for all that she had once been a wild child pop star, was now seemingly quite normal, and her husband Arthur and toddler Freddie were both lovely. Finn cooked an amazing risotto with vegetables and herbs from the Gunpowder Cottage gardens and they chatted about music and plants and all sorts of other things, and Jess remembered how nice it was to chill out with friends.

They were in the hall and Jess was putting on her coat and scarf ready to leave when Ethan drew her to one side. 'You know what we were talking about earlier,' he said, 'the ribbon you mentioned that had been tied round that old document? Have you got it with you?'

'It's here somewhere...' Jess rummaged in the depth of her bag, scattering tissues, a lipstick a couple of pens and her notebook. 'Did you remember something about it? Damn...' She tried to scoop up all the bits and pieces. 'I really must sort this out.'

'Hey, Jess, you dropped something.' Lizzie had come up to them, the piece of blue ribbon in her hand.

'Thanks,' Jess said, reaching out a hand to take it from her. In the same moment, she saw all the colour drain from Lizzie's face and she leaned against the wall and looked as though she was about to collapse.

'Shit!' Ethan said. He leapt forward and helped her towards a chair by the door. 'Sit down, Lizzie. Are you okay?'

'What happened?' Jess rushed over to them. Lizzie was now translucently white, her freckles standing out in sharp contrast, her gaze blurred. Jess wondered if she was pregnant or had eaten something that had made her ill, but Ethan appeared to know what was going on. He crouched down and held Lizzie's hand in a comforting grasp.

'It's all right, Lizzie,' he said. 'Come back to us.' Over his shoulder, he gestured to Jess to fetch Arthur, but the others were already spilling out into the hall. Lucy dashed off to fetch a glass of water.

'I'm all right,' Lizzie said. Her voice was thready, but her gaze had cleared and colour was starting to come back into her face. 'Sorry, everyone.' She managed a shaky smile. 'Just a Lizzie special. No harm done. Haven't had one of those for a while.'

Finn and Lucy exchanged a glance. Ethan didn't look particularly surprised, as though he'd seen this happen before. Arthur, who'd been jiggling Freddie in his arms, gave a sharp sigh. 'Damn,' he said wryly, 'just when I thought we were able to have a normal evening out like any other couple.'

'Sorry, darling.' Lizzie was sipping the water Lucy had brought. She looked at Jess. 'Sorry,' she said again. 'I didn't mean to startle you. I have this slightly weird gift...' She glanced at Arthur, who rolled his eyes. 'Sometimes when I touch an object, I get visions associated with its past. It's called psychometry and it can be a bit of a shock if it takes me by surprise.'

She saw Jess's look of astonishment. 'Obviously it's not something I broadcast,' she added dryly, 'but old friends know about it.'

'The ribbon,' Jess said, looking down at the old, frayed piece of material that was still in her hand. 'When you picked it up to give it back to me, it must have triggered something.'

'It did,' Lizzie acknowledged. She shook her head slightly as though the visions still lingered. 'How old is it?' she asked.

'We think it's seventeenth century,' Jess said. 'I'm so sorry, Lizzie, I didn't know.' She felt awful for inadvertently causing such a fuss. There had been something chillingly authentic about what had happened to Lizzie. Her reaction had been so spontaneous, so different from Francesca's calculated pronouncements.

'It's okay.' Lizzie's colour had returned now and she drained the glass of water, handing it back to Lucy with a word of thanks. 'It wasn't a bad vision, fortunately. Sometimes they can really shake me.' She took Arthur's hand and held it tightly. 'The ribbon belonged to a little girl', she said. 'Well, it belonged to her baby sister, but she wanted it for her red curls.' She smiled. 'So, she took it and she was very pleased with herself. I saw a cold room and snow outside and the girl was hungry, but she was also fine, if that makes sense. She was a resilient little thing.' Lizzie looked up. 'I could sense her character. I think she must have been very brave.'

'Wow,' Lucy said after a moment. 'Who was she?'

'Nell?' Ethan suggested, looking at Jess.

But Lizzie shook her head. 'No,' she said. 'Her name wasn't Nell. She was called Rose.'

18

ROSE – BECOTE MANOR, 1671

Throughout the autumn, Guy rode over from Ashdown to Becote twice a week to teach me to read. I was a terrible student. Accustomed to learning quickly and having little patience, I soon lost interest when I could not understand something. I was still grieving, so my mood would veer like the wind. Poor Guy would often be on the receiving end of my bad temper, and in some contradictory part of me, I knew I was trying him, pushing him away, seeing how far I could go. He never lost his patience with me, but sometimes he would get up and walk away when my bad humour became too much.

On fine days, we would sit at a table outside on the terrace, and if it rained, we would retire to the library, where there was a snug fire and comfy armchairs. Sometimes, Guy brought some books over from Ashdown with him. Lord Craven had books on an eclectic mix of subjects, for his interests varied from history to architecture to fiction. Guy read stories to me, then, after a while, he would give me easy pieces to read myself; at first, it seemed almost impossible, but gradually I started to recognise the shape of letters and match them to the sound they made. I used a tablet to write my alphabet and from there I tried to form them into words. There was something magical about it when it started to come together. There was an alchemy at work and it drove me to seek out other books; poems, romances and fables. I doubted that I would ever be able to write more than a passable hand, but my understanding of words was quicker now and I loved to read. I also gained an unexpected admiration for Nell, learning all the parts in her plays by rote. How much easier matters would have been for both of us had our mother sought to give us an education, but somehow, we had triumphed over the odds in our different ways.

One day, a carrier arrived from Oxford with a package for me from Templars the booksellers. I was beside myself with excitement. *Don Quixote* by Cervantes, Descartes' *Meditations on Philosophy* (a little ambitious for me, I thought), the latest fables by La Fontaine, another French translation, *La Princesse de Montpensier*, plus poetry by Shakespeare and Raleigh and many more. I shut myself in the library for hours as I laboriously read through them; Mother and Mrs Lambert were quite worried about me until they realised that in some way the books were acting as a conduit for my grief. They did not drive it away, but perhaps they allowed me to understand it a little better and I realised that there were others who had suffered what I had and had written about their experiences in beautiful words.

There were also many who had written about love. When Guy next came to work with me on my letters, I was distracted and could not concentrate. Instead, I watched him and the play of light over his face as he spoke about language and the beauty of words. I watched his hands and I remembered him holding me and the touch of his lips against mine. For the first time in a long time, I felt a frisson of awareness.

Idly, I spelt out some letters on the parchment in front of me. L O V E. And then 'My love for you is ever true.' It was trite compared to the sonnets of Shakespeare, but I felt the bottom drop out of my stomach when I realised that it was true. I loved Guy. I had loved him for a long time. I had rejected his kindness, I had tried to push him away, but he had waited with the patience he had always possessed and at last I saw the truth for what it was.

'Rose?' I looked up to find Guy's gaze on me. He had read the words upside down. Our eyes met and I could not look away. And as I stared at him, he stood up and started to come around the table towards me.

'Excuse me, madam.' Mrs Lambert was in the library doorway. 'I did knock, but I don't think you heard me. There is a gentleman here to see you. He says that his name is Sir Grey Cassells.'

I froze. What business could Sir Grey have with me now? I felt sickened as all my memories and fears came rushing back in, filling the space that a moment ago had seemed bright with promise.

'I'll deal with him,' Guy started to say, moving towards the door, but I stayed him with a gesture.

'This is my business,' I said. 'I will speak with him.' I put a hand against Guy's chest and felt the hard beat of his heart. I could see the frustration in his eyes. 'Thank you. But I feel I must do this.'

He stood back and I went past him and out into the hall. I was certainly not inviting Sir Grey into the confines of the parlour. I could see my mother hovering on the stairs and, in the doorway, Sir Grey Cassells, a man I had not met before but who had twice tried to purchase me for silver. He was tall, like John, and big, dressed in a fancy jacket with his family crest on the silver buttons and fashionable leather boots. His hair and moustache were greying, his face fixed in a disagreeable sneer.

He looked me up and down. 'I heard you had lost the child,' he said. There were no words of regret or consolation, no attempt at comfort. 'I came to see if the intelligence was correct.'

My throat closed. 'If you go to the churchyard,' I said, when I could speak, 'you will see her gravestone.'

'I have already been,' he said. 'There is no mention of her surname or that she was my grandchild. I wish you to change the stone to reflect her parentage or, failing that—' he looked at me contemptuously '—I will arrange for her body to be exhumed and reburied with her father in the family vault at Cassells Manor.'

Fury and outrage washed over me, emotion flooding back through me in a scalding tide. 'You will do no such thing!' I exclaimed. 'Why would you even care, when you disdained me as a wife for your wayward son and thought neither I nor my child was good enough? Harriet was mine alone. You have no claim on her. Now begone before I have my servants throw you out!' I could not really threaten to have old Ned horsewhip him from the house since he was too old and infirm to scare anyone, but I was tempted.

Sir Grey slapped his gloves against the palm of his other hand. 'I'll pay you,' he said. 'Fifty pounds to take her for reburial at Cassells. You would be wise to accept it. It will cost me less to bribe the priest to let me dig her up.'

I pressed hand to my mouth afraid I might be sick.

'Sir Grey!' Guy's voice rang out. He strode into the hall, his hand resting suggestively on his sword hilt. 'You are not welcome here, sir.' His voice was dangerously soft. 'I suggest you leave whilst you still may.'

'Ah, so the lover is here!' Sir Grey shot me a nasty smile. 'And there you have it, mistress, the reason I want no grandchild of mine near you or your kin. Already there are plenty of tales of how you, a widow of barely six months, lift your skirts for Lord Craven's agent. You and your sister are cut from the same cloth—'

Guy drew his sword and started forward, but in the same moment, my mother darted down the stair. She came up behind Sir Grey before he realised that she was there, and she lifted the china vase from the stand beside the first step and brought it down on the back of his head, where it smashed into several pieces with the most almighty crack. Sir Grey staggered, flailing wildly. I thought he would go down, but he steadied a little, then tottered forward towards the blade of Guy's sword. There was a terrible moment when I was afraid that he would impale himself on it, but at the last moment, Guy stepped aside and Sir Grey clattered out of the front door and down the steps. Guy slammed the door behind him. It was all over in an instant, or so it seemed to me. One minute there was mayhem and the next, silence.

I was shaking and crying. Guy picked his way through the shards of china, scooped me up in his arms and carried me through to the library. He sat down before the fire with me in his lap. I admit that I sobbed unrestrainedly into his shirt, soaking him.

'He is a vile, horrible man,' I wept. 'I wish he were dead!'

'Hush.' Guy stroked my hair gently. 'He will never hurt you or Harriet. I will never allow it.'

'He will go and dig Harriet up!' I struggled in his arms, driven mad with grief and anger.

'He will not,' Guy said, so definitively that it calmed me. 'I will speak to the priest, and ensure that Harriet is well-guarded.'

He tilted my chin up and kissed me. It was a kiss meant for comfort, such as one might give a child, but I kissed him back and it quickly turned into something else, something that made me tremble. After a moment, I drew back.

'You cannot kiss me when I have cried so much,' I said contrarily. 'I must look frightful.'

'You look lovely,' Guy said. He kissed me again to prove the point, then stood up, swinging me up into his arms and carrying me out into the hall.

The house was silent, Mother and Mrs Lambert having vanished most diplomatically. Up the stairs we went, to my chamber, which had seen so much grief and unhappiness but this late afternoon was bathed in a warm golden light that matched the joy in my heart.

'Wait!' I said, as our clothes went flying. 'You do know that I have not yet agreed to marry you?'

Guy paused. 'I'll work on that,' he said with a smile, 'as long as you are happy to take me now without benefit of clergy?'

'With all my heart,' I said, and drew him down into my arms.

* * *

I woke feeling happy. It was full dark, I was hungry, but I was also possessed of a sense of warmth and pleasure that was quite new to me.

'Well,' I announced, 'I imagined that quite differently!'

Guy, whose chest I had been pillowed on, rolled over slightly whilst keeping me close. A flint struck, and candlelight filled the room. He turned back to me and drew me deeper into the crook of his arm.

'Imagined?' he said. He raised a brow and I felt myself blushing. 'You have no idea how much that encourages me, Rose.'

'I think,' I reflected, 'that perhaps Nell was correct in this one matter. The skill of a lover, the effort he takes to please...' I smiled against his shoulder. 'It truly makes a great difference.'

'I am glad you think so,' Guy said. 'The effort a *husband* takes to please will be even greater.'

I laughed. 'I am willing to see if that proves true.'

He cupped my face in his hands and kissed me. 'Thank you,' he said.

'That makes me the happiest of men.' I felt his chest move as he sighed. 'All this time I have been coming here to teach you your letters, hoping against hope that with time and healing you might be able to look kindly on me again,' he murmured against my hair.

'You put up with my vile temper,' I said. 'That was very noble of you.'

'You were grieving,' he said simply. 'You still are. We all grieve the loss of Harriet and we always will. Yet, despite that, I hoped that your curiosity, your gallant spirit, would re-emerge one day and that you would find a purpose again.'

'I am not certain about my purpose yet.' I tilted my head to look at him. 'If I wed you – *when* I do – I will not be a conformable wife. I cannot. I need something to *do*.'

I saw the lines around Guy's eyes deepen as he smiled. 'You are not telling me anything that I do not already know,' he said. 'That is why I love you, Rose, for the woman you are.' He turned so that he could look at me properly. 'I told you that night in the inn at Oxford that I had wanted you from the start. That was true. But now there is a different truth – a better one, I hope. I *loved* you from the first moment I saw you, so fearlessly seeing off those loutish aristocrats with no more than your cunning and your little knife. I did not realise it then, but I know now. I love you, Rose Gwyn.'

'And I love you too, Guy Forster,' I said. 'I did not realise it either for I had never loved properly before.' The thought filled me with the greatest contentment.

'I did have a plan,' Guy admitted, 'if it meets with your pleasure.'

I raised myself on one elbow. 'Indeed?' I said.

'I thought to buy Becote Manor from your sister as wedding present for you. You are the eldest; it should have been yours. It will be held in your name and will be yours to do with as you wish.'

I looked at him. 'Truly?' I said. 'Mine alone?'

'Well,' Guy replied, 'I would like to live here with you when we are in the country, but it will be your name on the legal documents.' He smiled at me. 'You may read them for yourself and see that I do not cheat you.'

'You would never do that,' I said, 'but even so, I can scarcely believe...' I swallowed the lump in my throat. 'That is generous indeed.' Becote, my childhood home, a place of enchantment to me. I would keep Harriet near, but we could make a new life and a new story here. Already, I had ideas. 'I think we could get the manor to turn a profit again if it was well-managed,' I said. 'It is good land. But Nell may not wish to sell, of course. And if she does, she will fleece you for as much money as she can get.'

Guy laughed, his head bent close to mine, his breath gently stirring the strands of hair against my cheek. 'I would expect nothing less from her. I am sure we may come to terms.'

'There is just one other matter,' I said in a rush. 'The country is all very well, but there is a time for the theatre and the alehouse and the entertainments. It is very quiet here. I do miss town.'

I felt Guy laugh. 'You want everything,' he declared. He rolled me beneath him. 'Shall we return to London and get married?' he asked.

'Let's get married and then return to London,' I said.

19

JESS – THE PRESENT

'That was a seriously spooky thing that Lizzie did last night,' Jess commented. 'I was awake half the night thinking about it. Imagine if you could connect to the past like that. You wouldn't need to research in the Bodleian or the National Archives, you could just touch things and effectively go back in time.'

'I'm not sure it works quite like that,' Ethan said. 'But yeah, it's quite a gift. Lizzie's been like that since childhood, apparently. She's pretty good at controlling it now, but just occasionally... Well, you heard her. It can take her by surprise.'

They were driving into Gablecross police station in Swindon. Zoe had rung to let them know that the weapons expert, Marcus Wood, was dropping in that morning and to ask if they would like to come by to hear his thoughts on the finds that had been located with the skeleton. Ethan had rescheduled a meeting and picked Jess up from the hall. 'It feels important,' he'd said.

'It will be interesting to see if it ties in in any way with the Gwyn connection,' Jess observed. 'I feel we're getting closer to Nell and Rose, and from your family tree, it seems Rose might have been married to Guy Forster, but I'd like to find the proof of that. I'm going to take a look in the graveyard and at the church registers this afternoon.'

'There's one other thing I didn't get the chance to tell you last night with all the rest of the stuff that's been going on,' Ethan said. 'I looked up John Cassells, the highwayman who was Rose's first husband. There's not much information on him, other than that he sounds like a particularly bad lot, as my grandmother would have said, but there is one curious thing about him. Apparently, he was implicated in the 1671 attempt to steal the Crown Jewels.'

'The same attempt that was supposed to have a Beckett connection?' Jess said. 'Wow. I wasn't expecting there to be any truth in *that* legend!'

'There isn't, necessarily,' Ethan replied. 'After all, no one has turned up any missing jewels at Beckett in three hundred plus years. John Cassells was supposed to have been one of Thomas Blood's accomplices to the theft, but it doesn't appear he profited in the same way. There's no record of him after 1671, so perhaps he died and that was when Rose married Guy Forster.'

They turned into the police station, the barrier lifted and Ethan parked the car in the visitor spaces.

'I should have thought...' He turned to Jess. 'I hope this is okay for you? I mean, not triggering in any way after your experience with your ex?'

'That's really thoughtful of you,' Jess said. 'I can't pretend I like police stations, but I'll cope.'

Zoe was waiting for them in the reception and led the way down endless brightly lit corridors to a lab at the back of the building with a view of the railway line. It was functional, sparklingly clean and smelled of disinfectant. On a table at one side of the room was a motley collection of objects which Jess realised must be all the finds that had been unearthed with the body.

A man of about forty-five with a thick tattooed arms and a shaved head was enthusiastically examining what looked to Jess's untrained eyes to be a rusty piece of metal.

'Marcus,' Zoe said, 'meet Ethan and Jess. They're investigating the history behind the discovery of the skeleton.'

Marcus nodded to them, gesturing that he couldn't shake hands as he was wearing cotton gloves. 'Interesting finds, these,' he said. 'This is a small sword made of British steel, second half of the seventeenth century, but essentially a dress sword rather than a functional, military weapon.'

'You mean it was designed to be a fashionable accessory?' Ethan asked.

Marcus nodded. 'It could work as a weapon, but it was more for show. It's a high-status object.' He pointed to the blade. 'There's some nice work been done here to hollow out the edges of the blade to give that undulating "flaming sword" style. Plus, the pommel was originally very fancy and there's some initials chased on the inside and a coat of arms. Unfortunately, it's too degraded to be sure what it is, although we could do some more work on it. One of the initials is a G, but that's the best I can do.'

'I've asked Marcus to take the sword away and see what else he can find out about it,' Zoe said. 'Technically, I suppose all the finds belong to your sister,' she said to Jess, 'since they were found on her property and the police don't want them any more and they don't have any particular historical or financial value.'

'I'm sure Tavy would be interested in learning more about them,' Jess said tactfully. 'I'd be glad if Marcus could look into it. What about the other finds?' she added. 'The coins and suchlike?'

'There's a 1663 shilling of Charles II,' Zoe said, 'plus some trade tokens. In some towns and cities, they were issued by local traders in the place of small denomination coins,' she added, seeing Jess's mystification. 'They were popular during the Civil War when coinage collapsed, but they were abolished in 1672, which again is quite helpful in dating the body.'

'May I?' Jess took the proffered gloves and picked up one of the tokens. It was about the size of a penny and had a picture of an angel on it and the words 'His Halfpeny' on the back and the date 1666.

'It's from the Angel Inn in Cheapside in London,' Zoe said. 'All the trade tokens we found were from London, except for one from an apothecary's shop in Brighton.'

'Fascinating,' Ethan said. 'We're looking at a man of about thirty to fifty who was based in London or the South East and had a smart-looking sword. He may or may not have had the initial G.'

'Guy Forster,' Jess said, on a whisper.

'Who?' Zoe asked.

'Sir Guy Forster was the first of the line to live at Beckett Manor,' Ethan explained. 'We think he might have been married to Nell Gwyn's sister Rose, but it's all supposition at this point. We can't currently find a death date for Guy, but he would have been roughly thirty-five in 1671, as he was born around 1635. He was agent to Lord Craven for a while over at the Ashdown estate.'

'That would fit, then,' Marcus said, nodding, 'especially as he was of some social standing.' He pointed to the shreds of leather on the bench. 'Those probably came from a pair of smart boots originally.'

They thanked Zoe and Marcus and went out into the sunshine and fresh air. Jess took a deep breath.

'Okay?' Ethan asked, putting his hand on her arm.

Jess nodded. 'I'm fine, thanks. Just a bit sad if our story isn't going to have a happy ending.' She felt an odd, sinking feeling. 'I don't want it to be Guy Forster,' she said, almost to herself. 'Not if he was Rose's husband.'

'Let's not jump to any conclusions,' Ethan said. 'Not until we tie down Guy's dates and find out more about Rose.'

Jess turned her phone back on. 'There's an email from the Records Office at Kew,' she said, as she slid into the passenger seat of the Land Rover. 'They've found another document from 1682 that lists the estates that had been given by Charles II to Nell Gwyn.' She opened it up, scanned it and sat back with a sigh.

'What is it?' Ethan asked.

'Get this!' Jess said excitedly. 'The list shows all Nell's landholdings: Bestwood in Nottinghamshire, Drury House in Windsor, a place in Henley-on-Thames and Becote Manor in Berkshire. But...' She paused triumphantly. 'There's also a note in the margin, apparently, that says "previously the property of her father, Captain Thomas Gwyn".'

'So, we've got our link confirmed,' Ethan said with satisfaction. 'Becote was a Gwyn family property that was probably confiscated by Cromwell and restored to Nell by Charles II.'

'And—' Jess was almost exploding with excitement '—beneath *that*, it says "sold by Madam Gwyn to her sister Rose Forster, 1672".' She let out a whoop. 'That's so cool. God bless those pernickety seventeenth-century clerks who insisted on recording everything.'

Ethan started the Land Rover. He was smiling. 'I love your enthusiasm,' he said. 'You're really into this, aren't you?'

'I'm less excited at the thought that Guy Forster was the skeleton we found in the lake.' Jess had deflated quickly. 'I really wanted Rose to have her happy ending. After such a grim childhood and upbringing, imprisonment for theft, being married to a criminal and being "notorious", whatever the biographers meant by that, she deserved a break.' She wondered suddenly whether the kinship she felt with Rose was something to do with the way that Jared had treated her; it was a bond between them. She felt as though she *knew* Rose. 'Rose and Nell were both fighters in their own ways. I want them to have succeeded.'

'Don't lose faith.' Ethan put his hand over hers. 'We'll see what else we can discover.'

'You can drop me off in the village if you like,' Jess suggested, as they turned off the main road and headed into Beckett. 'I know you've got stuff to do. I'm going to grab a sandwich back at the hall, and then go searching for Rose and Guy at the church this afternoon. If they got married there, I should be able to find a record, and if they're buried there, hopefully I'll find a grave.'

'Best of luck.' Ethan pulled over into the layby by the arched entrance in the wall. 'I hope you find Guy lived to a grand old age and couldn't have been the body in the lake. Will I see you later?' he added. 'I could cook for you this time?'

Jess hesitated. 'Are we doing this, then?' she said. 'Seeing how it goes?'

'I don't see why not.' Ethan leaned forward and kissed her lightly. She could feel that he was smiling. 'If you'd like that.'

'I'd like it a lot,' Jess said.

'Okay then,' Ethan replied. 'My place at six?'

Jess waved him off and let herself in through the door in the wall. Wild daffodils were starting to show through the grass along the beech avenue, mingling with the aconites and wood anemones beneath the trees. The old house, on the rise above the lake, shimmered in the light. In the foreground, the sun was striking the corner of the fishing house, scattering coloured ripples along the water from the stained-glass window high in the wall.

Jess's phone pinged with a text from Ed. Tavy was in the US, he wrote, but Una had decided to come to Beckett for the weekend so that she could spend some time with Jess. Jess felt like a teenager who had arranged an illicit night out only to find that her cover was blown. But she was a grown woman of twenty-eight, she told herself. Her private life was none of her mother's business.

As she put the phone away, her eye was caught by a flash of blue down on the lake. Something, or someone, was in the water, in a nightmarish reflection of the moment when she and Ethan had seen the skeleton. Jess could see a flap of material, a shock of dark hair, a pale hand floating on the surface.

She started to run, feeling her legs shaking and her breath coming in short gasps that were part exertion, part panic. When she reached the little wooden bridge she almost stumbled in her rush to cross because she could see clearly that there was a body, bobbing slightly in the place where the bank had collapsed before. She fell to her knees on the muddy bank.

Not Mum, please... All Jess could hear were the words repeating themselves in her head.

With a sense of revulsion, skin prickling, she reached out and turned the body over, feeling the sickness rising at the same time as relief flooded her. She sat back on her heels and threw up. She couldn't help herself.

And then she heard her mother's voice. 'Jess? What's going on?'

She got up and stumbled into Una's arms.

20

ROSE – AUTUMN 1671

Guy and I married very quietly at the church in Becote. Mother and Mrs Lambert and Sam the watchman were our only witnesses and, after the service, I laid my wedding posy on Harriet's grave.

'Wish me luck, little one,' I whispered, and when the sun briefly pierced the clouds to illuminate the tiny purple cyclamen flowers that I had planted around her headstone, I felt comforted.

We had originally intended a modest wedding breakfast at Becote Hall, but when I had told Nell of our marriage plans, she had written back with glee to say that she and the King would be at Ashdown again, having a quiet sojourn in the country together before the rather more formal demands of Christmas at the court in London. She decreed that the Earl of Craven would host us all at a banquet and he seemed very amenable. He had already given Guy a fulsome wedding gift of fine silver, which I thought very beautiful but entirely impractical, though we could perhaps sell it to buy farming equipment.

Nell was by now seven months pregnant and I worried about her travelling from London, but she was so determined to claim the King for herself for a short while that she would happily have gone anywhere that was necessary. So it was that on the evening of our wedding, we went over to Ashdown, with me riding pillion behind Guy.

I had not visited Lord Craven's hunting lodge before and found it quite charming – a little square building of white stone set in the middle of a vast woodland that had originally been designed for hunting but now turned a tidy profit from forestry. I could see why Nell liked it, for it was extremely private.

Lord Craven himself greeted us at the door, a distinguished soldier with old-fashioned manners and a shrewd gaze. The house was stuffed with the most marvellous items from his time soldiering on the continent at the start of the century. Like him, it felt like a place full of relics. But there was nothing slow or foolish about the Earl. I could see in a moment why half of London went in fear of him, for not only was there his prodigious fortune, but he gave the impression of being the keeper of many secrets.

'Madam Gwyn is resting,' he told us, as he took my cloak. 'The travelling has fatigued her, but she and His Majesty will join us later to toast your marriage. My congratulations, Forster.' He slapped Guy on the back. 'I wish you much happiness.'

The Earl, Guy had told me, had never married, for he had been devoted to the King's late aunt Elizabeth, Queen of Bohemia, though the nature of their relationship was something of a mystery. On this, as on many matters, Lord Craven was as closed as an oyster, but the house was a shrine to his royal mistress, full of her paintings and hunting trophies. All these he showed me whilst the servants prepared a feast that had made my eyes pop: vast dishes of lamb and chicken and goose, pastries and pies, cauliflowers and spinach, trout from the river at another of his country houses, and a salmagundi with all manner of salad vegetables, eggs and meats.

We sat down to eat – I with the greatest relish. I was contemplating the next course of syllabub and whipped cream, when there was a thunderous knocking at the main door. The oak panels shook under the force of it.

'This is the sheriff! Open in the King's name!'

I giggled. I could not help myself. The sheriff of Berkshire, who was a self-important little pipsqueak called Thomas Vachel, was demanding entry to Ashdown House, where the King was in residence, in the name of the King.

'That noise is sufficient to wake your guests, my lord,' I said to the Earl of Craven, who threw down his napkin and strode out into the hall, just as the porter swung wide the door.

A whole host of men piled within. The hall at Ashdown was small and the ensuing melee was loud and confusing until the Earl raised his voice.

'Silence! I demand to know your business here.'

Vachel looked annoyed to be upstaged, but he was not cowed. He brandished a document in his left hand. 'We are here to arrest Guy Forster,' he said, 'for the murder of Sir Grey Cassells of Poynings, Sussex. I have a warrant from Sir Giles Pendreth in London.'

Pendreth, like Vachel himself, was a Puritan of the old persuasion who had turned coat sufficiently well when the King had been restored to get his old job back again. None of them liked Lord Craven, though, or his royalist friends such as Guy. I knew little of politics, but that I *did* know.

I gave a gasp. All urge to laugh at the situation fled. The last time I had seen Sir Grey Cassells had been that fateful afternoon six weeks before when Mother had hit him over the head, and he had staggered out of Becote Manor and disappeared. Truth was, once I had been reassured that Harriet was safe in the graveyard, I had thought little more of him because there were so many more exciting matters to think on. And yet here, suddenly, he was, and dead by the sounds of it.

I glanced up at Guy whose face looked as though it was carved from stone. He said nothing and squeezed my hand to indicate I should also keep silent. I realised that he must have been anticipating something like this and Lord Craven's next words confirmed it.

'You are a fool, Vachel,' Lord Craven said. 'I warned you not to trifle in this when you first came to me with your suspicions. You have no proof that Sir Grey Cassells is dead, let alone that Forster killed him. He had no reason to do so.'

I looked at Guy again, feeling fear clutch at my heart. All the time I had been feeling secure in the prospect of my future, this cloud had been looming on the horizon, and here was Vachel on my wedding day, ready to ruin everything. My happiness had been so fragile; surely it could not be snatched away so soon.

'Sir Grey Cassells never returned home to Sussex after his visit to

Becote last month,' Vachel said. 'There are witnesses who can place him in Becote village and attest to the fact that he visited the manor. His wife reported him missing. She is in despair.'

'I am sorry to hear that,' Lord Craven said, and he sounded as though he meant it, for his manners were so fine. 'However—' his voice hardened '—the man could be anywhere. And, I repeat, Guy Forster had no cause to wish grief on Sir Grey Cassells.'

'Sir Grey left Becote alive and well,' I said. 'There are witnesses who can attest to that too.' I was puzzled by Guy's silence and refusal to speak up for himself and I could not simply stand by and allow him to be accused. Perhaps it was an exaggeration to say that Sir Grey had been well after Mother had hit him over the head with a vase, but he had definitely been *alive*.

'The only witnesses are paid servants and the mother and sister of an infamous whore,' Vachel spat. His dark eyes glittered with Puritan fervour now. 'But we all know that you condone such licentiousness within your walls do you not, my lord?' He turned to Lord Craven. 'Very likely you are complicit in the plot as well.'

'Have a care, Vachel,' Lord Craven said coldly. 'My servants will horse-whip you from the house if you say another word.'

'I think not, my lord,' Vachel said. 'This time, you will not thwart me. You see—' he produced another document from the pocket of his coat with the flourish of a magician '—before he set out to confront Mistress Cassells – I beg your pardon,' his voice dripped contempt, 'Mistress *Forster* – at Becote, Sir Grey left a letter with his wife that he said should be opened in the event he did not return. This, she has given to me.' He waved it under our noses. 'In it, Sir Grey states that he had proof – signed statements from those involved in the late plot to steal the Crown Jewels – that Mistress Forster was not only guilty of taking part in the plot, which we all know is true, but that her sister, *Madam Gwyn,* was also implicated in the theft, that she gave one of the King's own gifts – a silver locket – in surety of her part in the deception!' His voice was rising with triumph and excitement at the same time that my heart was plummeting.

I remembered that Sir Grey Cassells had conspired with Thomas Blood to kidnap me to get his hands on Harriet. Thomas Blood must have told him all about his suspicions of Nell and in doing so he had handed him the means to bring us all down.

'Madam Gwyn then forged the King's signature on a pardon to release her sister from prison!' Vachel finished. 'Guy Forster knew this – he aided both his wife and her trollop of a sister! He had every reason to kill Sir Grey to keep him from revealing all he knew!'

'What an extraordinary story.' The voice, rich, low and full of amusement, came from above us, from the first half landing of the stair. I jumped violently and I think everyone else in the room did too. There, previously concealed by a wall hanging, was the figure of the King. He stepped forward into the candlelight thrown by the hall sconces. Dark and saturnine he stood, his expression impossible to read. 'Do tell us more, Vachel,' he said. 'Your story fascinates me.'

I looked around for Nell, but she was nowhere to be seen. Had she climbed out of a window and run away? Had the King locked her in whilst he got to the truth of what she had done? I remembered that months back, in the house in Pall Mall, I had thought it odd that the King had been out of town at Newmarket all week, and yet somehow Nell had produced a pardon bearing his signature. I remembered her telling me to make no mention of it when we met and certainly not to thank him for his generosity. I had not questioned her about it because perhaps, deep down, I had guessed what she had done and had not wanted it confirmed.

Oh Nell, I thought, *this is bad*.

Yet still Guy said nothing and I almost thought I could see a gleam of amusement in his eyes.

'Your Majesty!' Vachel was clearly shocked to see the King, but he recovered himself quickly. He gave a deep bow. 'I know that Your Majesty will want to know the truth of this matter,' he asserted. 'The shameful trick of impersonating the monarch, which is treason! I am only sorry—' he failed to look remotely so '—that I am the miserable conduit of such news about one whom you trusted, Madam Gwyn, and her notorious sister.'

I felt Guy move involuntarily then to hear me described so, and I tightened my grip on his hand. He gave me a quick reassuring smile and then his gaze returned to the King.

The King took a couple of steps down into the hall and held out his hand imperiously for the document, which Vachel reluctantly passed over to him. He perused it swiftly, head bent, the candlelight gleaming on the black hair threaded with grey.

Where was Nell? I wondered again frantically. If this went badly, very soon she and I would be back in prison, this time for treason, and Guy would be locked up on a charge of murder. I felt dizzy with fear.

'I see that Sir Grey's signed witnesses are Colonel Thomas Blood,' the King said after a moment, 'and a woman called Renwick, whom I believe used to serve Madam Gwyn but was dismissed recently when she was found to be a spy in the Duke of Buckingham's service.' He paused. 'It is hard to accept that a man to whom I have shown such favour would play me so false,' he said thoughtfully. 'I pardoned Thomas Blood, believing him worthy of a second chance, and he repays me by traducing the character of Madam Gwyn, whom he knows I honour above all women but the Queen. It is utterly shameful.'

I thought about the meeting I had had with Thomas Blood when he had threatened to blackmail Nell, and I had told him that if it came to a choice, I knew whom the King preferred out of the two of them. Looking at Charles now, I thought I could almost detect a twinkle in his eye and a flourish in the way he was acting his part. As I pondered this, a door opened above and a vision in white descended the stairs, ethereal, beautiful, playing the role of her life.

'God's death,' my sister exclaimed as she saw all the soldiers in the hall. 'What are all these long blades and longer faces? Sir Thomas Vachel – what do you do here, sir? I think you as welcome as the pox in this house.'

'Nell, my dear.' The King took her hand. 'Poor Sir Thomas came here to do me a service,' he said. 'He thought you had played me for a fool—' he pretended to peruse the letter again '—in some sort of plot, where you gave your precious silver locket as surety for treason.' His lips curled into a devilish smile. 'Surely that cannot be true?'

'What?' Nell's blue eyes opened to their furthest extent. '*This* locket?' She produced it from the bodice of her gown. 'Why, it has never been out of my possession, Majesty. It lives next to my heart.' She pressed the locket against her bosom to emphasise the point.

'So I thought,' King Charles said dryly. 'And the pardon that I signed for your sister...'

'The one that you had a clerk prepare before you left for Newmarket?' Nell raised her brows. 'You must recall, sire, that you asked me to have it delivered to the Marshalsea with due haste. You said that having shown clemency to Colonel Blood over the theft of the Crown Jewels, you wished to act with the same generosity to my dearest Rose.'

The King looked at me and smiled. 'Of course I did. My wretched memory. I recall it all now, my dear.'

'But Your Majesty...' Vachel had been turning steadily redder in the face as he spoke. 'The truth is here.' He pointed to the letter. 'The testament of Madam Gwyn's own servant and of the Colonel—'

Charles snapped his fingers. 'A woman in the pay of Buckingham and a man who is his puppet?' he said dismissively. He kissed Nell's fingers. 'I shall have to speak to the duke firmly and tell him to keep his lapdogs from barking. Their antics do not amuse me.'

'But what of Sir Grey Cassells!' Sir Thomas could see everything slipping away from him. I almost felt sorry for him. 'He is dead! Murdered—'

'What a pile of nonsense you have concocted, Vachel.' The King's words dripped contempt. 'Show me a body and I will consider opening an investigation. In the meantime, I suggest you restrain yourself from slandering an innocent man or he might have grounds to challenge you, eh Forster?'

'Indeed, Your Majesty,' Guy said. He bowed, his hand on his sword hilt.

'Come, my dear.' The King tucked Nell's hand through his arm. 'This fatiguing nonsense has made me long for some brandy. Craven?'

The Earl gestured to Vachel and the soldiers. 'You heard His Majesty. You are dismissed. Begone.' And as Vachel looked as though he might try to protest, he added, 'Do you really want me to remove you from my premises physically, Vachel?'

The sheriff did not. He and his men jostled their way out of the door hastily and it closed behind them.

'Forster.' The King clapped an arm about Guy's shoulders. 'Brandy?'

'Thank you, Your Majesty,' Guy said.

'Nell!' I grabbed my sister's arm and practically dragged her into the drawing room. She was still flushed with her victory and the excitement of the performance. She blew the King a kiss as the door closed on us and he laughed. 'Is it true?' I demanded. 'Was my pardon not worth the paper it was written on?'

'Oh Rose!' Nell's gaze slid away from mine. She was guilty, I thought. I'd known it at heart. 'I did it for you,' she said. The actress in her was rallying for an encore. 'In fact, I might ask for some gratitude from you. I put my own neck on the line to save you, but fortunately—' she preened in the cheval glass '—we have got away with it.'

'Well, you had best make good on it and ensure I get a proper pardon this time,' I said. 'I have no desire to be dragged off to gaol if the wind changes. And whilst we are about it,' I added, 'you did not do it for *me*. You did it because you needed me to find your necklace for you. You thought I was in league with John.'

Nell huffed. 'If you were concerned about the pardon, you should have asked more questions at the time,' she said, with impeccable Nell logic. 'What does it matter *why* I did it, Rose? You wanted to be free, didn't you?'

'Of course I wanted to be free,' I snapped. 'I wasn't going to ask any questions. I was glad to get out of the Marshalsea before they changed their minds!'

'Then it doesn't make any difference, does it?' Nell snapped back, and it was as though we were children squabbling again. 'You are free, so why are you complaining?'

For a long moment, I looked at her and she looked at me, and then we both burst out laughing and fell into each other's arms.

'Oh Rose,' Nell said, between tears and laughter, as we hugged each other. 'I hope you know I would do anything for you.'

'And I for you,' I said.

* * *

Later, in bed, back at Becote Hall, I asked Guy why he thought the King had been so indulgent with Nell when he must have known that, at the least, she had forged the pardon, even if he believed the other charges were untrue. 'He must care for her a great deal,' I said, 'to be so complaisant.'

'The King likes a rogue,' Guy agreed, 'and he has always admired your sister's wit and daring. I suspect that this escapade will only have made him like her more.'

I smiled. 'He is contrary. But he showed poor judgement in pardoning Thomas Blood, did he not? That man will always make trouble for him.'

I felt Guy laughing and propped myself up on one elbow to look at him. 'What is so funny?' I demanded.

'Dearest love,' Guy said, 'you can be so sweetly naïve. Have you never wondered just *why* the King was so generous to Thomas Blood in the matter of the theft of the jewels?'

'Frequently,' I said. 'But I thought it was simply his quixotic nature. What are you implying?'

'Merely,' Guy replied, 'that Thomas Blood got off lightly because his paymaster was none other than the King himself. Charles was short of money and conceived the idea to pay a thief to rob him of his own Crown Jewels. If Blood had succeeded, they would have split the proceeds and the King would have gained a fortune – and a new set of royal regalia paid for from the public purse. As it is, he freed Blood and bribed him with land and money to get him to hold his tongue.'

My mouth dropped open. All of a sudden, I remembered that day on the quayside by the Tower of London and Thomas Blood shouting, *'It was a gallant attempt! It was for the Crown!'* He had meant that literally, I realised. He had done it for the King and he was shouting it aloud, knowing his words would be repeated to Charles, a reminder of the hold he had over him.

I stared at Guy. 'And you know this – how?'

'Because I was a spy,' Guy said. 'Craven knows it too, and if the King had permitted Vachel to cart me off on that false charge of murder, he would have gently reminded him that it would be better to keep me on his side. Whilst no one could prove that the monarch tried to defraud his own people, it would make for a troublesome tale. Many of those who do not love the monarchy would seize on it.'

'Well,' I said, 'it seems that no one does anything out of the goodness of their heart. It is all blackmail, bribery and self-interest. I am shocked.'

'That is true in politics, I fear.' Guy pulled me down beside him and kissed me. 'But be assured,' he whispered, 'that when it comes to you, I do everything out of love.'

21

JESS – THE PRESENT

This time there was a body in the lake, it was different. This time, there were police everywhere. The house was searched, the grounds closed off. There were questions and interviews, endless repetition of the same themes:

'Did you know Jared Carter was intending to abscond from Bright Hill?'

'You saw him less than two weeks ago. Were you aware of his plans?'

'Did you arrange to meet at Fortune Hall?'

'Where were you between nine o'clock and twelve this morning...'

Una had called Ethan, who had called Lizzie, who had arranged for her cousin, Juliet Carey, a hotshot lawyer from London, to come and represent Jess. Jess was incredibly touched that someone she'd only met once had put herself out for her, but they were a tight-knit group of friends and she suspected Lizzie was doing it for Ethan as much as for her. When Juliet arrived, she wasn't taking any nonsense.

'You do realise,' she said to the police inspector, 'that there were no signs of foul play on the body and that my client has an alibi for the time in question, which includes CCTV from *this* police station? She has told you repeatedly that she knew nothing of Jared Carter's plans and, in terms of his conviction for fraud, she was interviewed extensively at the time and was cleared of any involvement.'

After that, the police let her go.

'There's nothing to charge you with,' Juliet said, as she whisked Jess out of the station. 'They're just fishing. Sorry, that's a tactless analogy under the circumstances. But it's clear that it was either an accident or Carter took his own life. He might even have chosen to do it at Fortune Hall to cause trouble for you. Sadly, that's a well-known phenomenon, suicide prompted by rage and revenge.'

Jess didn't know what to make of that. She was bone-weary and faint with hunger. She hadn't eaten since breakfast and it was going on for nine o'clock. It was dark outside and a forest of light bulbs popped in their faces as they came out of the doors of the police station.

'Piss off,' Juliet said to the journalists, who were shouting questions.

Ethan was waiting; her mother was in the car. Jess almost cried when she saw Ethan. She didn't want him to be dragged into all this.

They bundled her into the car, Juliet giving her a hug.

'I'll keep in touch,' she said. 'Hang in there, sweetie.'

'We're staying with Lucy and Finn tonight,' Jess's mother said. 'They're lending us Gunpowder Barn, or at least Lucy's aunt is. I didn't think you'd want to go back to the hall, and it's all in a mess anyway, with the police turning it upside down.'

'How awful.' Jess shuddered. She was racked by shivers and felt so cold. She kept thinking about the moment she had turned Jared over in the water and his bloated face had stared up at her. An accident or suicide, Juliet had said. But Jared was surely too self-obsessed to take his own life, and what was he doing at Fortune Hall anyway?

She remembered him asking if he would see her again and telling him it would never happen. Why had he come looking for her? What could have been important enough to him that he would walk out of Bright Hill prison to do it? She did not flatter herself that Jared had been so in love with her that he had wanted to see her one more time. There had to have been some other reason.

The street lights stopped as they drove out of the village heading for Knightstone, the dark countryside whipping past. In the front, her mother and Ethan were talking quietly. Jess's mind, unable to rest, ran over the events of the day again: the walk back from Beckett village, approaching the lake through the tree-lined path, reaching the bridge, seeing the body in the water... Her mother, who had arrived at the hall ten minutes before, had told the police she'd come out to meet Jess when she saw her coming towards the bridge. She'd not seen Jared's body because of the way the land sloped down towards the water. She seemed to be holding up remarkably well for someone who had, like Jess, stumbled into a complete nightmare.

'We're here, darling.' Her mother's voice cut into Jess's thoughts and she realised that they were outside the house and Lucy and Finn were waiting for them.

Lucy hugged her and took them all inside. Jess had a blurred impression of the barn conversion being an amazing space of high ceilings and huge windows, but she was too tired to take it in properly. She felt as though she needed to sleep for a week. Her mother hurried her upstairs and into a cosy room where the lamps were already lit. She plonked a suitcase down on the bed.

'I've packed a few things for you,' she said. 'I'm going to put the bath on for you now, sweetie, and make you some toast.'

It was lovely to be so cosseted. It reminded Jess of her childhood, living above the pub, when Una would tuck her and Tavy up in bed with hot chocolate, and she would drift off to sleep to the sound of the regulars in the bar laughing and chatting. Her mother had packed one of Tavy's extraordinary miniscule and sheer nighties for her rather than her own pyjamas, but she would have slept in a sack, she was so tired.

She fell asleep only to dream of endless dark corridors and police questions and Jared's dead, staring eyes. She woke up shaking and realised that she must have cried out, because Ethan appeared in the doorway looking ruffled and unkempt from sleep. He came across to the bed, sat down beside her and put his arms around her as naturally, as though he had always done it, and she felt a huge rush of emotion. 'It's okay, Jess,' he said. 'You're safe. It's only a dream.'

For a moment, Jess struggled against the overwhelming knowledge that she needed him. She had been used to looking after herself, both when her family had fallen apart years before and after Jared, when she'd sworn not to let her guard down again. She knew that when things righted themselves again, she would be fine. But she also knew she wanted Ethan around because it felt right. So really there was no dilemma.

'Stay,' she said. 'Please.'

* * *

When Jess woke up, Ethan had gone and the room was filled with bright morning light. She appreciated his tact in giving her the time and space to work out what she wanted to do next. She could pretend the night had never happened, that they hadn't made love and she hadn't fallen asleep in his arms feeling safe and comforted. She could thank him for his chivalry and never mention it again. Or she could talk to him. This whole Jared thing was a mess, but Ethan had hung on in there and that meant a lot. It meant he wanted to be there for her and she'd be the one acting like a coward if she pushed him away.

On the table beside the bed was a note in Ethan's writing, short and sweet:

Gone to work. I'll ring later. E.

Jess found she was smiling.

* * *

'The police rang,' her mother said, as Jess rather listlessly ate a bowl of yoghurt and fruit. 'You can't have toast all the time, sweetie,' Una had said. 'It's not healthy.' Much as she appreciated her mother's renewed interest in her life, Jess wasn't sure she wanted dietary advice from her, particularly not at the moment when she needed comfort food. 'There's no evidence of foul play, they said,' Una continued. 'No marks on the body at all. The initial conclusion is that Jared must have fallen into the water of his own accord. Which is great, isn't it!' She bustled about the cottage's open-plan kitchen, humming as she tidied up.

'I suppose it is good news in a way.' Jess felt that her mother's summary of the situation was somewhat simplistic. 'But it's grim for Jared's parents.'

'Yes, poor them,' her mother said vaguely. 'But he was a scumbag, darling. He treated you very badly. I told him so when I went to visit him last week.'

'What?' Jess put down her spoon with a clatter. 'You went to see *Jared*?'

'It was the day I was in Oxford,' Una had stopped cleaning and stood like a statue in the centre of the kitchen, the dishcloth forgotten in her hand. 'I took a taxi. Bright Hill isn't far from Oxford, so it was no problem. I'd asked to see him and he agreed.'

Jess was feeling sick all over again. 'What did you say to him?' she asked.

'I just told him what I thought of him,' Una said. 'Treating my girl like that.' Her blue eyes were suddenly sharp and clear. 'When I saw you again and realised what he'd done to you, pet, I couldn't keep quiet. He needed to be told what a douche he was. So, I told him.'

Jess swallowed hard. 'Erm... I appreciate that, Mum, I really do, but...' She cleared her throat, hardly knowing where to start. 'I assume the police know all about this?'

'Of course, darling,' Una said. 'It was all on the CCTV. There's no problem. I just wanted you to know.' She came over and gave Jess a tight hug. 'I love you,' she said to Jess as she squashed her to her bosom. 'We're chalk and cheese, but I really do.'

'I know Mum,' Jess said. 'I know.'

Una released her and started cleaning again. 'Super place Lucy's aunt has here. She was off on a tangent in typical fashion. She should lease it to the production companies for reality TV shows.'

'Mum,' Jess said wearily, 'not everyone wants to be involved with TV.'

'Quite right,' Una agreed comfortably. 'Don't look at the papers or the social media today,' she added. 'It's lurid.'

Jess sighed, remembering the huge fuss when Jared was arrested. 'Nothing could induce me to look,' she said.

Una's phone rang. 'It's Tavy,' she said. 'How are you, babes? How is LA?'

Jess could hear a squawking at the other end of the phone, which indicated that Tavy was talking very loudly and very quickly.

'Right,' Una said, after a few minutes. There was an odd note in her voice that Jess hadn't heard before – was it apprehension? She couldn't be certain. 'Are you sure—' Una still sounded hesitant. 'Of course... But you've checked with the lawyers? Well, you know best, babes.'

Unusually, she was silent when she ended the call.

'Is everything all right, Mum?' Jess asked.

Una didn't answer for a moment, then, 'You'd better go to Tavy's Instagram channel,' she said. 'She's about to make a big announcement about the discovery of Jared's body.'

'What?' Jess was startled. 'But she wasn't even here.' She crushed a feeling of irritation that her sister could be turning the latest drama in their lives into a public spectacle. 'Is this a good idea?' she asked. 'Has she spoken to the police? They might not want her to do this—'

'This *is* her speaking to the police,' Una said heavily. Her hands were shaking a little.

Jess grabbed her and held her tight. 'Mum?' she repeated, with more urgency. 'What is it? What's happened?'

But Una only shook her head and tapped on the Instagram icon.

Tavy had already started. She had clearly recorded the video earlier as she was sitting beside a strip of golden sand beneath a stripy beach umbrella. She looked tanned and beautiful in a plain white T-shirt, her hair blowing in the sea breeze, her blue eyes wide and serious. 'I want to address the stories that are currently circulating about the discovery of my former brother-in-law's body at the house I own in Oxfordshire,' Tavy was saying. 'I know there is a lot of interest in the press and I want to set the record straight.'

'He wasn't your brother-in-law,' Jess muttered through gritted teeth. 'We weren't married.'

'There has been speculation that Jared Carter went to Fortune Hall to try to see my sister, who is working for me at the moment,' Tavy said. 'I can assure you that this is wrong. Jess is completely innocent in all this. In fact, Jared came to see me.' She stopped for effect.

Jess felt her mouth drop open. 'WTF?' she said faintly.

'A number of years ago, *before* the fraud, I invested in Jared Carter's company,' Tavy continued. 'It was an error of judgement on my part and I regret it deeply. I cut ties with him two years before the company was investigated, but I realise that people will still be disappointed in me – and rightly so. I let you all down. I fell below my own high standards.'

'Bless her,' their mother said fondly. 'Always thinking of others.'

'For God's sake,' Jess snapped.

'Yesterday,' Tavy continued, 'when I heard of the tragedy at Fortune Hall, I discovered that Jared Carter had tried to contact me to tell me he was coming to see me there, but because I was out of the country, I had not received his message in time.'

'Establishing her alibi there,' Jess muttered.

'I immediately informed the police,' Tavy said, 'but by then it was too late and he had suffered this terrible accident. I have no idea why he wished to speak to me. He did not say, but it may have been to do with the book he was intending to write about his experiences. Jared's body was found by my poor sister, who is in deep shock. I beg you to give her the space she needs to heal. I shall be returning to the UK at once and will, of course, be happy to assist the police further if I can. But I beg you to respect the privacy of my family whilst we come to terms with this. I wanted to put the record straight—' Tavy gave the camera a blinding smile '—so that neither I nor my sister should live under any shadow of doubt. Thank you as always for your love and support, guys. You are the best.'

'Well, hell,' Jess said blankly. Her thoughts were in a complete daze.

Somewhere, she could hear her phone ringing urgently. She checked the caller ID and saw with relief that it was Ethan.

'Are you okay there?' His voice was sharp with concern. 'I just heard Tavy's announcement. What the hell? Did you know she had invested in Carter's firm?'

'No,' Jess said. 'Neither of them ever mentioned it.' No wonder Tavy hadn't wanted to talk about Jared, she thought, remembering the way her sister had brushed aside her attempts to apologise for dragging her into the debacle. If only she'd known. Tavy had already been knee-deep in it all, and no doubt Jared had been going to announce that in his memoir. 'Oh God,' she said. 'What a mess.'

'I'm coming over,' Ethan said. 'I can cancel this meeting—'

'No,' Jess interrupted. 'Thank you, but I refuse to let either of our lives be derailed by Tavy. I'll see you later.'

She went to find her mother, who was taking a private call from Tavy. 'You must come back at once,' Jess heard her say. 'We don't want the police issuing an international warrant for your arrest, although I suppose it might be good publicity.'

'That isn't going to happen, Mum,' Jess snapped, although she wished someone would arrest Tavy simply to keep her quiet for a bit. 'Tavy isn't guilty of anything.' *Except ludicrous self-promotion*, she added silently.

'I *am* coming home, Mum,' Tavy said. Una had her on speaker now. 'Is Jess there?'

'Yes, I am,' Jess said.

'Chin up, babes,' Tavy said. 'We'll face all of this together as a family.'

Before Jess could ask her what the hell she had been thinking getting involved with Jared in the first place, and then never even mentioning it to her, Tavy cut the call.

22

ROSE – LONDON, JANUARY 1672

The last time I had been to Nell's house in Pall Mall I had been a fugitive from the Marshalsea prison, filthy and starving, throwing myself on her mercy. This time, I had called to deliver various Twelfth Night gifts for my new nephew, James, who had been born on the twenty-fifth of December, to much rejoicing from Nell and the King, though I suspect it had spoiled Queen Catherine's Christmas.

The new baby was as healthy and cherubic as the brother he had joined in the nursery, and after I had admired him and Nell had opened his presents for him, I left her to rest and went along the corridor to see our mother.

That morning, I had consulted Nell's physician and he had confirmed what Guy and I had hoped was true; that in six months' time, God willing, a new baby might take its place in the nursery at Becote. He or she could never replace Harriet in my heart or my memories, but it would be a fresh start and I wanted to share the good news with my mother.

It was a dark winter afternoon and the candles were already lit and the curtains drawn when I knocked on the door of her chamber. The maid who was chaperoning her slipped out, giving me a smile.

'She is quiet this afternoon,' she said. 'There has been no trouble.'

Mother appeared not to hear me come in. Her head was bent, the candlelight showing threads of auburn and gold in her dark hair. A half-empty bottle was at her elbow and the room smelled of brandy. I felt a helpless exasperation knowing this would never change. Whilst she had been staying with us at Becote, she had been sober much of the time, but that partial improvement had not lasted. As soon as she had returned to London with Nell, she had gone back to her old ways.

Mother was playing some sort of game with counters, rolling a dice and moving the counters toward and away from one another in a complicated but precise pattern. When I looked more closely, I saw that they were trade tokens from various alehouses in London: The Rose and Crown, The Red Dragon, The Hind's Head – places she had drunk in, I supposed, but then I also saw others I recognised: The White Hart that John had patronised and Peg Cherry had been the barmaid, and his other favourite hostelry, the Lamb and Flag.

I felt a flutter of intuition then, a sense that there was something I had missed. Mother looked up; her eyes were awash with drink, and yet somewhere within, there was a spark of knowledge.

She held out one of the tokens to me. It was from Beacon Court, with apples on one side and a flaring torch on the other. 'This one is for Nell,' she said. 'The orange girl.'

I looked at it, not understanding. 'Those are apples,' I pointed out, 'not oranges.'

She laughed. 'Golden apples,' she said, 'for Helen of Troy.'

'Of course.' I remembered the stories our father had told us as children, of the Greek myths and heroes. Our mother Helena, and Nell in her turn, had been given a name that meant a bright, shining light. A beacon. I turned the little coin over. On the other side the golden apples glowed. 'The Greeks called oranges "golden apples",' I said.

I thought of Nell, with her love of puzzles and her wit and her facility with words. From whom had she inherited those skills? It was so easy to dismiss our mother as a drunkard, lost in her own world, but she had not always been so. Once, she had been pretty and witty too. I looked at her, Helena Smith Gwyn. For the first time, I glimpsed the woman who had captured the heart of the gallant soldier Thomas Gwyn, with her beauty and strength, her character and determination. Her spirit lived on in Nell and perhaps in me too.

Mother spoke again. She was smiling, happy I understood. 'The Rose coin is for you,' she said, and held out a token that had roses on one side and an oak tree on the other. The tree, I realised, was the family symbol of the Forsters, who had once upon a time been royal foresters and taken their name and coat of arms from their profession.

To my surprise, I felt tears close my throat. 'All our stories are here, aren't they?' I picked up the coins one by one. The red dragon for our Welsh ancestors, the ox and ford for the city of our childhood, and the May blossom and bells for our parents' wedding.

'This is for your new baby,' Mother said, holding out a coin with a stork on it. Her gaze was sly. 'I know you are expecting. I recognise the signs. I've seen them many times.'

'Is it so obvious?' I was smiling a little, and she smiled back.

'You are starting to feel happy again,' she said. 'I am glad.' She sighed, her head drooping a little, and I started to rise, thinking it was time to leave her. But then she uncurled her fingers very slowly to reveal the last coin that was in her palm. It was a halfpenny token for a butcher's shop in Cheapside showing the picture of a castle. 'This is John's coin.' She let it fall from her hand. 'He deserved to die.'

I caught my breath on a gasp.

Mother looked up and her gaze was very clear. 'He hurt you too much and too often,' she said. 'Then he threatened Nell. My Gwyn girls. I could not let him do that to you both. I could not let him live.' She looked into the fire. 'I asked him to meet me at the Cock and Hen. I bought him gin. The rest was easy.'

I put my hand over her gnarled one where it rested on the table. 'Mama,' I said.

'I didn't protect you enough when you were young,' she said. 'I am sorry. You will be a far better mother than I ever was.'

I hugged her then, feeling the fragility of her bones beneath the withered skin. I wanted to beg her to take no more drink, to give herself the chance to recover, to let Nell and me care for her so that we could have more time with her and start afresh. But it was too late. The physicians had said she would not live much longer. 'Oh Mama. Never think that you have failed us.'

She did not reply and I simply held her whilst the candle burned down and the firelight lit the room for the two of us. I wondered then about Sir Grey Cassells and what had happened to him after he had stumbled out of Becote Hall having made those threats against me and Harriet. I would not ask Mother. I did not want to know. John was dead and his father missing. I would let both of them go.

Sometime later, Mother released me and reached for the bottle of brandy. Her gaze was cloudy again as though she had already forgotten what we had been talking about.

I gave her a last hug and stood up. I could feel the tears running down my face. I needed fresh air, I needed Guy.

'She is drinking again, I fear,' I said to the chaperone who was waiting outside the door, nodding sleepily on a stool, 'and her speech rambles. I could not understand her.'

The maid shook her head sorrowfully. 'She is often that way. Whatever she says, I do not regard it.'

'Thank you for taking care of her,' I said. 'I will be back to see her soon.'

I went down the stairs and out into Pall Mall, where the snow lay on the ground and the link boys were passing with their torches. Guy had just arrived with the carriage to take us back to our lodgings at Lord Craven's house in Drury Lane.

'I am so glad to see you,' I said, throwing myself into his arms, heedless of the servants' supercilious looks and the passing nobility.

'What is it, Rose?' my husband said gently, holding me close. I breathed in his scent and felt safe and secure.

'It is nothing,' I said. 'I am only happy to have so much.' And in my pocket, I held close the little bag that my mother had slipped into my hand as I left her, the one with the missing Crown Jewels.

23

JESS – THE PRESENT

Jess was back at Fortune Hall when the phone call from the bookseller in Oxford came through. She was packing the suitcase she had only unpacked ten days before; Lucy had told her that she was welcome to stay at Gunpowder Cottage until she got herself sorted out as Jess had confided she needed to be away from both her mother and her sister.

'I love them in my own way, but I can't live with them,' she'd said.

'And Ethan?' Lucy had asked. 'Could you live with him?'

'Maybe,' Jess had replied, 'but we haven't talked about that.'

She smiled a little as she reached for the phone now.

'Jess?' the voice at the other end said. 'It's Sue here, at St Philip's Booksellers in Oxford. I thought you'd like to know that I've heard from Dr Craig at the Ashmolean.'

For a moment, Jess's mind was blank and then she felt a flicker of excitement. 'Sue!' she said. 'That was quick!'

'The mills of academia grind fast when they are excited about something,' Sue said dryly. 'And they are very excited about your horoscope. Or, I should say, about Rose Gwyn's horoscope.'

Jess sat down very quickly on the side of the bed. 'Rose Gwyn?'

'It's a match for the Nell Gwyn horoscope that they already have in the museum, to the extent that they are certain it was cast by Elias Ashmole

himself, just as Nell's was.' The enthusiasm in Sue's voice was clear now.
'They'd like to meet you as soon as possible to discuss where it was found
and negotiate a price to buy it. It's important for them to have the pair. This
is a marvellous discovery, Jess,' she added, as Jess was struck dumb with the
news. 'I hope you realise how significant it is? Not only will it be fascinating
to study the two documents side by side but it may also tell us a lot more
about Rose, whose life has been totally overshadowed by her sister. At the
least it will foster great interest in her.'

'Yes,' Jess said. 'Yes, I'm sure it will.' Then, as her brain caught up: 'Wow,
this is so extraordinary. I can't believe it!'

Jess wrote down the details of the museum curator who would be in
touch. When Sue rang off, she texted Ethan, since she thought he was probably the only person who would appreciate how excited she was. In a
moment, she would go down to tell her mother and Tavy, but given the lack
of enthusiasm with which Tavy had greeted the news of Nell Gwyn's
connection to Fortune Hall, she wasn't expecting much interest.

'I was hoping for more than just a few dry documents,' Tavy had said,
when Jess had mentioned the papers that confirmed Nell had owned
Becote. 'We can't do much with *that*.'

As she folded the last jumper into her case, Jess heard raised voices
from below. Most people weren't around, as filming had stopped pending
the investigation into Jared's death. Only Una, Tavy, Ed and Francesca were
in the house and Jess was fairly certain it was Tavy's voice she could hear, or
Tavy crying.

She hurried down the stairs, through the kitchen and into the hall, the
sobs getting louder the closer she got to the living room.

'Babes,' Jess heard her mother saying. 'Don't. He isn't worth it.'

'What's going on?' Jess said.

Tavy was sitting curled in a ball on the sofa, hugging a cushion and
sobbing her heart out. She was not crying in her usual way, dabbing carefully at the corners of her eyes, but with great big sobs, her make-up
streaming down her face with the tears.

'I've made such a mess of everything,' she wailed. 'I mean, I knew
Hunter behaved like a jerk sometimes, but we did look good together and it
wasn't like it was going to last forever. But to be cheating on me with Olive

Crew! She's only a model. She's not even got her own show! He's ruined everything and now he has the nerve to go on television and beg me to ring in to forgive him!' She buried her face in her hands. 'I hate him! He's such a liar!'

Jess looked across at the TV, which was showing Hunter in an earnest debate about himself with two presenters on what was obviously a daytime TV chat show. He did look good – regretful, penitent, humbled, all of the things that should melt an audience's heart. She pressed the remote and turned him off.

'Don't do that,' Tavy said, muffled. 'I need to hear what he's saying.' She reached for her phone.

'Oh, Tavy, no!' Jess said, as she flicked the TV back on again.

'I'm not going to take him back,' Tavy said fiercely. 'I'm going to ring in and tell him what a scumbag he is. Where's Mum gone? I need her!'

'We have a caller,' Faye Frost was saying excitedly as the camera cut away briefly from Hunter to focus on her. 'It's...' She paused. 'Oh, it's not Tavy, but it is someone you know well, Hunter.'

Hunter mimed surprise.

'Hunter Blair!' Their mother's outraged tones rang out down the line. 'You should be ashamed of yourself, treating my baby girl so badly!'

There was a gasp of shock from the audience.

'It's Tavy's Mum!' Faye said, looking ready to expire with delight. 'Una, welcome to *Celebs in the Morning with Frost and Poole*! Is there anything else you want to say to Hunter? He's right here!' The camera got in close to Hunter's face. He quickly shut down the sneering grin he was sharing with the male co-presenter and tried to look comically nervous.

'You've disrespected Tavy and you've disrespected her fans.' Una was getting into her stride now. 'Tavy is a wonderful girl – she lives to make other people happy. She adored you, Hunter, and you treated her and all those other lovely people like sh—'

'Well, Hunter,' Rich Poole broke in hastily, 'you've heard how upset Tavy's mum is. How can you defend yourself against those accusations?'

Jess missed Hunter's undoubtedly insincere response as Tavy, who had been staring frozen at the screen, suddenly shrieked, 'Oh my God, Mum!' and ran off down the corridor towards the kitchen.

There was some confusion in the TV studio and then Rich interrupted Hunter urgently. 'Sorry, Hunter, but we're hearing that Tavy has gone live on her Instagram to talk about your interview and her mum's intervention. Cutting to that now.'

Jess had the surreal experience of seeing her mother and her sister, in the next room, crying and hugging each other on Tavy's Instagram feed as seen via an audience member's phone on the TV.

'I have an announcement to make,' Tavy said. 'I'm well rid of Hunter Blake. He's a creep and he's got a tiny—'

'Tavy.' Ed's voice cut authoritatively across the live feed. Jess hurried after her mother and sister and found him in the kitchen doorway, standing in unusually assertive style, hands on hips, tie loosened, suit jacket undone, his hair ruffled. He looked, Jess thought, quite hot, and it seemed Tavy had suddenly noticed it too because her mouth hung open and a speculative look came into her eyes.

'Ed!' she said, in the tone of someone who has had a miraculous vision. 'I—'

'I'm not doing this in public,' Ed announced. He took Tavy's phone, turned it off, tossed it aside and took her in his arms.

'Wow,' Jess said blankly to their mother. 'I didn't see that coming.'

'He's a lovely boy!' Una was beaming – and filming – as Tavy and Ed embraced. 'I'm so happy for them!'

Jess made for the back door. It wasn't that she wasn't happy for Tavy, but she felt as though her head was in danger of exploding. She grabbed her shoes from the porch and stepped out into the open air with relief. She doubted that she would ever look at life the same way that Tavy and Una did, but perhaps it didn't matter. She, her sister and her mother accepted each other the way they were and that was the best she could hope for; all she had wanted, in fact, when she had first arrived at Fortune Hall.

Her phone buzzed with a text. It was from Ethan and it said simply:

Meet me in the graveyard, E x

She smiled. She took the car as she wasn't yet ready to walk past the place where she'd found Jared's body, and parked in Church Walk between the lime trees. She could see Ethan sitting on the wooden bench outside the church, elbows resting on his knees, gazing out across the fields. He looked good – crisp white shirt, walking trousers, boots. When he saw her, he straightened and got slowly to his feet.

'You old romantic,' she said when she reached him. 'You know all the best places.'

Ethan smiled at her. 'How are things?' he asked.

'Oh...' Jess sighed. 'It's the usual melodrama at the hall. Tavy has discovered that Hunter has been cheating on her, Mum called him out on live TV, Tavy is filming it all on her Instagram feed and has thrown herself into Ed's arms. I can't cope. I'm moving out to Gunpowder Barn for a few weeks until I decide what I want to do next.'

'It's been a fast few days,' Ethan agreed. 'We've discovered two bodies, found a seventeenth-century horoscope and traced the history of Rose Gwyn. Meanwhile, your sister has dumped one boyfriend and gained another, broken her ankle and revealed her connection to a convicted fraudster.'

Jess giggled and slipped her hand into his. It felt easy, right. 'I prefer our week,' she said, and Ethan turned and kissed her, warm and sure. 'Was there any particular reason you wanted to meet here?' Jess asked.

'There's something I wanted to show you,' Ethan said. 'I know you didn't want Zoe's skeleton to be Guy Forster because he was Rose's husband and you wanted them to live happily ever after together.'

'It's not such a big ask,' Jess protested, 'not when you've had to struggle for your happiness, like Rose.' She thought of the carefully formed letters. *My love for you is ever true.* She had only had the tiniest insight into Rose's life through the snippets of biography, and the words she'd written and the horoscope, but she felt she knew her, that determined little girl who had stolen her sister's blue ribbon for her own red curls and had carved out her own life. She wanted fiercely for Rose to have been happy in whatever way was important to her.

'Well, everyone dies of course,' Ethan said, 'but it turns out that Guy and Rose both lived to a ripe old age, had four children and were buried in the same grave.' He was leading her over towards the yew tree that dominated the western corner of the churchyard. 'The reason we couldn't find them before was because they weren't buried with the rest of the Forsters in their part of the graveyard. They preferred to be over here for some reason.'

The tomb was very simple. Jess knelt in the freshly mown grass to trace the words that had, centuries before, been carved in the stone. *Sir Guy Forster, Knight, and his dearly beloved wife, Rose. Death cannot part them.*

'Oh,' she said. She found her face was wet with tears and rubbed them away. 'I'm glad for them. Glad that they had their time together.'

'They were married here as well,' Ethan said. 'I found the entry in the church records. They were the first of my family to live at Becote in the house that Rose, not Guy, owned. There's this as well...' Ethan's voice was a little hesitant. 'This is one of the lost graves they rediscovered only recently.' He squatted down by Jess's side and brushed aside the grasses that had almost swallowed up the tiny stone that stood at the foot of Rose and Guy's tomb.

'Harriet,' Jess read. 'Rosebud.' She looked at Ethan. 'That's all there is?'

'There's a carving,' Ethan said, pointing. 'I think it's a rose.'

'Oh,' Jess said. 'Oh, Rose.' She thought she understood now why Rose and Guy had chosen to be out here in the open air, beneath the yew that had probably already been old in their time.

'In the registers she is recorded as Harriet Cassells, stillborn child of the widowed Mrs Cassells,' Ethan said, echoing her thoughts, 'but, evidently, Guy must have cared for her too. He is recorded as having paid for the plot and the stone and, rather oddly, for a man to stand watch over the grave for six months after she was buried. I can't imagine why.'

'There's so much we'll never know for sure,' Jess said, 'the gaps in history that can only be filled with imagination. But at least it seems certain that the skeleton in the lake wasn't Guy's.'

'No,' Ethan confirmed. 'Guy Forster lived well into his seventies and died peacefully in his bed.' He looked at her. 'Rose's former father-in-law, Sir Grey Cassells, disappeared sometime in the mid-seventeenth century. It was a mystery that was never solved. But as his estates were in the South East, I don't suppose there was any connection.'

'They weren't anywhere near Brighton, were they?' Jess wondered, thinking of the trade token with the sign of the angel on it that Zoe had showed them, which had been found with the coins and the sword.

'His estate was at Poynings,' Ethan said, 'just five miles from Brighton, actually.'

'G for Grey,' Jess said thoughtfully. 'The initial engraved on the sword,' she added, as Ethan looked puzzled. 'I wonder? Maybe Rose and Guy bumped him off for some reason and threw the body in the lake.'

'Now you really are in the realms of imagination,' Ethan remarked. 'You might as well suggest that Rose stole the lost Crown Jewels from her first husband and hid them at Becote Manor.'

'Perhaps she hid them at the fishing house,' Jess said, 'where I saw her ghost walking.'

Ethan's brows shot up. 'You saw *what?*'

'I thought I saw Rose walking beside the lake a couple of times,' Jess admitted. 'Then there was the scent of roses. You smelled it yourself,' she reminded him, 'that day we were in the fishing house and you showed me the stained-glass window.' She stopped, remembering the play of the light across the water the last time she had walked down the beech avenue, and the way the colours had rippled on the surface in a jewel-bright rainbow.

The words from the book about Becote came back to her: *There is a stained-glass window in rather naïve style on the west side of the building. This was added later in the seventeenth century...*

'Oh my God,' she said faintly. Could Rose have played some huge cosmic trick on everyone and hidden the gems in plain sight? It would be in character, she thought. That bright, brave, indomitable woman who had lost and gained so much in a lifetime full of adventure. The other Gwyn girl, whose life had been equally as vivid as her sister's.

Jess could see Rose now, her blue eyes alight with mischief, her lips curved into a smile.

'There's something I need to show you,' she said to Ethan, scrambling up, tugging him towards the lychgate. 'I think we may have found the Crown Jewels.'

And for a moment she imagined she could hear Rose's delighted laughter follow them out into the rest of their lives.

ACKNOWLEDGEMENTS

A huge thank you to everyone who reads this book. History and storytelling are two of my favourite things and sharing them with people is such a joy. I hope you enjoyed reading about Rose Gwyn who, like the women in my previous books, was a real person from the footnotes of history. Her fascinating life was a pleasure to research and I hope I have done her justice.

I would also like to give heartfelt thanks to my editor Sarah Ritherdon and to Boldwood Books, for believing in my writing and supporting me with such enthusiasm, energy and excitement. It's a privilege to be working with so vibrant and committed a team of professionals. A very special vote of thanks goes to fellow Boldwood author Louise Douglas, for her 'matchmaking'!

Much love goes to my friends and family for helping me through the tough times and into this exciting new chapter. To all the readers, reviewers, friends and colleagues who have been with me for all or part of my twenty-five-year writing career, thank you so much for your time, generosity and support. You are the best.

ABOUT THE AUTHOR

Nicola Cornick is the international bestselling and award-winning historian and author of over 40 novels featuring women from the footnotes of history, and has been translated into 25 languages.

Sign up to Nicola Cornick's mailing list here for news, competitions and updates on future books.

Visit Nicola's website:

Follow Nicola on social media: www.nicolacornick.co.uk

 x.com/NicolaCornick

 facebook.com/nicola.cornick

 instagram.com/nicolacornick

 bookbub.com/authors/nicola-cornick

Letters from
the past

Discover page-turning
historical novels from
your favourite authors
and be transported
back in time

Join our book club
Facebook group

https://bit.ly/SixpenceGroup

Sign up to our
newsletter

https://bit.ly/LettersFrom
PastNews

Boldwood

Boldwood Books is an award-winning fiction publishing company seeking out the best stories from around the world.

Find out more at www.boldwoodbooks.com

Join our reader community for brilliant books, competitions and offers!

Follow us
@BoldwoodBooks
@TheBoldBookClub

Sign up to our weekly deals newsletter

https://bit.ly/BoldwoodBNewsletter